LOVE TORMENTED

To Cathy
It's never too late
to follow your dreams!
Enjoy
Sara Pickering

LOVE TORMENTED

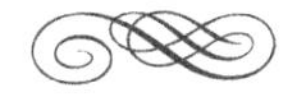

Lana Jean Pickering

Contents

Love Tormented

Cover design by Nadia Morel.

ISBN-13: 978-1-7753735-1-3
Print Version

Dedication

To my Dad, and my biggest fan.
I miss you every day.

"We all have some experience of a feeling that comes over us occasionally, of what we are saying and doing having been said and done before, in a remote time - at our having been surrounded, dim ages ago, by the same faces, objects and circumstances."

-Charles Dickens

I

Maggie hollered over the racket in the kitchen, "Why the hell didn't somebody tell me George wasn't here yet with the damn order?!" She hung her head while the throbbing in her temples continued. The clang of pots and pans and the whirl of a blender caused ringing through her head like a drill bit through heavy steel.

Shaking her head, she looked around at the efficient space. Didn't they realize that without that order there would be no food to prepare for tonight? And if there was no food to prepare, they couldn't feed their guests. And if they couldn't feed their guests, they would stop coming to stay here. And if guests stopped coming to stay here... they'd all be out of a Goddamn job!

Dressed in his white chefs' uniform and toque, Urbain walked up beside her with the ever-present grin on his mocha-colored face. He had the most intriguing eyes, dark brown with a light grey rim outlining the iris and in them a twinkle of mischief. "Ah *Cher*, don't you go frettin' none. George will be here in a quick minute. He won't leave me hanging when he knows I needs me the ingredients for the best étouffée in this here city. And to do so, I needs the makins' of the Holy Trinity. Don't you worry none, he's comin'."

As if conjured by Urbain's calming words, the back door opened and in walked George Dufrain. Dressed in his usual dark blue uniform with his name patch over his heart, he sauntered in as if he had all the time in the world. As his eyes landed on Maggie, his ebony black skin crinkled around his eyes and his smile grew wider. Maggie shook her head at him. "You're late, mister."

"Now Maggie, I'm never late. I'm always right where I want to be. And now I'm here looking at the prettiest face in N'Orleans."

She knew George was a notorious flirt, and it was probably why he was late. But he always brought her the best produce in the Crescent City, so she couldn't complain. "Yeah, yeah, I bet you say that to all the girls. Better hope your wife doesn't catch you flirting. She's got relatives who can put a curse on you."

George's eyes widened and then he looked sheepish. "Aww now, you know I love her more than anything. I might flirt a bit, but my sunshine Louisa is all I need."

Maggie smiled, then called over Carlos, the new kitchen hand, to help get the order unloaded. Turning back to Urbain she could see he was beaming. "You see *Cher*, I told you not to worry."

He was the head chef at the Colonial Hotel for the past three years and had turned the whole place around for the better. She should have known he was on top of it. "You're right, I need to have more faith, I guess."

What she needed was a solid night's sleep. Maybe then she

could focus on her job instead of being as irritable as an alligator with an empty stomach.

"*Cher*, what's eatin' you?" Urbain had a sense about what people were feeling, so it didn't surprise her when he asked.

"Sorry, I've been having the craziest dreams. When I wake up I feel like I haven't even slept. They're so vivid it feels like they really happened."

Urbain cocked his head to one side, a puzzled look on his face. "Hmm, sounds to me like someone's tryin' to tell you something. Maybe you need to pay a visit to a mambo, maybe she can tell you what they mean."

At the mention of a mambo, Maggie remembered the first time she'd seen Emeline when she was only twelve. Wow, it had been a long time since she thought about that day. Shaking off the thought, she decided she wouldn't be thinking about her today either. "Thanks Urbain, but I just need Grandma to whip me up some of her sleeping tonic to make sure I get a good night's sleep."

Looking at her with brows drawn down, Urbain said, "Don't ignore what the dreams tell you, Maggie. Dreams are not always just dreams; sometimes they're memories from the past." He nodded his head. Turning, he strode over to check on preparations for the breakfast service.

She stood, rooted to the spot as Emeline's words from all those years ago floated through her mind. "You've lived many times, but every one's ended in tragedy. But I swear to ya, on all the graves of my ancestors, I'll see ya happy in this one, Maggie. We needs to alter your destiny if you're ever goin' to be with your true love. Pay mind to your dreams, sweet child, for they will tell your story."

Coming out of her thoughts, she made her way back to her office. Sitting behind her desk, she took a deep breath and wished she could have stayed in bed. And why of all days was she focused on Emeline? She had a million things to get done, and important guests coming.

She had been the general manager of The Colonial Hotel for the last few years. Only six months after getting her Masters in Hospitality and Tourism Management degree from the University of New Orleans, she'd been lucky to land such a great job. She knew her boss, Damon Guidry, hadn't wanted to give her a chance. However, when his last GM left and there was no one else to fill his shoes on such short notice, he didn't have a choice.

Maggie had worked at the Colonial in several positions while she attended school. She needed the extra cash she made to supplement the scholarship she'd received. This worked out well as she learned about every job in the place, and it made sense that Damon hired her for the role. Between her experience and education, this was exactly the job she'd been working towards.

Working for Damon wasn't exactly her ideal situation, but she decided it could be worse. He was your classic rich guy with good looks and a pompous attitude to match. He seemed to waffle between making advances, which were highly inappropriate, to being super condescending. She knew it was his way of trying to make her quit.

However, it would take a lot more to make her step down from this job. He just couldn't grasp the idea she could do this job and do it very well. And the thought of them ever being an 'item' was laughable. Damon was rich, and she was not. He would never understand what it was like for her to work so hard to get where she was. He had been born into wealth and it showed.

Her grandmother raised her after a car accident took the life of her parents when she was only five. Damon could never relate to her life and she had no desire to be part of his. Sure, he was handsome with his honey-blond hair, sky-blue eyes and lean swimmer's body, but he didn't appeal to her. The man of her dreams was tall, dark and handsome, with a wide smile and dark denim-blue eyes. Or at least, the man who was frequenting her dreams most nights looked like that. And now she was daydreaming. Yeah, she needed to get some sleep.

But not right now. They were short-staffed, which had kept her busy the last couple of months. She needed to check with Genevieve to see if those welcome baskets she ordered had arrived. A follow up call to the florist was on her agenda regarding some special flower arrangements, as well as reviewing the linen order, since her head of housekeeping was off sick. One of her special guests, a very high-profile movie star, was hoping for tickets for the New Orleans Saints game on Sunday, so she needed to call in a few favors. He was an amazing guy, and she didn't want to disappoint him.

It was just the start of the day and it felt like she'd been here for eight hours. However, she could handle whatever came her way, and hoped tonight she'd sleep like the dead, or maybe something not so creepy. But for now... coffee.

* * *

Liam sat in the cramped airline seat and wished, not for the first time, that he could have booked a seat in first class.

At six-foot two-inches with a muscular build, he felt like a sardine squished against the window, while the guy next to him snored and leaned closer. What he wouldn't give for just another foot of room. He didn't mind flying, but he detested sitting in coach. Unfortunately, he needed to get down to New Orleans ASAP to meet with the owner of the Colonial Hotel. His company accepted a contract to do a complete review of the old building. Since historical architecture and restoration was his passion and specialty, he said he would do it. His boss, Paul, had sent him the specs and told him to call by the end of the week.

Liam leaned a little further away as the gentleman snored and then shifted to face the aisle. Traveling from New York to New Orleans, Louisiana had been a frequent occurrence for many years as he'd grown up in NOLA, and his parents had lived there until about four years ago, when they moved to Arizona. He and his sister both moved away from home once they left to go to university. His sister, Caroline, lived in Fort Worth, Texas with her husband James and two-year-old son, Jonathan.

He still traveled to New Orleans on occasion to visit his family, especially his Aunt Nora, one of his favorite people in the world. When he was a kid growing up, he would sneak over to her house for the best bread pudding ever. It was also the place he would go if he was in trouble with his parents. He spent countless hours sitting on her back porch listening as someone played guitar or running around the backyard of her home with his cousins, Owen and Walker.

Sometimes he missed those easy days when life seemed simple. Now his whole life was about deadlines and contracts.

He still loved his job, but what he wanted now was to settle down in one place. At first, he loved the constant change, experiencing new places, seeing different architecture styles and meeting all kinds of people. Traveling for his job had been great until about two years ago.

Now he wished he could put down some roots. As he got older, most of his friends and even his sister had settled down. He had stayed away from committed relationships because he never knew where his job would take him. It's hard to be in a relationship when you're flying around the globe all the time.

But, if he was honest, he'd never met a woman who had made him want to stay. He wasn't a player by any means, but he'd been with several women. None had come into his life that made him feel anything other than lust. Not one had ever made the earth tilt under his feet. He'd always hoped he could find someone to ground him. At thirty-three, he guessed it would happen when it happened.

The guy beside him shifted again, bringing Liam's thoughts back to the present. Looking at his watch, he groaned. He still had over an hour left in this tin can. Reaching under the seat, he pulled out his carry-on bag and took out his earbuds and phone. He could at least listen to some music instead of the chainsaw coming from his neighbor. Flipping through his playlist, he chose Mumford and Sons, loving the mix of instrumental and harmonic voices.

Next, he pulled out his laptop to read his file on the hotel. He reviewed the documents from the New Orleans historical society. As he read, his mind wandered back to how his love of old buildings started.

It began the day his father took him on a tour of the

French Quarter when he was about twelve. The beautiful Spanish-style homes with their ornate wrought-iron railings and secluded courtyards inspired the need to explore and learn their history. Every building held a unique story of love, hope, death and despair. He loved the stories of the haunted houses the most. To this day, ghosts fascinated him and he knew on the day of that tour, one spoke to him.

They started their tour in an old historical house on Royal Street. Its soft salmon color and grey shutters made it stand out from the others. As they walked through the thick wood framed door of the house, the whole atmosphere changed. His father was speaking to his friend Barnes, who was the real estate agent trying to sell the place. The two of them wandered to an adjoining room, leaving Liam to wander from room to room alone. Looking around at the hardwood floors and high-vaulted ceilings, he noted the architectural details of the crown molding and the wide marble mantel. After walking through several rooms, he climbed the wide staircase, letting his hand run along the carved banister. Looking up, he stared at the brilliant crystal chandelier hanging from the ceiling, each gem reflecting rays of light in every direction.

Reaching the top of the stairs, he felt a cold breeze creep along the floor and up his bare legs. It seemed to come from down the hall. He thought it was strange considering the windows were open and, with the July heat pouring in, it was hot enough to melt metal outside.

His rubber soles squeaked on the hardwood until he came to an open door at the end. He tentatively pushed open the dark-paneled door and stepped into a bedroom. Blue and green flowered wallpaper covered the walls, and on the tall windows hung dark blue velvet curtains. A white gossamer canopy topped the four-poster bed. The layered material billowed like clouds, which pooled to the floor. It smelled of old musty fabric, and he crinkled his nose.

A large six-drawer dresser took up the space along one wall. Above it hung an enormous, oval mirror. Resting on the dresser was an old-fashioned silver hairbrush. It had a thick handle, with an oval brush head, and an intricate design of a butterfly on the back. Picking it up, he felt the cold of the silver seep into his skin. As he held the brush, he could feel a cool breath on his ear as a female voice said, "*Watch over her, as she is your true happiness. Distraction could destroy her. You are the only one who can save her.*"

Liam dropped the brush and backed away. Looking up into the mirror he saw an apparition reflected behind him. It was a woman in a white dress, with a pink flower in her dark hair and glowing grey-green eyes. He watched as she reached out her hand and placed it on his shoulder. A chill ran down his arm and she whispered, "*She is of the river.*"

As if coming out of a trance, he shook his head and ran from the room, and didn't stop until he was standing out on the sidewalk. Pacing back and forth, he tried to reason with himself. It must have been something other than a ghost. But no explanation could rid him of the fear or the thrill he felt, or the unexplainable need he had to figure out what the cryptic message could mean.

His father found him sitting on the front steps and once they said their goodbyes to Barnes, they left. He'd never spoken of the incident to anyone.

Dragging his thoughts back to the present, the Captain's

voice came over the intercom and announced they would land in ten minutes. As Liam packed away his things and prepared to leave the plane, he had an overwhelming feeling of relief to be here. Like something was waiting for him, calling to him almost. Shaking his head, he chalked it up to being homesick. He was looking forward to spending some time with his aunt and cousins. It had been a while and he could use someone to fuss over him, as she always did. He had texted his flight information to her a few days ago, and she said someone would be there to pick him up. Mmm, he could almost taste the warm bread pudding.

* * *

Maggie woke with a start. Frazzled, she looked around her room and wondered why it was so bright. Rolling over, she stared at her alarm clock, then sat bolt upright and yelled, "Shit!"

It was eight twenty-five, and she had to meet with her boss at nine. Factoring in the twenty minutes it would take to get through traffic, she had no time to get ready. Whipping back the covers, she ran into the bathroom. Finishing in record time, she glanced at her face in the mirror and could see pillow creases. Great, now she would have to cover those up. This was not going to be a day she could wear her hair down. What a rat's nest! Grabbing an elastic, she pulled her hair into a messy bun. Then, she splashed some water on her face and brushed her teeth.

Argh, of all days to be late! But the crazy weekend at the hotel had left her exhausted. As she dressed, she thought back to the disaster of Saturday night and the equally horrible Sunday, which she'd spent cleaning until two this morning.

The weekend started out just fine. Friday was just a regular day, and she had scored some fantastic tickets for her special guest. However, the same could not be said about Saturday night. The nights little adventure started with a newlywed couple deciding to have their first domestic disturbance right in the lobby of her hotel.

She'd been home for thirty minutes before she rushed back to work. Rosie called her, saying the police were on their way. Arriving back at the hotel, she could see several people watching as the new bride screeched at her husband, while the guy flinched at her every word. Maggie wasn't sure what prompted the argument, and with the high decibels the wife was reaching, she couldn't make out what was being said. She watched as one of her security guards, Maxon, and two policemen, one of whom she'd dated for a while, stood back, trying to figure out if they should engage or not.

Just then, the bride flailed her arms and shoved her husband. Maggie watched as the poor guy landed right on his ass. The two officers moved forward, but before they could get close enough, the bride grabbed a vase off one of the side tables and threw it at her husband. It hit him right in the head, shattering into a million pieces. He started yelling as blood gushed from his forehead. Not wanting to draw more of a crowd, Maggie decided to step in. She could see that this bride was not going to let this go anytime soon.

Maggie made her way over to the husband after snagging a clean cloth off the maid's cart nearby. Bending down by the man on the floor, she pressed the cloth to his head then turned on the woman.

"OK, I think that's enough. I don't know what's going on here, but I will not stand by and watch this kind of behavior happen in my hotel. I will ask Officer Hebert here to take you up to your room where you can pack your things. We do not need any further drama here tonight."

She then turned to her staff, who were waiting for her instructions. "Eloise, call the hospital and see if they can send an EMS unit over to have a look at him. Georgina, get your cart. We need to get this glass and blood cleaned up before someone slips. Amy, why don't you run over to the kitchen and get this man a bottle of water while he gives his statement to Officer Beauregard." Turning to the crowd, she spoke louder, "OK, nothing more to see here. Everyone have a good night."

The crowd moved along and even the bride looked shocked, until she started sobbing all over Officer Hebert, saying her husband never treated her right and she didn't think she could live with someone who didn't treat her special. Yeah, Officer Hebert had his work cut out for him.

Looking down at the husband, as blood seeped through the cloth on his face, Maggie gave him a soft smile and said, "They say the first year of marriage is the hardest. Only three hundred and sixty-two more days to go." The husband groaned as Officer Beauregard came over to help him up. Maggie knew the officers weren't happy with how she'd stepped right in, but damn it, she had a hotel to run!

She'd dated Kenneth Beauregard for about eight months last year. They'd gotten along fine, but secretly, she called him Kenny 'Choir Boy' Beauregard. At over six feet, he was handsome with dirty-blond hair and a dimple in his right cheek, which would bring most women to their knees. He was sweet, maybe too sweet. And the attraction just wasn't there. Neither was his imagination.

"We had it under control, Maggie. You walked right into a volatile situation. I thought you were smarter than that!"

"You call that under control? This poor guy is bleeding all over my hotel floor! Any more under control and she would have stabbed him in the jugular with her high heel."

Shaking his head, he frowned. "Maggie Rivard, you're lucky I don't arrest you."

"Arrest me for what?! Trying to keep the peace in my hotel?" She could feel her anger rising.

A slow smile spread across his face. "Now, Maggie May, don't go gettin' all riled up. I'm here to serve and protect, which means protecting you, too. What would have happened if she'd come at you? Then, I would have had to protect you *and* him. Next time, just let us do our job."

He turned to head towards the EMS personnel who had just arrived but turned back. "And, Maggie... it was great to see you again." He winked as he hauled the poor husband off to get bandaged up.

Maggie was about to head home when a bunch of rowdy, drunken guests arrived back at the hotel after a fun-filled booze fest on Bourbon Street. One guy had enjoyed the night a little too much and vomited right in the middle of the lobby. Unfortunately for Maggie, by this time, all the housekeeping staff were gone. This meant she had to clean the mess herself. So, early Sunday morning at about one thirty, she finally made it home, only to be back at work for seven to help with the setup for the Ladies Auxiliary luncheon.

Things were going well until there was a backup in the plumbing, and the toilets in the West wing flooded. She called the emergency plumbers into fix it. She'd been telling Damon some repairs were necessary, he told her to hold off. While the plumbers fixed the issue, they had to redirect all the ladies to the other facilities within the hotel.

Once the plumbers and the ladies had left, Maggie made a call to a company she dealt with many times to come and steam clean the carpets. Between the clean-up crew, the housekeeping staff and herself, they got everything under control around ten o'clock.

She then dealt with a panicked guest who had lost their passport, and another one who had forgotten to bring their medication. She sorted out the passport and then called her pharmacist, who was a friend. It was twelve-thirty in the morning when she headed home and collapsed into bed, forgetting to set her alarm. If Damon would let her hire another concierge, she wouldn't need to handle all the extra stuff. Unfortunately, she didn't see that happening anytime soon.

Now it was Monday morning, and she was late. Grabbing her purse and briefcase, she tucked a pair of high heels under her arm and stuffed her feet into some flip-flops; she would slap some makeup on in the car. As she backed out of her driveway, the clock on her dashboard said eight forty-five. Crap! Hitting the call button on her steering wheel, she asked to call Rosie. When it connected, she didn't even wait for Rosie to say hi before she said, "I will be late. Can you take Damon to the tearoom? Set up for coffee and tea and have Emily put some of those butter scones and peach preserves in there. I'm starving. And PLEASE, for the love of all that is holy, do not let him go to the West wing. It will still smell musty in there."

Rosie's voice squealed on the other end of the line. It was loud and high enough to make dogs bark. "Oh. My. Gosh. Maggie! You will not *believe* the man who walked in with Mr. Guidry. He is gor-ge-ous. I'm so jealous! You get to spend the next hour staring at those dreamy eyes."

Shaking her head, she huffed out an exasperated sigh. Damon hadn't even mentioned he was bringing someone to their meeting. Wait, did Rosie even hear a word she'd just said?

"Focus, Rosie. Please get the tearoom ready. I need coffee, tea, scones and peach preserves. And do not let them go in the West wing."

Rosie was quiet for a moment and Maggie could hear the smile in her voice when she said, "Yes Ms. Rivard, right away." Then, in a hushed whisper she heard, "So lucky!" And the line went dead.

Great, just what Maggie needed today, an unannounced guest of Damon's. She wondered if this guy was as pompous and chauvinistic as her boss. He was always putting her on the spot to see if she would slip up. He was such an ass sometimes.

By the time she pulled in, she was only about five minutes late. However, when she went to pull into her reserved spot, a car was there. A red Toyota Civic with local plates sat mocking her. Letting out an impatient huff, she stared at the car. This was all she needed now. She didn't have time to drive around in circles looking for another spot. Giving up, she parked in front of the hotel. René was standing by the valet desk and dashed over to get her door.

"René, I hate to ask, but I'm late. Can you park my car somewhere and tow the car in my spot?" She winced, as she hated to ask people for favors.

He smiled so wide his gums showed. With his thick French accent, he said, "Ah, *oui* miss. Consider it done."

He spun around and yelled over to Julian as he took her keys. She waved at them both as she ran for her office. Hopping around on her feet, she slipped off her flip-flops and pulled on her heels. Hopefully, Rosie had moved Damon and his guest to the tearoom. All she needed was two minutes to get focused and she could pull this off.

2

Grabbing the handle of her office door, she shoved it open just as someone pulled from inside. Before she could stop her momentum, she ran headlong into the most beautiful denim-blue eyes she'd ever seen. Then she face planted. Right. At. His. Feet. Taking in a deep breath, she felt arms scoop her up and set her upright. Those dreamy eyes came back into focus, and just like that she'd gone speechless.

She fumbled for words when the man said in the most delicious, deep voice, "Don't think I've ever had anyone fall for me like that before. Miss Rivard, I presume."

Maggie could feel her face grow hot as her mouth opened and closed, but no sound came out. Then she heard Damon say, "Can't say I've ever seen her speechless before. She usually talks my ear off."

Damon's voice pulled Maggie out of her stupor. "Well, just doing my job is all." She looked over at Damon with a glare. Then, in a gentler tone she said, "So, who have you brought here today, Damon?"

Looking back at the stranger, she realized he was staring at her, so she fidgeted. Rosie wasn't wrong when she said he was gorgeous. Dressed in a dark blue polo shirt and beige khakis, this guy could pull off business casual like a magazine model.

Thick, dark brown hair, great panty-melting smile and just a touch of stubble, which made her fingers itch to touch it. His bottom lip was nice and plump; the kind you'd want to suck into your mouth and give a bite. Whoa girl, she thought to herself; she didn't even know his name.

He seemed to realize he was gawking and stuck his hand out. "Sorry, I'm Liam Kavanagh. I'm a Structural Engineer with the engineering firm of William, Douglas and Stephenson in New York."

As if in slow motion she slipped her hand into his. The large warm hand enveloped hers and the tingling shock ran right up her arm. She was sure her heart did a triple beat as she stood staring at the hand holding hers.

Damon walked over saying. "Now Liam, I'm the one you need to impress, not her. Why don't we move this meeting to a better location?"

Maggie's face flushed with embarrassment at the comment. Pulling her shoulders back and giving Liam her best smile, she said, "You might not need to impress me, but the Colonial is like my home. Whatever goes on here is very important to me. Why don't we head over to the tearoom? The staff has set out some coffee, tea and scones. Hope you're hungry, Mr. Kavanagh. Emily makes the best butter scones in the state. Right this way, gentlemen."

Rosie was standing just outside her office, a wide grin splitting her face. Rolling her eyes, Maggie smiled and made her way to the tearoom. What she wouldn't give to have two minutes to get her thoughts pulled together. She had not expected Damon to show up to their weekly meeting with an engineer. He'd talked once about wanting to tear down the hotel and buy the adjacent properties. Maggie knew it would be almost impossible as you needed to jump through hoops to get approval from the historical society. Besides, Damon's father, the real owner of the building would never allow it to happen. Maybe he planned to start on the many renovations and restorations which needed to be done. By the end of this meeting, she hoped to have a better feeling about what this meant. That was if she could focus on the meeting long enough with Mr. Bedroom Eyes in the room. She wished she'd dressed up today. Maggie was sure she looked like a train wreck. Oh well, no time to dwell on it. What she needed now was coffee.

* * *

Liam watched her walk ahead of them as Damon droned on beside him. She had a great walk which gave her curves lots of sway. He liked curves and her forest green skirt accentuated them. He estimated her to be about five-foot four-inches, but those heels gave her tanned legs just the right amount of length. At over six feet, he usually dated taller women. Shorter, smaller women always seemed too dainty. However, even with her clumsy fall in her office, Maggie didn't seem the least bit fragile.

As she walked, he wished she'd turn around so he could see her eyes again. They were the most exotic grey-green color, highlighted by the slightest hint of makeup. His eyes drifted down to her butt again, and as if she could feel his stare, she turned her head. Yep, now she caught him checking out her ass. She didn't frown, but she didn't smile either. Turning away from him, he watched as she stiffened her spine and continued forward.

He could tell she'd haphazardly pulled her hair into a bun, but the dark brown locks were shiny. His fingers itched to be buried in it, allowing him to pull her head back to devour her neck. With those kinds of thoughts, he'd have her undressed in his head if he didn't behave himself.

Thinking back to the touch in her office, he realized it was like nothing he'd ever felt before. The shock from her hand had given him heart palpitations. He could still feel how soft her skin was as she slipped her hand into his. In that moment, looking into her face, it was as if they were the only two people on the planet. Then Damon had ruined it with his snarky comment.

As they entered the tearoom, her scent surrounded him. She smelled like magnolias and citrus. It reminded him of his Aunt's backyard in the spring and he loved that smell. Walking further into the room, he could see the antique furnishings which gave the room a cozy feel. Brocade high-backed chairs sat by the window, their gold threads picking up the light. She moved towards the window where a silver tea service waited and the aforementioned scones. His stomach growled at the sight.

Taking their seats, Maggie crossed her legs and Liam almost groaned as her skirt shifted to show more of her leg. She leaned forward as she started pouring coffee, and he could see the top curve of her breast as her white blouse shifted. Looking away, he repositioned himself in the chair and tried not to think about her body. She would think he was a pervert if he kept it up. But it would take all his willpower to do so. There was just something about her that intrigued him. She nodded to him motioning to the coffeepot she had, and he nodded back.

Damon sat down beside Maggie, and, clearing her throat, she said, "Damon, why don't you start off by telling us what your plan was when you hired Liam's company to look at the building?"

Liam could tell by the tone in her voice she hadn't known the reasons prior to this meeting. This was not what he had expected at all. Usually with the contracts he worked on, everyone was in the loop regarding expectations and a full plan was in place. He sat back waiting to hear what Damon told her.

Taking a cup of coffee from Maggie, Damon said, "I decided it would be a good idea to have a firm come and evaluate the building. I want to understand its historical authenticity and how structurally sound it is. That was one reason I went with Liam's company. I'd heard that he is one of the best in the business for this kind of project, and with his background in structural engineering he is the perfect fit for this job. I mean, I need to know my investment is sound."

Liam watched several emotions pass over Maggie's face. First, there was concern. From what Liam knew of business, whenever you heard a businessman say he wanted to make sure his investment was sound, it usually meant he wasn't confident that they were. Knowing rich men as Liam did, he knew if it wasn't a sound investment Damon would think about cutting his losses and selling. He could appreciate good business and making sure you hadn't tied yourself to a sinking ship, however, it might have been a good idea to talk to his operations manager prior to the meeting. Then she wouldn't be sitting here nervously wondering what was going to happen to her position here at the hotel.

Clearing her throat, she nodded and smiled, "I see. I hadn't realized you thought the Colonial was not a sound investment."

"Don't go jumping to conclusions, Maggie. I love the hotel. I just want to have Liam check it out. Then I'll have a better understanding of what needs fixing," Damon said.

Liam decided not to say anything. He'd worked for companies that were all about the bottom line. If the place would drain every cent out of their bank accounts, they would get rid of it as soon as possible. He wasn't sure if this was where Damon wanted to go. He'd wait and see once he had a look and told Damon what he found.

Damon looked at Liam. "Why don't you give us a quick overview of what your general procedure is to complete an assessment. Maybe then Maggie will realize I'm not up to anything underhanded."

Liam frowned. Why would Maggie think he was doing anything other than wanting to restore his hotel? He logged the comment to ask Maggie later. "I should tell you that I specialize in historical preservation and restoration, so the Colonial is in good hands. I usually complete a condition survey, which includes a visual inspection and materials testing. For the testing, I would do an analysis to find out what the cause is of any deterioration or distress. I would make inquires to the Historic District Landmark Commission, as well as the local Council on Environmental Quality about stresses in the environment. I was born and raised here, so I have connections to people and local businesses."

Liam watched as a brief look of concern passed over Damon's face. Making a note of the look, he continued, "I realized that to some, adhering to New Orleans historic heritage can seem like a road block, but knowing what I do from other cities, it is one of its strongest assets. Wouldn't you agree?"

He stared intently at Damon's face, waiting to see any flicker of disapproval. When Damon's face remained neutral, Liam decided he must have mistaken what he'd seen. Both Maggie and Damon nodded, and he finished outlining his work. "After completing the consultations, I make recommendations for repairs and restoration. I will also recommend if a business should or should not renovate. I can be part of the renovation process, manage the repairs or renovation and sign on to provide long-term monitoring. As part of my service, I look to eliminate safety hazards, and also review and correct structural deficiencies. I do this in keeping with the historical integrity of the building."

He watched as Maggie's interest grew with everything he said. She seemed encouraged that his focus was on restoration and keeping with historical preservation. It made him think again about what Damon might have said to her to make her think otherwise.

Chuckling, Liam said to Maggie, "All that to say I will be in your hair for the next week or more, and if Damon wishes I could be here for longer still."

Maggie smiled and Liam felt his stomach flip. When she smiled her whole face lit up. The sparkle in her eyes was one of the most distracting and beautiful sights he had ever seen.

Damon cleared his throat and a deep V formed between his brows. "Once the assessment is complete you can recommend to me, not only the possibilities for restoration, but you can also tell me if it's even worth doing anything, correct?"

Liam nodded and watched Maggie frown again. He could tell the two of them were not on the same page for The Colonial. He would need to find out more about this tension between them so he understood what he was getting himself involved in.

"That sounds great, Liam." Damon placed his mug on the table and sat back. "I'll let my secretary know the paperwork will be coming. What do you need from me? Or, I should say Maggie, as I'm not on site." Damon nodded his head towards Maggie.

"I guess the only thing I need is free rein over the hotel to do my inspections. I'll talk to the employees as they're the ones who will know the things that I might need to look into while I'm here."

Maggie spoke. "Will you need to stay at the hotel?"

Liam watched her face, but she gave nothing away. "I'm staying with my aunt at the moment, but I wouldn't mind staying here if it's OK."

He directed the question to Maggie, but Damon barked out, "Of course it is! Maggie, give him the best room we have."

"I don't need the best room; just a place with a desk and a bed is fine with me. I'm just thrilled to have a bed. A few of my jobs I've had to camp in tents. And while I'm not against camping and being in the wilderness, the locations were so remote it created some difficult challenges." Liam winced at the thought of waterlogged laptops and lumpy bed rolls.

Damon grunted, "You'd never catch me in a place like that. Way too rustic for me. I need my king-size, ultra-firm mattress and my three thousand thread count sheets to sleep."

Liam watched as Maggie held back a chuckle. She was probably thinking the same thing he was. This guy hadn't roughed it a day in his life.

"You won't need your sleeping bag here. The only issue you might run into is Suzanna," Maggie said as her eyes sparkled. Damon shook his head. "Geez, Maggie, need you bring that up? I'm sure an intelligent man like Liam doesn't believe in something as hokey as ghosts."

Well, this was intriguing. "Are you saying there is a resident ghost here?" Liam asked.

"We have a couple. Damon here doesn't believe in ghosts, but many guests and most of the staff have witnessed at least one." Maggie's eyes took on a look of mischief.

Damon shook his head again. "I've stayed here a hundred times and I've never seen a single one."

"Perhaps they just have nothing to say to you. Or maybe, you're not Suzanna's type." Maggie's smile grew.

"Don't go filling his head with nonsense of ghosts and spirits and any of that hocus pocus voodoo crap either," Damon said, a frown creasing his brow.

Liam watched as Maggie cringed at what Damon said, so he jumped in. "Well Damon, to tell you the truth, I'm pretty open minded about things. Having been born and raised here in New Orleans, I've heard all the tales and if I were you, I wouldn't call voodoo hocus pocus. Someone might just put a spell on you."

Maggie's eyes sparkled at the comment. "You might not

know right away if you see her. Suzanna was a maid at the hotel back in the late 1800s. It was the Lumbers Hotel back then. As the story goes, the married owner of the hotel fell in love with her. He used to sneak in to see her every chance he could. One night, in a rage, his wife came to the hotel and caught him with Suzanna. The wife grabbed an umbrella stand and threw it at the two of them and it cracked Suzanna's skull. She fell to the floor and died while the husband and wife struggled. The police came and pronounced her dead. To this day people see her cleaning rooms and walking the corridor on the third floor of the east wing."

Liam nodded, excited by the prospect. "How about you book me a room on the third floor in the east wing? Perhaps I'll get to see if the stories are true."

Damon just frowned. "I would have given you the fanciest room in the place, but you want the spooky floor? To each his own." He stood up. "Well Liam, it was nice to meet you and I'm looking forward to your report. I've got another meeting to attend. I'll leave you in Maggie's hands. Don't skimp on the service Maggie. Give him anything he wants." Then he left without a backwards glance.

Liam watched as Maggie frowned at Damon's back. She turned to him and said, "Not to worry, I won't skimp on you. Anything you need, our staff is always willing to help."

Just then her stomach growled, and she looked mortified. "Sounds like someone missed breakfast this morning," Liam chuckled, and a blush crept into her cheeks. Her tanned skin with the added rose hue just about took his breath away. She was beautiful.

Maggie looked at him with a slight frown. "It was a crazy

weekend here at the hotel, and between you and me, I didn't get home until the wee hours. I was dealing with a plumbing issue. Since you're about to find out all of our secrets, I might as well tell you. So, no breakfast this morning and I'm not sure when I'll get lunch today either. Why don't we continue to chat about the hotel while we take advantage of the scones? They are amazing."

They talked about the hotel and its history while they both enjoyed coffee and scones. When the conversation slowed, he moved the conversation to her. He found out about her education and how she came to be the general manager at The Colonial Hotel. She also told him she lived with her grandmother. They shared a house; she was upstairs and her grandmother had the ground floor. He mentioned his aunt, and Maggie said that she knew her. His aunt and her grandmother attended the same church, and sat on a few charities together.

"It's a small world." Maggie finished her second scone with peach preserve, and Liam watched as she licked a dollop of preserve off the end of her thumb. He held back a groaned at the simple act. Never in his life had he ever wanted to be a thumb more than in this moment. "When would you like to check in?" she asked.

He shook his head, trying to pull himself out of the dirty fantasy he was having about her mouth. "I told my aunt I would stay tonight, but I can come tomorrow." He set down his cup and grabbed his portfolio.

As Maggie wiped her hands on a napkin she nodded and said, "I'll check with reservations and set you up."

They stood up and walked out to the lobby. It was a beautiful hotel. He could feel the history ooze from the walls and floors. Excitement crept in as he looked forward to checking this place out. And if he got to spend some time with Maggie, so much the better.

Maggie stopped and faced him by the front entrance. "It's been a pleasure, Liam. I look forward to having you here. Again, let me know if there is anything you need for your stay. Here's my card." She put her hand out and if Liam was honest, he wasn't sure whether he wanted to touch her again. But he reached out and took her hand in his, and this time there was only a slight tingle, but in a good way. She had the softest skin, and he lingered longer than necessary while holding her hand.

"I'll be here tomorrow, and I'll let you know if there is anything I need. I'm looking forward to it." Regrettably, he let go of her hand and she smiled. Turning, he headed out to where his aunt's car was parked.

3

Maggie watched as Liam exited the hotel and if she'd been any less of a professional, she would have thrown her hands in the air and screamed like a lovesick teenager. Instead, she turned and walked over to the reception desk to talk to Genevieve about Liam's reservation.

Rosie and Genevieve were watching her with crazy maniacal smiles on their faces. Rosie was almost breathless as she said, "Oh. My. God! You are so lucky getting to spend time with him. He is so yummy."

She smiled at the two young ladies. They had both started at the hotel just after Maggie took over as general manager and she loved them from the start. The two of them could have passed for twins, with their curvy bodies and light brown skin, except Genevieve dyed her hair a bright blond and Rosie always left hers black with cornrows. Their smiles were genuine and many of the guests told her how wonderful they were. They were both hard workers and understood how much the hotel meant to her. It helped too that they weren't much younger than she was. They were great people, and they felt like family. Actually, all her staff felt like family. "You'll get to see him again because he's coming to stay at the hotel tomorrow. I need a room on the third floor, east wing."

Both the girl's eyes widened as they gasped. Rosie leaned forward and in a conspiratorial voice said, "The Suzanna floor? How can you put him there? What if she shows up?"

Rosie had experienced Suzanna. She'd been helping with some paintings Maggie brought in over a year ago, and when she went into room 309, it was ice cold in there. She put the frame on the floor and was about to unwrap it when a movement caused her to look towards the window. An apparition of a woman in a maid's uniform floated across the floor and, Rosie swears, smiled at her. The poor girl freaked and refused to go back in the room.

"I told him about her and the third floor. He said he wanted to stay there. If room 310 is available, please reserve it for him. It's the nicest room on the floor and it has the living room suite which will work for him."

Nodding, Genevieve started keying in the request right away, but was listening as Rosie spoke. "So, what was the meeting about?"

"Damon hired his firm. Looks like he will be looking at the building and providing an assessment on repairs and possibly upgrades to the architecture," Maggie responded.

Smiling and waggling her eyebrows, Rosie asked, "How was the meeting?"

Maggie couldn't help but think about those amazing blue eyes. "He seems passionate about his work and I hope he can encourage Damon to invest further in completing some upgrades."

Genevieve rolled her eyes, looking bored. "We don't care about his credentials and resume, we want to know if you think he's hot."

Looking down at her hands, Maggie pretended to look at her fingernails, a tiny smile curving her lips. "As your boss it would be unprofessional of me to comment. However, in my opinion, I'd have to say he's hotter than my Aunt's Vi's spicy creole shrimp gumbo."

"Does she use Louisiana hot or andouille sausage in her gumbo?" A deep baritone voice said.

Maggie's eyes whipped up to Rosie and Genevieve to see they were both trying to keep straight faces. The voice had come from behind her and she knew who she would find when she turned around. She felt heat crept into her cheeks as she turned to find Liam standing there, a huge smile spread across his face. She wished she could disappear.

"Oh, hhhheeeeyyy, Liam. I was just doing you – I mean, getting you a room, for your stay, for tomorrow. I wanted to get you a good room." Her face flamed and she knew she was rambling but couldn't seem to stop herself.

He smiled wider and said, "Thanks, I appreciate it. I was wondering if you could help me with something else."

She fidgeted with embarrassment and decided she'd help him with just about anything if it meant he would leave so she could get over her humiliating comment. "Sure, absolutely. What can I help you with?"

"Here's the thing. When I drove in this morning, I saw Damon and he told me to park out front. He said it wouldn't be a problem, but now my car's missing."

Flustered, Maggie's stomach clenched with dread as she realized she towed Liam's car. Crap. "Oh well, you know what, just let me check with the valet and see if they can help.

Maybe they just moved it." She knew that was a stupid thing to say, but she needed to stall for time.

Just as she turned, Liam said, "Moved it? How could they do that if I have the key?" She turned around to see him dangling the keys from two fingers, a small smile curling his lips.

Letting out a long breath, she looked him in the eye and her shoulders sagged. "Here's the thing, Liam. The space you parked in is a designated staff space. The car had a local license plate, so I had it towed. I am so sorry. Let me see about getting it back. It will probably take about half an hour, but let me see if I can't pull a few strings."

Liam frowned, but she could see a slight glint in his eyes. "You had my aunt's car towed?"

There was an awkward pause before he continued. "I had some stuff to get done this morning. Well, I guess I can hang out, but I think I need some compensation for my lost time. I think it's only fair that if my car isn't back in, let's say, thirty minutes, you have dinner with me tonight."

Maggie's mouth fell open. Was he seriously trying to blackmail her into having dinner with him? What the hell? Well, she would see about that. He didn't know who he was dealing with. Narrowing her eyes, she stared at him. "Fine, but if I get it here within half an hour, no dinner. And you have to show me your report before Damon sees it." Two can play the blackmail game.

"I don't know if I can do that. He's paying me to do this assessment. I guess I could give you a little peak... if you win. Guess you better see if they can bring it back." He smiled and her heart betrayed her with a flutter.

She spun around and hit the front doors at a run. She zeroed in on René and almost tackled him. "You need to get the car back I asked you to have towed, and I need it back in less than thirty minutes! It is *very* important. Can you do that for me?"

René started nodding right away, pulling his cell phone out of this pocket. "Let me call Roch. I'll see if he can get it back here pronto."

Maggie nodded, feeling better already. René hit a number on his phone and started speaking rapid fire French. She took in a deep breath and yelled out to René, "Tell him if he has it here in twenty-five minutes, I'll comp him a dinner at our restaurant!"

There was no way she wanted to sit through a dinner with Liam after the 'hot' comment. It's not that she didn't think he was hot, because he was. But now he knew how she felt and she didn't like not having the upper hand in any situation. She had to deal with enough of that from Damon.

She watched René hang up and nodded. Perfect, the last thing she wanted after these last few crazy days was to have dinner with Mr. Kavanagh. She wanted to go home after work and get into her pajamas and continue her binge watching of Sons of Anarchy. Charlie Hunnam was super-hot in leather. She also wanted to drink her favorite Merlot and finally, drift dreamlessly off to sleep.

Turning around, she went back into the hotel. She found Liam sitting at the lobby bar talking to the bartender, Albin. He looked over at her and held up a mug in a cheers motion. She shook her head and walked back to her office to wait for the moment she could gloat that he'd lost. Then not only would they not be having dinner, but she would get to see the report before Damon.

Once seated at her desk, she turned on her computer and prepared to start her day. She waited about twenty minutes before she, hopefully, would watch as Liam got in his aunt's car and drove away. Maggie walked out to see him still sitting at the bar. She glanced towards the front entrance, but saw no sign of the tow truck. There was still time before she needed to panic. Walking over to the front counter, she stopped there so she would have the perfect view of Liam as his little deal backfired.

As she looked over at the door, Rosie whispered behind her. "Maggie, what the heck? Why wouldn't you want to have dinner with him? If he would have given me that deal, I would have taken twenty-five minutes just to walk out and ask René to bring it back."

Maggie laughed. Maybe she was crazy for making this deal, but damn it, she hated not being on a level playing field. It was for the best. Her track record with men was total shit. She dated some losers and had sworn off dating on principle that all the men she met were assholes or didn't make her heart flutter. Plus, she didn't want to deal with anything awkward as she had to work with Liam for the next week.

Glancing at her watch, she was getting a bad feeling. Twenty-seven minutes had already passed. Her eyes moved over to Liam and she realized he was watching her. She smirked at him. Deciding to get this over with, she walked over, and his eyes never left her. His gaze started at her toes and traveled up, a smile spreading across his face. If she had any doubts about his attraction to her before, they vanished.

"Miss Rivard, time's ticking and I still don't see my aunt's car. Where would you like to go for dinner?" Liam asked.

Oh, he was so cocky! She couldn't wait to wipe the smug smile right off his face. She heard the door open and saw René walk in. Making his way over to her, a frown on his face, he said, "Maggie, I feel terrible. Roch just called to tell me there is a traffic jam on the Esplanade. He is sorry, but he cannot make it back in time. It will take about twenty more minutes."

Well crap. Nodding to René then turning back to Liam, she watched as his smile widened. Double crap! "As I was saying, where would you like to go for dinner? Here's my card with my cell number. You can text me your address. I'll pick you up at seven," Liam said, an unmistakable smug look on his face.

She took the card and could see her pajama, wine and TV date with the very delectable Charlie Hunnam disappear.

"I'll let you figure out a place for dinner," she said. Now if you'll excuse me, Mr. Kavanagh, I have a hotel to run."

Spinning away, she marched back to her office. Perhaps she should have said she would choose. Then she could have picked the most expensive place in town and made him pay through the nose for all his smugness. That little thought made her smile.

* * *

Liam received a text from Maggie with her address at six o'clock. He couldn't have been more impressed with himself. He felt slightly guilty for what he had done, but as they were about to go for dinner, he could deal with the guilt. Now, a gentleman would have just asked the valet to call the tow truck guy, who happened to be René's cousin, and ask him to bring it back. However, when he found out Maggie had it towed, he turned the situation to his advantage.

He hadn't lied. Damon *had* told him to park in her spot. In fact, his exact words were, "Just park there. Maggie can park around back. Women need to work on keeping their girlish figures. The walk will do her good". So, he parked there. It surprised him when Maggie had fallen at his feet because while she wasn't rail thin, she was curvy and far from the overweight woman Damon had alluded to.

So that part was true. The part he hadn't mentioned to her was René had told him he was under an order to have it towed. René also told him it would be at least forty-five minutes before he would get his car back. That's when Liam set his plan in motion. He paid René and the other valet each fifty bucks to keep the forty-five minute return time to themselves. When he'd walked up behind her as she was telling the ladies she thought he was hot; it couldn't have been more perfect. Watching her blush again had sent his blood draining south. He hoped he got to see more of that tonight.

Pulling up in front of the address she'd sent him in the Garden District, he looked out to see a beautiful late-eighteen-hundreds classic house with light blue siding and white cast iron railings. White shutters framed each window, and long columns supported both the main floor and second storey. There was also a black cast iron gate along the front yard of the house.

No sense waiting any longer, he thought. Liam couldn't wait to see her again. Getting out of the car, he made his way around to the front gate. Just as he stepped onto the sidewalk, he noticed two ladies sitting on the porch, their eyes glued on him. He wasn't sure what to think of this situation. Meeting relatives was something he didn't have a lot of practice with. Before he had time to change his mind and wait in the car, one lady called out to him. "Well, come on in now. Let's take a look at' cha." He grinned and opened the front gate.

Walking up the wide front steps, he saw the two women and he would have known Maggie's grandmother right away. She wore a flowing, flowered skirt and a white blouse, her feet in strappy sandals. The eyes and smile were the same as Maggie's, and he couldn't mistake the look of mischief on her face. Her salt and pepper hair was up in a bun and for an older woman, she was beautiful. Liam now understood where Maggie got her beauty from. The other lady was black with the most amazing ebony skin, a friendly smile and the kindest eyes he'd ever seen.

"Well Gladys, this one looks quite civilized. That smile could make just about any woman sell her soul. My, my, my, would you look at the shoulders on this man? My Henry had shoulders like that. Look at those dark blue eyes. Hmm, that girl sure is in trouble with this one, *Mmm hmm.* And look at how handsome he is when he blushes," The older woman said.

Liam's face heated the moment the assessment began, and he could feel his embarrassment right down to his toes. Shaking his head and moving forward, he held out his hand to Maggie's grandmother. "It's a pleasure to meet you ma'am. My name is Liam Kavanagh." He then shook the other lady's hand.

"You can call me Margaret. Oh my, Gladys, did you hear that voice? He could be a radio announcer with that deep smooth bourbon voice. Tell me Liam, what do you do for a living?"

Clearing his throat and preparing for the inquiry, he stated, "I'm a Structural Engineer, specializing in historical restoration. Mr. Guidry hired me to assess his hotel."

Gladys spoke this time. "We hear you're from New York, son, but that ain't no Yankee accent you got there," she said.

"Yes ma'am, I live in New York, but I was born and raised here. Moved away to go to university and I'm based up north now."

Margaret raised her eyebrows. "An Engineer you say? Isn't that just fancy? And did you say historical restoration? If that is your specialty then why aren't you based back here in New Orleans? You can't get any more historical a place than right here. Do your parents still live here?" She peppered him with questions.

"No ma'am, they live in Arizona now. But my Aunt Nora still lives here. Maggie mentioned the two of you know her. Nora Mouton."

Nodding her head, she smiled. "Oh yes, Nora and I have been on the church fundraising committee going on about five years now. She is such a sweet woman, and her sons are such good boys. Now Liam, where are you plannin' on takin' my girl tonight for dinner?"

Liam laughed. "I do have an idea, but I wanted to see if she had any favorite places."

Gladys frowned. "Now if she tells you she wants to take you to her favorite place, she'll take you to some hole in the wall po' boy place and believe me honey, you don't want that. You'll have indigestion all night."

From behind him he heard someone clearing their throat. He turned to see Maggie walking out of the house and his whole mouth went dry. She was wearing a plum-colored dress which was form fitted over her breasts and then flowed down just below mid-thigh. Not only did the color highlight her tanned skin, but it made her eyes seem lighter, making them sparkle. Her hair was back in a clip leaving it to flow down her back. To say she was beautiful was not even near close enough.

He realized he was standing there gawking when he heard Maggie's grandmother. "Looks like you stunned him, Magpie. Snap your fingers in front of his face to see if he'll come to."

Laughing, he said. "Sorry about that. Maggie, you look amazing."

"Thank you. You look great too. I, ah, hope these two weren't asking too many questions. They are ever vigilant in their pursuit to marry off their daughters and granddaughters. They want to fill their walls with pictures of their grand babies," Maggie explained.

Liam tore his eyes away from Maggie to look at the ladies. They both smiled and shrugged.

Maggie turned to Liam and said, "Gladys is my grandmother's best friend and my best friend Lolita's mother." Turning to Gladys, she said, "Heard she'll be home in a few weeks."

Liam watched the pride shine in Glady's eyes. "You heard right. My baby girl's coming home! She's not sure when she's deployed next, but I will enjoy having her home while I can."

Maggie looked sad for a moment. "Yeah, I can't wait for her to come home. I miss her, too."

She turned toward Liam and her eyes were mesmerizing. "I guess we better get going. I was thinking maybe you'd be all right if I took you to my favorite place."

Liam smiled and looked over at Gladys, who shook her head subtly. "If you don't mind, I thought maybe we'd go to a place downtown."

"Sure, that'd be fine," she replied. He watched as Maggie walked over and gave her grandmother a kiss on the cheek. Then she walked past him to the stairs.

"You have a good night, Magpie. Take care of my girl, Liam."

Liam followed Maggie and called out, "Yes ma'am."

He walked past Maggie and opened her door. She smiled as she got in and he caught the smell of her magnolia scent again and it stirred something deep within him. He wanted to gather her in his arms and breathe her in.

Walking around to the driver side, he got in the car and started the engine. He looked over at her. She was looking out the front window and everything about her drew him in. The warm smile, the bright eyes, the tanned skin that he could seriously see himself kissing every inch of, and the dark brown hair that he wanted to gather in his hands while he kissed those plump lips. She overwhelmed him.

Without looking his way, Maggie said, "You keep staring at me like that while my grandmother is watching, she's liable to come down here and give you a lecture on proper dating etiquette."

She looked at him then and smiled. He liked that sassy mouth. He could think of many things to do with that mouth.

"We better get moving then. Don't want to make your grandma mad, Magpie."

"Hey, no one calls me that but her. She's called me that my whole life and only she is allowed to do that."

"Fair enough, I get that. My sister calls me jerk face sometimes. I'm not sure why, but it's her thing." The sound of Maggie's laughter filled the car and he loved the sound of it.

4

Driving into the French Quarter, they talked about the city and how much it had changed since he'd lived there. It fascinated Liam, hearing her talk about New Orleans, and could see how passionate she was about it. He felt envious of her love for what she did and the place he had once called home.

Living in New York suited him well enough. He had a few friends, most of them colleagues, who he would see when he was home, which wasn't often. If he was honest, he hadn't had time for them as his job kept him busy. The thought of his lonely apartment was not a place he missed at all.

They parked the car and got out. As they walked, they heard the faint sound of the steamboat whistle coming from the river. Liam stopped in front of a place with a wooden sign hanging over the door. It was a very upscale restaurant, and his cousin Owen had to pull some strings to get him a reservation for tonight.

"Looks like someone has connections. It's hard to get reservations on short notice here. I'm impressed, Mr. Kavanagh." Liam smiled to himself, glad he'd impressed her.

They entered the restaurant and within minutes they were following the hostess to their table. As they did, Liam realized several men in the place had their eyes on Maggie. Jealousy rippled through him like a wave, and he glared at each of them. He quickened his step and pressed his hand into the small of her back. He knew it was a possessive move, but he didn't care.

Ever the gentleman, he motioned for her to sit and pushed in her chair. As Liam sat down, he watched as she looked around the restaurant and the waitress asked if they would like anything to drink. Liam looked up to see the waitress staring at him. He looked to Maggie to see if she had any recommendations. Maggie had a small smirk on her face as she said, "Anything Merlot."

Liam told the waitress to bring their best Merlot. The waitress lingered just a few seconds too long and Liam wondered if there was a problem. Maggie looked at the young lady with a smirk. "Well, run along sweetheart, we're only getting thirstier by the second."

The waitress walked off and Liam saw Maggie shake her head. "She was watching you like she wanted to take a bite out of you."

"What are you talking about? She just asked about the wine and waited for our choice."

"No, she asked *you* about the wine and her eyes never left your face. And she lingered because she was hoping you'd look up and notice her. Geez, you probably get that all the time and just don't realize it."

"Maggie, all my attention was on you, not the waitress. And if we're taking notes, you probably didn't even realize that at least five men checked you out as you walked in.

That guy over there in the red shirt even got a slap from his wife for looking your way," he explained.

She laughed. Liam wanted to hear more. "Ah, so *that's* why you manhandled me as we walked in. Not sure if I'm a fan of the strategic pawing, but I guess I understand. I'm not usually aware if people notice me. I mean, I don't seek attention." She flushed slightly.

"First, that wasn't even close to a manhandling. When I do, you'll know it. Second, men throughout the ages have always staked their claim. I know that makes me sound like a caveman, but not doing so means some other schmuck will just waltz right in. Please forgive my instincts to make sure these men knew you were with me," he grinned.

Maggie laughed again, and it made him want to just stare at her all night. He was just about to continue to make her laugh when the waitress came back and poured their wine. This time Liam made a point of looking at her to see if she was showing any sign of interest as Maggie had claimed. She took their order and the whole time Maggie spoke, the waitress never once looked at her. Her focus was on him. *Damn.* Maggie was right. As the waitress walked away, she did a backwards glance at him.

They both picked up their glasses and clinked them as Maggie said, "Wow, she's only got eyes for you, city boy." She smirked and took a sip of her wine. "But hey, it's not like I haven't played second fiddle before. Plus, you already know what I think about how you look, so I can't blame her."

Liam watched as she bit down on her bottom lip and then winked. He was taking a sip of his own wine and almost choked. After coughing and wiping off his face he smiled and blushed. He wasn't expecting the wink. The waitress arrived with their salads and Liam chose not to look at her this time. Maggie should never feel like she's second fiddle to anyone.

They talked about all kinds of things, starting with where each of them had gone to school while growing up in New Orleans. Maggie had gone to high school in the Garden District, while Liam had gone to one in Mid-city. As they talked about the people they knew and places they had been, Liam wondered why they'd never met before. However, in a city with a population ranging between four-and five-hundred-thousand people, maybe it wasn't so hard to believe. It's funny how life works. They grew up in the same city, but fate had not brought them together until now.

Their meals were fantastic. Maggie had the Cajun Cioppino and Liam settled on the linguine and manila clams. They both agreed the bread pudding they had for dessert was amazing. As they sat sipping their wine and discussing their time at university, Liam couldn't believe all the things that Maggie had accomplished and how hard she'd worked to get where she was.

Thinking about her life, he saw the roots she had here and the pride in her job, and the contributions she had made within the community. It made Liam feel like he was missing something in his life, like there was something just out of his grasp. "I wish I could be as happy as you are in your job." Liam watched as Maggie's eyes grew big.

"By the sounds of what I heard today, I thought you loved your job?" she asked, perplexed.

"I did in the beginning. I mean, I love what I do, but the traveling is getting tedious. Don't get me wrong, I've been to some amazing places, but it would be nice to be in one place for more than a week or two at a time. Most of my friends are at the stage of having kids and buying houses, and I'm still flying around the world."

Maggie leaned across the table. "Tell me something. If you quit your job tomorrow, what would you want to do? I mean besides take a week to just lie around all day and binge on your favorite Netflix action series. What else do you feel passionate about?"

Liam smiled and looked away. She would probably think it was stupid, considering what he did now. "The work I do as part of the restoration aspect is my favorite. But, it's never enough. I've always wanted to be the one to do the actual restoration, you know. Getting in there and getting my hands dirty, not just overseeing other people's work. Being able to go into a building and restore from top to bottom would be amazing. When I was in university, I worked on some construction jobs to earn money for school and I loved it."

Maggie hadn't looked away from his face the whole time he'd spoke. "That sounds amazing. What's holding you back?"

Liam grimaced and shrugged. "It was hard to change as I'd started down one path and then altering it seemed impossible. I chose the career I wanted and followed it through. Now I'm not sure it was the best decision."

Maggie nodded. "I understand. There was a time when I wasn't sure if my choice was the right one. But I love my job now and I'm good at it. However, sometimes you need to step back and figure out if it's still what you want."

He smiled and loved the way the lights made her eyes shine. He was just about to ask if she was up for a stroll around the Quarter, when a man walked up to the table and stared right at Maggie.

Dressed in olive color chino pants, saddle strap brown loafers and a cream color cotton button-down shirt, he looked sharp. His hair was dirty blond, which was all one length to his chin. Liam watched as the man leaned down and said, "Maggie May, is that you? Long time no see, sunshine!"

Maggie looked up at the man and a smile broke across her face. She was up and out of her seat in a flash wrapping her arms around the man. "Bobby Joe!" As they hugged Liam wondered if this guy was someone she'd dated. Maggie pulled away from Bobby and looked over at Liam. The man then turned to Liam and he could see the heat in this man's eyes.

He'd been trying not to pull another caveman move, but the look in this guy's eyes was making it hard. Liam stood up, a small frown creasing his forehead. "Maggie, introduce me to your friend."

The guy's eyes went wide as he smiled, showing all his very white teeth. His eyes roamed over Liam with appreciation. Um, that was unexpected.

"Oh Liam, this is Bobby Joe. Bobby, this is, ah, my boyfriend, Liam."

Boyfriend? OK, he was now very curious about this little white lie.

"Boyfriend? Damn Maggie, you would nab this sexy slice of pie, wouldn't you? That is a total shame girl. I think he is far too good looking to be straight. It's a good thing you told me before I started hitting on him. Liam, if you ever change your mind and want to switch over to the dark side baby, you look me up." Then he winked at Liam.

Bobby pulled back and gave Maggie the once over. "But it's no wonder he's all starry-eyed for you. You are smokin' hot in that dress. Is that from Roxanne's boutique? The color is perfect on you. Liam, don't you think so?"

"Absolutely, she looks gorgeous." Liam let his eyes roam over her.

Bobby Joe's eyes lit up. "Wow, that voice sounds like warm caramel, all sexy and sweet, isn't it Maggie?"

She smiled at Liam and he could tell she was loving this whole situation. "Oh yes, I believe Grandma referred to it as 'smooth bourbon'."

"I've always said your Grandma is one of the smartest women I know. How's she doing?" Bobby Joe asked.

"She's doing really well. Her doctor told her to take it easy, but you know what she's like, stubborn as a mule. She knows I am worried about her though, so she at least tries for me."

Listening to Maggie talk about her grandmother he could see the absolute love and adoration she had for her. It was nice to see this side of her, like a stolen glimpse of something private.

"Bobby, I thought you moved up to Baton Rouge. What brings you back to New Orleans?"

"I got some gigs lined up down here, so I'm back. I'm playing over at the Spotted Cat on Thursday night. You and Liam should come on over for a drink."

Before Liam could say anything, Maggie spoke up and said, "We'll see what we can do."

"You do that, sunshine. I would love to have you come and see us. Then I can secretly covet your boyfriend as I play. You know Stan would love to meet him too."

Maggie laughed. "Oh boy, do I. I can't make any promises, but if we're available, we'll drop by."

Liam smiled too. Looked like he might wrangle another date with Maggie, which was more than fine with him.

"Well, Maggie, my girl, I must get going. So much to see, and so many men to do. If you're coming, shoot me a text." Bobby looked at Liam. "And Liam, it was my pleasure to meet you. Don't be a stranger around town now." He winked again and was gone.

The two of them returned to their seats, and he stared at Maggie. She just smiled as she picked up her wineglass and downed the last few swallows. He didn't rush her; he just let her take her time. When she finished, she leaned towards him. "Guess you're wondering why I lied."

"Maybe, a little bit." Liam watched as her eyes danced with mischief.

"Let's just say it was for both our benefits. It saves me from Bobby Joe trying to set me up with all his relatives and straight friends. And I just saved you from having him hit on you, hard. Since he thinks we're together, he knows you're not interested in men and I am blissfully attached. See? Win-win."

Liam couldn't help but laugh. "Then let me say thank you very much. I guess it should flatter me." He shrugged and Maggie laughed.

Once the check was paid, they made their way outside. The whole evening was wonderful, but he didn't want it to end yet. However, he also knew she had a busy week and didn't want to keep her out too late.

Driving back to her place, she talked about how she'd met Bobby Joe. He'd worked at the hotel restaurant while he played at bars and nightclubs. It sounded like Bobby was talented and was starting to make a name for himself.

Liam pulled up out front of her house and turned off the car. Looking at the front porch he wondered if he would see Margaret again.

"If you're wondering if you'll have to answer more questions, she's out tonight. My grandmother has many suitors and I believe it was her bowling night with Hank." Maggie gave him a warm smile. "Thank you so much for the dinner, Liam. I guess I'll see you tomorrow."

She grabbed the handle and Liam panicked and said, "Wait. Let me walk you to the door. It's the least I can do."

"Oh, you don't need to. I can make it to my door alone. It's a nice neighborhood. I know every single person who lives on this street." She grabbed the handle again, but Liam wasn't going to give up.

"That might be so Maggie, but as I'm a nice city boy with deep southern roots, I wouldn't feel right about having you go to your door alone."

Maggie frowned, her forehead creasing. "You're pulling the southern gentleman's card? You haven't lived here in over twelve years."

"Ah, but a man should always remember his roots and his manners." Liam gave her his sweetest smile.

"Fine then, let's go." She huffed out a breath but remained in her seat.

Liam got out of the car and walked around to the passenger side. Opening the door, she got out and gave him a shy smile. She opened the back gate which had steps to the second story. At the top, there was a small deck with two lawn chairs and a small table. He could imagine her coming out here in the mornings with a cup of coffee, before the sun got too hot, just enjoying some quiet time, listening to the sound of the city as it woke.

She looked at him and cleared her throat. "Thanks again for dinner."

The soft glow from the moon highlighted her hair and made her skin look luminescent. She was exquisite. As he watched her, he had the strangest sensation, like he'd looked into those eyes before. It was an overpowering sense of déjà vu. But it wasn't possible, he had just met her.

He stepped towards her and she looked up into his face. Her sweet smell surrounded him and he watched as she licked her lips. Those beautiful, full lips. He knew if he kissed her she would taste exotic and he craved it more than his next breath. As he looked at her face, her mouth opened and he decided that was enough of an invitation.

Cupping her face in his hands and stroking his thumbs over her cheeks, he leaned in and kissed her. Her lips were so soft. Pulling back, he rubbed his lips back and forth over hers, loving the friction. Then he took the kiss deeper and ran his tongue along her bottom lip. A small moan escaped her and he could feel his blood heat. Taking one hand away from her face, he pulled her closer. Maggie responded by wrapping her arms around him, pressing up against him.

Liam could feel her breasts as she leaned in and his dick thickened. It had been a while since he had been with anyone, so the taste and feel of her made his senses go crazy. She was an amazing kisser and the way she moved against him was pure sin. Walking her backwards two steps he leaned her against her door and their kiss continued, deeper and more demanding. He felt lost in her and, God help him, he did not want it to end.

Somewhere off in the distance a dog barked, and it seemed to pull them both back to reality. He gave her one last lingering kiss, then stepped back so he could see her face. He watched as her tongue came out and licked her bottom lip, as if savoring his taste. It almost made him want to reach for her again.

"Well, that was... Yeah, um... I'm gonna... go. You know, gotta get up for work in the morning." She turned and opened the door.

He wasn't sure what it was, but she drew him in. She'd ignited something in him which he'd never felt before. Just seeing her move away from him, he wanted to pull her back into his arms. But she was already across the threshold. "Good night, Maggie. I'll see you tomorrow."

She nodded her head and let the door close. He felt like he could fly. His heart was light and as he went back down the stairs, he whistled the last song they'd heard on the radio before bringing her upstairs. Thinking about the evening, he wondered when he could see her again. Maybe he could talk her into going to see Bobby Joe on Thursday night. He hoped he wouldn't need to trick her into a date next time.

5

Peeking through her window, she watched as he trotted down the stairs. Oh. My. God! What had she done?! She knew she shouldn't have let him kiss her, but his mouth was *so* tempting. He'd looked so sexy in his black jeans and his dark grey button-down shirt, which emphasized his chest muscles. Every time he laughed or smiled; her heart melted. And that kiss was better than anything she'd ever experienced. When he'd rubbed his lips back and forth across hers and licked her bottom lip, her whole body had quivered right down to her toes. The smell and taste of him had her wanting to wrap her legs around his waist and yell, "More, please!"

Her grandmother had been right when she said he would be trouble. He was trouble with a capital T, and he was sexy with a capital Sizzle. She better try to limit their interactions to those related to work only. It was for the best. She shouldn't encourage him. He needed to focus on his project at the hotel, and she had plenty of work to keep her occupied. If he needed anything, she was sure Rosie or Genevieve could help him out.

She moved away from the door and went into the bathroom to get ready for bed. After such a busy weekend, she needed to get some rest. Maggie completed her evening routine and laid out her clothes for the next day. There was a conference starting on Wednesday and there were some last-minute arrangements which she needed to deal with. Maggie thought back to Liam and hoped he was enjoying his room on the third floor. Her own experience with their resident third floor ghost was much creepier than Rosie's.

It was her last year of university, and they scheduled her to work in housekeeping. She was working in one of the third-floor suites, bent over, scrubbing the tub in the bathroom. Turning on the hot water to rinse out the suds, the steam built in the room. The sound of the water hid the slight creak of the bathroom door closing on its own.

Humming to herself as she finished wiping down the tub, it took her a moment to realize that the room was thick with steam. Making her way to the door, she grabbed the handle and pulled. It didn't budge. Tugging hard, the door still didn't move. Maggie called out, "If this is someone's idea of a joke, it is *not* funny! Open the door!"

No voices or sounds came from the other side of the door. There was a slight tingle down her back, as if someone touched her. All the hairs stood up on her arms and as her breathing picked up, she whispered to herself, "Stop. You will get out of here. Now calm down." Her head turned towards the mirror, and words formed in the foggy reflection. Breathing in through her nose and out through her mouth, she could see the words,

He will come from afar for your heart.

She didn't understand what it meant, but at that moment

she didn't care; she just needed out. Taking a deep breath, she said aloud, "OK, Suzanna, I got your message. Please let me out." When she twisted the handle, it opened.

Thinking back to that day she realized Suzanna hadn't meant to scare her; she had just been giving her a message. Every time she'd been in that room since, she wondered what the spirit had been trying to tell her.

Maggie crawled into bed and set her alarm. Her mind was all over the place today. Thoughts of Emeline, Suzanna, and all the strange dreams she'd been having. She was sure a psychologist would have a field day with her. And it wasn't because she was having dreams about spiders or flying or even showing up naked at work. Her dreams had seemed almost like memories. She would be in a strange time and place, and her feelings were real in each dream. The pain and sorrow were tangible. Many times she had awoken with tears on her cheeks. There were also times she would wake up flushed with passion, her body trembling from a dream encounter with a lover. The emotions were genuine, and it was as if she'd lived it all. But it wasn't possible.

Curling up on her side, she hoped she'd sleep the whole night. She was just getting comfy when her phone chimed. Sighing, she unlocked the screen and saw Liam's name.

Hey Maggie, I just wanted to say thank you for the fantastic company tonight. Looking forward to moving in tomorrow. Sweet dreams.

She couldn't help but smile. Why, oh why did he have to be

so adorable? It would be much easier to stay away from him if he was an asshole. Shaking her head, she texted him back.

It was my pleasure, Liam. Pleasant dreams, see you tomorrow.

Pulling up the covers, she smiled to herself, thinking about how much she loved Liam's eyes. Before she could lecture herself on needing to stay away from him again, she fell asleep.

* * *

Her heart raced as she ran through the field. Panic rose within her, keeping her moving away from her home and ever closer to where she needed to be. The sun was just setting, and the shadows crossing her path made her fearful that she'd been caught. The leaves of the cane plants slapped against her skin, making it sting and burn. But she couldn't stop — no matter what. She had to keep running! Before the night fell, she needed to see him.

Continuing through the fields, she made her way to the back of the neighboring farm. She crept along the back of the barn and hoped no one saw her. This was against the rules. They told her not to go, that something bad would happen, but she didn't care. She needed him.

Hiding beside a barrel, she crouched, waiting for darkness to fall. He'd sent a message telling her to meet him here. As she sat, her whole body trembled with fear that anyone other than Tomas would find her. She leaned against the barrel, feeling the fatigue set in. Running her hand over her stomach, she could feel the mound she'd been trying to hide. It was getting harder every day.

Lydy knew they'd broken the rules. They could never be together.

She was the property of the man who owned the plantation she worked on. And he'd been forcing her to be with him. Mr. Blake was a married man, but he liked to have her do things. He hadn't forced himself into her yet, but she was sure it would happen soon. If he found out she was with child, he would be angry. Mr. Blake had told her many times how she belonged to him.

But her Tomas meant everything to her. They'd known each other for many years when he'd been working at the Blake farm. That was, until Mr. Blake saw Tomas and her together. He'd sold him a week later. The night after Tomas had moved away, Mr. Blake had beaten her and told her if he ever caught them together he would kill Tomas. She'd tried to stay away for Tomas's sake. She would never forgive herself if something happened. But he came and found her one night to talk, and they'd been doing so ever since. Mr. Blake had gone away three months ago for business and she'd met with Tomas. That night he told her he loved her, and he wanted them to be together.

Lydy loved being held by him. Touching his ebony skin, his hands caressing her. He'd made her feel things she'd never felt before. When she looked into his eyes, she could feel how much he wanted her and she couldn't deny him anything. His hands glided over her body and every part of her longed for him to touch and taste her. He was generous and sweet. Tomas told her he wanted to be with her, and she told him yes. It had hurt when he entered her, but the pain eased away and all she knew was him. The way he kissed and loved her body that night was more than she could have ever dreamed.

When they went their separate ways at the end of that evening, she missed him something terrible. When her bleeding didn't come, she knew something was wrong. She'd been listening her whole life to women talk, and she'd learned what it meant when you had a baby growing inside.

Now she needed to tell Tomas. She hoped he could help her, tell her what she should do. Lydy'd never told him about what Mr. Blake made her do. He would be angry, and she didn't want to risk him doing anything. She'd kept it to herself as it would do neither of them any good.

Hearing a faint rustling sound, she pushed herself as low as she could. When a hand reached out and stroked her cheek, she almost screamed. A hand covered her mouth, "Shh, sweetness, it's just your Tomas."

Turning, she wrapped her arms around his neck and breathed a sigh of relief. He returned the embrace and held her tight. She was overjoyed to be here with him, her heart filled to bursting. Tomas pulled away and held his finger to her lips to let her know she needed to be quiet. They made their way back into the field by the light of the moon and walked a short distance so they could talk.

He touched her shoulder, then pulled her against his chest. "I'm glad ta sees ya, Lydy. It's been too long. But why did ya risk comin' ta sees me?"

She reached up and stroked his cheek, and he held her hand to his face. Just knowing how much he cherished her touch had her heart breaking. Now that she was here to tell him, Lydy was unsure. What if he got angry and pushed her away? She couldn't bear it. But she couldn't hide it any longer.

"I needs ta tell ya something." She paused, not wanting to speak.

"Lydy, what is it? Ya can tell me anythin'." He rubbed his thumb over her cheek and she could feel the tears fill her eyes.

"Please, don't be angry." She took a deep breath, stealing herself for the rejection. "I'm with child, Tomas."

He seemed stunned for a moment, and she braced herself for the worst. She could only wonder what he thought. Was he going to hate her for letting this happen? What would she do if he pushed her away? And how was she going to be with Tomas when she knew Mr. Blake would never let her go?

She worried when his silence continued, but then he looked down at her stomach and dropped to his knees. The moon shone down on him as he pressed his cheek to the slight mound of her stomach. "Oh Lydy. Ya carryin' my baby." Then, he pulled her down to hold her close and kissed her.

"Lydy, I'm gonna tell Mr. Johnson. He's a good, kind man. I'll tell him. I'll sees if he'll buy ya from Mr. Blake. He's a good family man, Lydy. Let's me ask him if he would do it for me. Mr. Blake knows I'm gonna be free soon, but I's can stay to do extra time. He'd let me do that, Lydy, so's we can be together. You havin' my baby."

Leaning back, he rubbed her stomach. Tears streamed down her cheeks, and happiness filled her heart. This was better than she could have hoped. He wanted them to be together. But as he held her, she realized she hadn't told him everything.

"Tomas, I needs ta tell you somethin' more. Master Blake won't sell me." She had his big hand in hers, rubbing her fingers over his calloused palm.

"I'm sure Mr. Johnson, well he be willin' to pay good money for ya. I'll tell'm how hard a worker ya are. He'll pay for ya."

Shaking her head, she looked into his face, the moon gleaming in his dark eyes. "Master Blake... well... he toll me I could never leave."

"Why'd he say that, Lydy? You gonna be free someday."

"Oh, Tomas, he won't. He... he... toll me so. He likes me." She swallowed, trying to clear the lump in her throat. "He likes ta... touch me. He says I belong ta him and I won't ever be able to leave."

Tomas was quiet- too quiet- and she regretted telling him. But he needed to know that it wouldn't be as easy as asking Mr. Johnson. She leaned forward, her voice urgent. "Tomas, he toll me if he saw us together, he'd kill you. Tomas, I'm so sorry. Please, I don't wantcha to die! I'll tell him when I went to visit mama, someone grabbed me and forced me, but I don't see who. I won't tell him it's you, Tomas."

He was still and hard, like a stone. She didn't know what he was thinking, but it scared her.

"Tomas, please speaks ta me. I needs ya safe. Please." She took his hands and brought them to her face, and more tears filled her eyes. The happiness she'd felt just moments ago seeped away, like rain into the soil under her feet. Now, she was forced to watch it all slip away because she wouldn't risk him. Tomas looked at her then, a lost look in his eyes. Her heart broke further, and she had no way to make this easier for either of them.

The anguish in his voice broke her. "Lydy, he's been touchin' you? Why didn't ya tell me? He can't be doing that, Lydy. It's not right. You're mine. I'm your Tomas. And you havin' my baby." He pulled her face closer and she could see the tears in his eyes. "I won't let him touch ya again, Lydy. Ya can't go back there. That's my baby."

She cried as he pulled her in tight against his chest. This was harder than anything she'd ever suffered through. All the long, hot days in the field, all the times she'd gone hungry, and all the beatings she'd lived through. They were nothing compared to not being able to be with him.

They heard rustling through the cane plants and someone whispered, "Tomas, ya gotta git outta here. There's a man from the farm down yonder lookin' for ya. He's yellin' that ya stole one of his..."

A young boy burst through the canes and came to a halt. He stared at the two of them. "Tomas, is this here Lydy?"

"Gilles, where dis man?" Tomas pulled Lydy with him as he stood.

"He's up at the big house. He toll Mr. Johnson he was comin' ta git her back. I thinks you should run, Tomas." Gilles was wringing his hands, looking between Tomas and Lydy.

Lydy turned to him and nodded her head. "Yes, Tomas! Run and hide. Make your way ta the swamps. I'm gonna go back. If I go back, he won't come for you no mo'. I'll say I was visitin' Arita, and I lost track."

Tomas looked at her, anger on his face. "No, Lydy. You're with child. My child. I won't let ya go back there, ta that man." Grabbing her hand, he started walking towards the big house. Gilles struggled to keep up and protested as they moved.

"Tomas, don't go back there. He's lookin' for ya. He looks wild angry. You gotta go. Go hide like Lydy said, just till he ain't lookin' for you no mo'," Gilles said desperately.

"Gilles, he can't have her back. She's carryin' my child. I needs to tell Mr. Johnson." Tomas was walking straight towards the plantation owner's house, determination in his stride.

The statement seemed to stop Gilles from saying anything further. Lydy panicked, knowing Mr. Blake would see Tomas and her together. Tugging her hand, she tried to pull away, but she felt weak. She didn't have the strength to get away and run. Coming up to the main house, she could see torches and lanterns had been lit. Many people watched from their small homes. Women were standing on the front porches, holding babies on their hips. Little children were holding on to their mother's legs, wondering what all the noise was about. She started feeling sick, sensing something bad was coming.

As they walked up, Mr. Johnson was standing there, looking at

Tomas. "Tomas, Mr. Blake is out front. He's sayin' you stole his slave. Is that right?" he asked gruffly.

Still holding her hand, he looked right at the man and said, "No sir. I never stole her. She and I are goin' to get married. She's carryin' my baby."

"Tomas, this might be a problem. Mr. Blake is furious, and he thinks you stole her," Johnson said, looking back over his shoulder towards the front of the house, concern written on his face.

"Mr. Johnson, do ya think you could buy her? I'll stay here and work for ya for as long as ya want. We just wanna be together, ta be a family," Tomas negotiated.

Mr. Johnson looked at Tomas with understanding and pity. He was just about to answer when there was movement coming from the side of the house. Mr. Blake rounded the corner, and he looked like he was out of his mind.

"You bastard, get away from her! She's mine!" His words sounded slurred, and Lydy knew he must have been drinking. When he drank, he often came out to find her. Mrs. Blake must have gone to bed with one of her headaches. Now he had come looking for her. She never should have come here.

Tomas didn't back down. He stood his ground as Mr. Johnson raised his hands. "Now, John, I'm trying to get this sorted. Why don't you just wait and I'll bring her back?"

"I'm not waiting a damn minute. He took what's mine." He spat back. Mr. Blake was so angry his face was red and saliva clung to the corners of his mouth.

It was then Lydy saw the rifle and her body went cold. As if in slow motion, Mr. Blake raised the rifle and pulled the trigger. Tomas had no time to react. The shot pushed his body back into hers. His weight pulled her down, knocking the air out of her lungs.

She could hear Mr. Johnson yelling, and several men were running. Once she pulled herself free, she could see Tomas, a gaping hole in his stomach. Scrambling forward, she grabbed the bottom of her long skirt and tried to press it into the wound to stop the flow of blood. She wrapped her arm around his shoulders, pulling him up, but he was a big man and there was no way she could hold him.

His hands trembled as he touched his stomach and looked as if he wasn't sure what had just happened. Then he turned his face towards her. More people came running up to him carrying torches, while others were pressing more cloth to the wound. Looking into her eyes, he said in a raspy voice, "Lydy, take care of our baby." He tried to reach up to touch her face as he said, "Mine always." His head slumped to the side; all life leaving his dark eyes.

Shaking him as hard as she could, she yelled, "Tomas! Tomas! Come back. Don't leave me, please! Oh God, no. No, no, NNNNOOOO!" She cried over and over, her heart shattering. As people tried to pull her away from him, she screamed.

* * *

"Oh God, Maggie, please wake up! Oh Lord, this must've been a bad one."

Tangled in her sheets, body shaking, and face soaked with tears, Maggie struggled to pull herself together.

"Magpie, sit up now. Let me get a damp cloth. Look at me baby, that's it. There's my girl," Margaret said, soothingly.

Coming to, Maggie watched as her Grandmother shuffled into her bathroom and came back with a cloth and a glass of water. "Honey, drink this down now. You were screaming so loud your throat must be raw."

Maggie took the glass in her shaking hands and drank it all. Her grandmother was right, her throat hurt.

"OK, there you go. Let me have that glass." Grandma sat on the edge of the bed and wiped her face, just like she'd done many times over the years.

Taking the cloth, Maggie finished cleaning up the streaks of tears off her face and took her first full breath since she woke up. Shaking her head, she couldn't believe how real the dream was. They all seemed real, but this one had been terrible.

"Maggie, I know you don't want to talk about it, but sweetheart, this has been the worst one. I've heard you before. You wake up talking or crying sometimes, and this is an old house. I can hear you through the air duct in my room. Oh, don't look so worried. If I know you're up here with someone, I cover it up. But honey, this is scaring me. I know you don't want to, but you need to see her. Emeline says the time is coming, and she needs to see you." Margaret explained.

Shaking her head, Maggie said, "Grandma, please, not this again. What is she going to do? She'll pull out her creepy chicken leg rattle and make me one of those weird *gris-gris* bags that smells like a wet dog. Then, she'll want to come here and hang stuff around our house, warding off evil spirits." Maggie shook her head again.

Her grandma looked at her with raised eyebrows. "You better not let her hear you say that. She can help you, babe. That's all she wants to do, is help."

Pulling in a deep breath, she blew it out. "Let me think about it. I just want to get back to sleep, if I can." Maggie said.

"How 'bout I get you some warm milk?"

Maggie shrugged and nodded her head. It couldn't hurt. Her grandmother smiled and pushed Maggie's hair away from her face before making her way to the kitchen. When they'd renovated the upstairs, they made it into an open concept so you could see the whole apartment, except the bathroom.

"How was your date?" Her grandma used the last of the milk to fill a mug and put it in the microwave to heat. She must have known Maggie would not talk about Emeline anymore.

"It was nice," she said nonchalantly. Maggie straightened her sheets from the twisted mess they'd become from the dream.

"Just nice? By the looks of that boy, I would think it was better than nice," Margaret said. There was nothing getting by this woman.

"It was fine." She didn't want to talk about Liam and the way her heart flip-flopped when she thought of him.

"Oh, come on now, Magpie. That boy was hotter than a Louisiana summer! And from what I could see, he was quite charming. So, unless he was a total bore on that date, it must have been better than nice or fine." Her expression indicated she knew there was more that Maggie wasn't telling her.

Rolling her eyes, she said, "OK, fine. It was great. He's funny, interesting, smart, kind, sweet. He's everything a girl could hope for. And he's leaving soon. He's not someone you could forget. Liam is the guy who sneaks into your daydreams and sets up shop. Then you can't get him out of your head."

Looking over, she saw her Grandma smiling at her. "He kissed you, didn't he?"

Maggie rolled her eyes again. Of course her grandmother would ask that. "Yes," she said reluctantly.

"And..." Grandma's eyes sparkled with mischief.

"It was amazing. He cupped my face and stroked my cheeks, and it felt incredible. When he touched his lips to mine..." She put her hands over her face, thinking back on the kiss.

"Oh my! He is trouble, isn't he?"

"Yeah." Her Grandmother made her way over with the warm mug and sat back on the edge of the bed. Maggie took a few sips of the creamy milk, letting it settle in her belly and spread its warmth.

"So, what's your next move, Magpie?" Her grandmother fussed, tucking Maggie's hair behind her ear.

She shrugged. "I think I'm just going to steer clear of him. I'll help him with the things he needs for his report and then when he's finished, he'll move on and go tour the world looking at other old buildings."

"Life is hard sometimes, isn't it? Baby girl, you have overcome many hurtles. Looks like there's more to come." Standing up, she leaned over and kissed Maggie on the forehead.

"Try to get some sleep. I'll see you later."

"I'll try, and thanks Grandma."

"Anytime. Oh, and Magpie, I hate to tell you this, but from the look on that boy's face, there ain't *no way* you're gonna shake him. He's already in it... with both feet." She winked at Maggie and giggled. She closed the door that took her downstairs.

Maggie sat and sipped her milk and thought about what her grandmother just said. Well, she couldn't control his feelings, but she could control hers. If her plan was to steer clear, then she would. She thought about his dreamy blue eyes and she almost lost her resolve. If she couldn't hold it together when she was alone in her room, how the hell was she going to do it when they were together?

Finishing her milk, she set the mug on her nightstand and turned off the light. She would need more rest if she was to fight off the delicious man she would no doubt see a lot of over the next couple of days.

6

Liam strolled into the hotel around nine-thirty the next day. He'd taken his aunt out for a nice breakfast to thank her for having him, and then she dropped him off at the hotel. He told her they would get together for dinner one night before he left to go back to New York.

After he checked in, he looked around the lobby but didn't see Maggie anywhere. He shouldn't have expected to, as he knew she was a busy woman. He'd track her down later. Taking the elevator up to the third floor, he found his room.

It was impressive. She must have given him the nicest room on the floor. It was a living room suite, complete with a sitting area, a large fifty-inch television and a huge desk. It was a corner suite with a view of the main road and another window facing the alley. All the furnishings were rich in texture and color. Walking into the bedroom, the large king-sized bed dominated the space. Being a tall man, he appreciated a big bed. He unpacked his suitcase, then laid out his work supplies on the desk with the printer he had requested. Connecting his laptop and laying out his files, he felt ready to get started. He hadn't dressed in anything fancy as he wasn't sure where his review might take him. Keeping it casual, he was wearing jeans and a button-down shirt.

Portfolio in hand, he made his way to the lobby and over to the front desk. Genevieve, as the name tag stated, was sorting through some paperwork as he walked over. Her eyes settled on his face as she smiled. She was a pretty girl. Sunny, blond hair, warm brown skin and a friendly smile. "How can I help you today, Mr. Kavanagh?" she asked.

"Mr. Kavanagh? That's my Dad. Just call me Liam," he said smoothly.

"OK, Liam, what do you need help with?"

"Who would I see about getting access to all 'authorized personnel only' areas?"

"Oh, you'll want to go down to the security office. If you walk down the hall to the left, you'll see some administrative offices. The last door on your left is the security office. Nelson is our head of security. If you're looking for access or information, he's your man," she said.

Liam smiled and thanked her. Following her directions, he came upon the security office and knocked on the door. A large black man with wide shoulders answered the door, a stern look on his face. He had short cropped hair with grey at the temples. His security uniform looked pressed, and his shoes were shiny. Something told Liam this man had probably been in the military at some point.

"Can I help you?" His voice was gruff as he looked Liam over.

Liam held out his hand. "Hi, I'm Liam Kavanagh. I'm doing a structural assessment on the hotel. They told me you were the man to see about getting access to restricted areas of the hotel."

The frown left the man's face. He took Liam's outstretched

hand and shook it firmly. "Yes, Ms. Rivard told me to expect you. I'm Nelson Bernard. Come on in. It's not spacious up in here, but we make do." He ushered Liam inside.

Liam walked in and could see the banks of monitors against the wall. As he watched, he could see many areas on display. The main entrance, valet area, lobby, reception desk, the front and back parking lots and delivery area. There was also a screen facing down the hall where Maggie's office was. As if his thoughts had called to her, she stepped out. The screens were all in black and white, so he couldn't see what color she was wearing, but she looked amazing.

Nelson told him a bit of the history of the hotel. The other security guard came in and Nelson took Liam on a tour of the hotel. When they got down to the basement, a chill ran right down Liam's spine. The basement itself was fine; there were sections for storage areas and utility blocks, with a designated portion for underground parking. But he got a weird vibe, like someone was watching them.

"You feel it too, don't cha?" Nelson was watching Liam's face. "You can feel the change in the air down here; the heaviness of it. Lots of the staff flat out refuse to come down here. It's not my favorite place in the hotel."

"Do you have any stories to go along with the eerie feelings?" Liam asked, though he continued to feel anxious as he looked around.

Nelson smiled and nodded. "As the story goes, back over a hundred years ago, there was a man who was a gambler, a drunk and a notorious womanizer. There was a casino in the basement and a bar upstairs in the hotel. He would go to the bar and drink, then come down here to gamble. One night, he came down for a poker game. He wagered over his bank roll and lost. An argument broke out and he got stabbed. The women who work here are skittish to come down here. Some have even said they've felt hands touch them. A young girl who used to work in the catering office came down here about a year ago. She ran screaming upstairs. After that incident, Maggie changed the storage areas upstairs so that no one needed to come down here. Well, except for electrical and maintenance."

Leaving the basement, they covered more areas of the hotel. Nelson was knowledgeable and had a story about everything and everyone. Liam enjoyed spending time with him, and he knew he'd be coming back to ask questions again. He said his goodbyes to Nelson and went to grab a bite to eat at the restaurant. Liam had compiled a list of reports and documents he wanted to look at, so he went to find Maggie. Ever since their kiss last night, she hadn't strayed far from his mind.

Walking down the hallway to her office, he stopped in front of her door. He knocked and heard her say 'come in'. Opening the door, he saw her sitting behind her desk. With papers spread across the top and the phone up to her ear, her fingers flew over the keyboard. He walked in and took a seat in front of her desk. Her distraction allowed him time to watch her. Her hair was down today, brushed poker straight. As he looked at her face, he could see the dark circles she'd tried to cover up. But even with the tired eyes, she was a beautiful woman and his blood heated just looking at her. "Yes, I understand. Let me look at our bookings and we'll get back to you. OK, I'll try my best. Talk soon. Bye." Maggie made a few more notes on her computer, then clicked her mouse. Taking a deep breath, she turned her attention to him and gave him a genuine smile.

"Liam, how are things going? Finding everything you need?" she asked.

"Yeah, it's been great, and Nelson has been fantastic. But I was wondering if you might have time to go for a coffee, or maybe even get some dinner tonight. I would love to pick your brain about a few things."

He could have just asked her the few things now, but he wanted to have another opportunity to go out with her. Liam watched as she looked away from him and back to her screen. "That sounds lovely, but I'm swamped. I also have a committee meeting tonight that I can't miss," she said.

Shot down at point blank range. Ouch. He thought it best not to push. "No worries. We can chat at some point tomorrow if that works. Although, I'd love to take you out again."

She laughed, but the humor didn't reach her eyes. "Is there anything you need for your report?" she asked.

"Yeah." He opened a folder and pulled out a sheet of paper. "Here's a list of documents I'd like to look at. If possible, I'd like to get them by the end of tomorrow."

As he watched her look over the list, he tilted his head to the side. "I don't mean to pry, but are you feeling all right? I mean, you look tired. Sorry, that's not to say you look bad, just tired."

She looked up from the list and shook her head. "I'm fine, just have a lot on my mind."

Jokingly, he said, "Might any of it be about me?"

Her smile was tight as she said, "I have a lot people on my

mind, Liam. I have a hotel to run and people depend on the decisions I make."

Liam winced. "Sorry, I was just joking Maggie. I've spent most of the day looking around your hotel, and I can tell how hard you work. If it helps you sleep better, everyone here thinks the world of you."

She looked apologetic as she said, "No, I'm sorry for my rudeness. It's been a long day, and it's not finished yet. I'm just cranky. Thank you for sharing what my employees said. I'm very lucky to have such great people to work with."

He nodded. "Let me get out of your hair. I've got some email and stuff to do. See you tomorrow."

She looked over at him and nodded. "Yeah, I have to go soon. I'll get those documents pulled together for you. Have a good night, Liam."

He walked out and decided he would work on his notes from today. He also needed to do some follow-up emails on some other projects. It might be a good idea to try the gym at the hotel to work off some of his sexual frustrations too.

* * *

After finishing some work and going for a workout, Liam went back to his room to shower and order dinner. He flicked on the TV and watched the news and some random sitcom while he ate. As his eyes grew heavy, he decided to go to bed. Stripping down, he crawled into the big king-sized bed. Within seconds he was out.

Sometime later he awoke. Sitting up, he looked around to see what had disturbed him. As his eyes adjusted to the darkness in the room, he saw nothing until he looked towards the window. There stood a female figure wearing a maid's uniform. There was a light glowing from within her, which illuminated her face. Her long hair was loose and seemed to float around her shoulders. All the hair on Liam's neck stood on end as she stared at him. The apparition moved toward him and looked Liam right in the eyes. "*She needs your help. The gilded hunter will destroy her.*"

He'd run away the last time he'd encountered a ghost. This time, Liam was a man, and he wanted some answers.

"Who is she, and who is trying to destroy her world?" he demanded. He held his breath as he waited for her to answer.

Suzanna stood silently until she started fading away. "*She is of the river*," she intoned.

How could Suzanna have known this wasn't the first time he'd heard that phrase? That was the same verse said to him when he was twelve. Heaving out a sigh, he muttered, "So not helpful." Lying back on the bed, he thought back to the two ghost encounters. How could they have been speaking of the same person? This made no sense at all. Maybe he was mistaken about what they'd said?

Frustrated and unable to fall back asleep, even though the clock read four-thirty, he got up. No sense laying there staring at the ceiling. He might as well be productive. He got showered, dressed, and made his way down to see if he might get some breakfast.

The hotel was eerily quiet at this time of the morning. There were no carts or housekeeping staff out and about, and even the lobby was vacant, except one desk attendant. He made his way to the restaurant, but found the doors closed. *Damn.* Maybe he could sneak in the back.

Following a hallway around, he saw a door which looked promising. Opening it, he saw ovens, stainless steel counters and refrigerators. The smell of fresh-baked bread drew him in further.

"I'd ask if you were sleepwalking, but the drool on your lip makes me think you just followed the smell."

Liam turned to find a tall black man with a white uniform and a chef's hat on. He had a big smile on his face and very shiny eyes. He walked over and looked at Liam with curiosity and held out his hand. "We haven't met yet, but I've seen you round here. Liam Kavanagh, right?"

Liam shook his hand. "Yeah that's me. If we haven't met, how do you know me?"

The man laughed, a booming sound which reverberated throughout the kitchen. "Nothing happens in this place I don't know 'bout. Plus, Nelson gives me the scoop on everything."

Liam nodded as the man spoke again. "I'm Urbain Valcour, head chef here. And by the growling sounds your stomach is making, I'm assuming you're looking for some food?"

"Yeah, I woke up early and thought I'd get up and get some work done. But my stomach had other ideas." Placing a hand over his stomach, Liam hoped Urbain took pity on him.

"The restaurant doesn't open for a while, but come on over here to the back, and I'll sees what we can rustle up for ya."

The two men wandered back and as Liam sat, Urbain got out a frying pan and a few ingredients. Liam let his eyes wonder around the large kitchen. Stainless steel counters stood in rows in the middle of the room and appliances lined up against the walls like military soldiers just waiting for their time to serve. The kitchen gleamed and shined, and he could tell Urbain ran a tight ship.

"You up for an omelet?" Urbain asked, smiling at him.

"An omelet would be fantastic. Thanks."

"OK, one deluxe omelet coming up. The deluxe means whatever I have in the fridge to throw in." Liam laughed, and watched as Urbain mixed and diced and whipped everything together. The hot pan crackled as he poured the mixture in. Next, he dropped bread in the toaster, and a plate and butter appeared. Liam was amazed at the efficiency of the man, and the smell of the omelet had him almost drooling.

Urbain plated it up with a side of toast and a cup of coffee. Then he dropped into a seat across from Liam and sipped his own cup. "You're doing a report on the hotel, I hear," Urbain said.

Between bites, Liam said, "Yeah, Mr. Guidry hired me to assess the hotel. It's a great place. Nice people, too. It must be a great place to work?"

"One of the best I've worked in, and I've worked in some amazing places. Now, Mr. Guidry is not what you'd call... nice to the working folk. In fact, I don't think he's ever spoken to anyone in the hotel, except Maggie. He's more worried about the bottom line than the people. But Maggie, now she's the one who cares. She's about the nicest, sweetest person on the planet. She cares 'bout all of us. It helps she's worked here while she went to school. She knows this place inside and out. Not only that, she is generous. Supporting any cause and not just because she feels she should. She does it because she wants to."

Liam raised his eyebrows. He wasn't expecting to get the

lowdown on Maggie, but he'd take it. Leaning forward he asked, "What things does she do?"

"You name it. She donates her time to several children's charities and goes at Christmas time to the hospital and gives out gifts. She goes at least twice a month to the soup kitchen over on Rampart. Pitched in all she could during the Katrina clean up. The list goes on. She's generous with her time and her money. Everyone loves her.... here."

With the last statement, he realized Urbain was telling him something. "So, is this the part where you tell me I best not be interested in taking her anywhere?"

Urbain smiled and shook his head. "You're a sharp one. I won't lie; the rumors are flying because you took her out to dinner. Nothing but nothing gets by the employees of this hotel, especially when it comes to Maggie. But you look like a smart man. I'm sure even you can see how much people love her."

"I agree she's done a great job with running the hotel. She's efficient and has a head for the business. And I don't intend to take her away from here." Liam replied as he rubbed his fingers along the top of his coffee mug.

"So what are your intentions, if I might ask?" Urbain had a questioning look on his face.

"To be honest, I don't know. I know I enjoyed spending time with her the other night. She's funny, smart, easy to talk to. I won't lie, I think she's beautiful; her eyes can draw you in and take your breath away. The first time we met she just blew me away," he said earnestly.

Looking at Liam with a frown, Urbain shook his head. "Oh boy, sounds like you got it bad, son."

Liam smiled and shrugged. "I can't say I've been trying hard to resist either," he said.

Urbain laughed a big belly laugh and said, "And how does she feel about you?"

"One moment I think I'm gaining ground, the next she's pushing me away." He wished he knew how she felt.

Standing up, Urbain took Liam's plate and cup. "Well, Liam, as long as you don't take her away, I'm gonna root for ya."

"Good to know. Hey, I have a question for you? Have you ever had an encounter with the ghost on the third floor?"

Coming back over, Urbain said, "I haven't had reason to visit any of the floors in my line of work. I know a lot of the housekeeping staff have and some kitchen staff who deliver room service have. Nothing bad though. They see her in the hall, looking like she's cleaning. But that's it. Why, you see her?"

Liam nodded. "Yeah, I think she woke me up this morning. Or hell, I don't know what woke me, but I think it was her. She spoke to me."

Eyes going wide, Urbain leaned forward and whispered, "What'd she say?"

"She said 'she' will need my help, and then something about a gilded hunter destroying her. I don't understand what it means. I don't even know what woman she is talking about or who the gilded hunter would be."

Urbain just looked at Liam and cleared his throat. "If I was you, I'd see a mambo. Maybe she'd be able to tell ya why this spirit spoke to you. In all my time here, I don't think she's spoken to anyone else. But don't ignore the spirit; she is trying to tell ya something important."

Liam thought about this and nodded. "Well, I'll think about the mambo. I don't know what message she is trying to tell me. Maybe she's trying to tell me something will happen to one of the women in my family." Thinking his mother or sister might be in danger made his heart clench. He'd call them today and check in. Hell, maybe he'd check in with his aunt too, just in case. "Thanks, Urbain, for the breakfast and advice. I'll keep you posted."

"You do that, Liam. And I'm here most every day at four. If you get up early again, come on down and see me."

Liam waved and made his way out through the door to the restaurant.

While he and Urbain had been chatting, a few employees had come in and started their shifts. He made his way over to a small table by the window and opened the file he'd brought down to review, putting on his reading glasses.

The conversation with Urbain kept playing on his mind. Should he see someone about the encounter? He wondered why he was the only one she'd talked to. Shaking his head, he decided that it could wait. What he needed now was some quiet and another coffee. Waking up at four-fifteen meant coffee would be his best friend today.

7

As Maggie drove to work, she reflected on the conversation she had last night with her best friend. Lola called right after she got home from her charity committee meeting. After waking up crying and not being able to fall back asleep, exhaustion was setting in. But when she answered the phone in her usual greeting for Lola, she didn't let it show. "Yo, Yo, Lo Lo! You better not be calling to tell me you're not coming home. I don't care how big your commanding officer is, I will take him down."

She could hear her friend laugh. "Hello, Magnum. I'm not calling to tell you anything of the sort. I just thought you needed a call from me."

The voodoo blood ran deep in the genes of that family. "Now why would you think I needed you to call me? I'm doing just fine. Not that I don't love hearing your voice," Maggie said. Now, she might have been able to pull this off if she hadn't yawned the biggest, noisiest yawn right into the phone.

"Really, you're fine? Is that why you're yawning at nine-thirty? The Maggie Rivard I know is a night owl and never has a problem staying up."

"The Maggie you know is getting old and needs her beauty sleep."

Maggie could almost hear the smirk on Lola's face as she said, "Oh yes, you need your beauty sleep, because I hear someone's got a new beau?"

"No, no, and no! He is not my new beau, he's not my new anything except a colleague. There is nothing going on." Maggie should have known she couldn't get off that easy.

"Now I *know* something is going on because you're too adamant. If you thought it was nothing you'd say, 'Lolo, I'm just havin' me some fun'. But here you are, spouting denial, and that throws up a big red flag for me, Magnum. I should inform you my Mama told me all the dirty deets on Mr. New York hunk. All six feet, dark hair, blue-eyed, stubble-faced, bourbon-voiced, handsome yumminess. Those were my mother's words, not mine. She said when you walked out of the house it stunned him into silence. Mama also mentioned that back in her day, if a boy looked at a girl the way he looked at you, he'd get arrested." Lola said with a hint of a laugh in her voice.

Maggie rolled her eyes at the comment. "First, it *is* nothing. We're working together for a week, maybe two, and then he's leaving. Second, I think your mama might be a cougar, or whatever animal name they have for elderly ladies who eye up younger, attractive men."

"You admit he's attractive?" Maggie could hear the smugness in Lola's voice.

Damn her! Lola should have been a lawyer instead of a soldier; she could always slip her up. "Fine, yes, he's attractive. OK, more than attractive, he's super sexy and muscled."

There was a gasp on the other end of the phone. "You kissed him, didn't you? I know you did, I can tell."

Lola knew her better than almost everyone except her grandmother, so she might as well answer. "No, he kissed me."

"OOOOOHHH, was it THE kiss? The one that starts with soft caresses and slowly simmers in your belly? Or was it a back-of-the-head grab with lips locking and passionate fireworks?" Her best friend was a notorious lover of love. She loved romance novels and sappy romance movies. Maggie figured it was because Lola's army career was so serious and violent that she needed the soft outlet.

"If you must know the details, he cupped my face and rubbed his lips over mine, then kissed me." Maggie rubbed her fingertips over her lips as she remembered the amazing kiss.

"Oh my God, it was *the* kiss! It sounds amazing. When are you seeing him again?" Lola was breathless.

"At work, tomorrow, which is the only place I will see him from here on out. There's nothing there to pursue. I have my world, and he has his. I don't want to talk about him anymore," Maggie said, adamantly.

There was silence on the phone until Lola said, "OK, let's talk about something else. I hear your dreams are getting worse. You can't resolve this on your own, Maggie. I'm worried about you. You need to talk to her. You know Emeline talks to my mama every day. She's saying the time to do something is *now*."

"Hey, want to talk about Liam again?" Maggie did not want to talk about Emeline.

"Nope, too late. Just tell me why you won't see her. The truth, Maggie, no jokes."

"The truth? Fine, I don't believe in destiny. I don't believe something, or someone controls my life path. If I see her, she'll tell me things I don't want to hear. I'm not saying past lives are not a thing, but I don't want to believe this is how it works for me."

"Oh Maggie, did you hear yourself just now? You first said you don't believe, and then you switched to you don't *want* to believe. This tells me that somewhere in the back of your mind you believe. You're just too stubborn to accept it. Look, all I will say is, I love you like a sister, and I don't want anything bad to happen to you. If you love me, you'll see her. This is important, Mags."

Hanging her head, she knew she would have to say something to appease her friend. "I love you; you know I do. You were the only girl in first grade who ever picked me to be on your team. Even though you knew I was total shit at baseball. For that, you have my undying devotion. What if I say I'll think about it?"

"Fine, guess I have to settle for that. Anyway, I gotta go. I need to fit in a quick call to Mama or she'll fret. Take care of yourself and I'll see you soon. Goodbye, Magnum PI. Love ya."

"Stay safe and keep your head down. See you soon, Lola Loon. Love you, too."

After the call, Maggie crawled into bed and had a fitful night's sleep, filled with dreams about floating in a wooden boat down the bayou. Spanish moss hung down, brushing over her face, and alligators watched her with gleaming, evil eyes from the shore. She'd woken up tangled in the sheets again; thinking cottonmouth snakes were crawling on her.

Now, here she was in her car, wishing she had a bucket of coffee or three more hours of sleep. She faced another full day, and Nelson messaged her last night to tell her he wanted to see her this morning.

Pulling into her spot, she got out and pulled her purse and briefcase from the passenger side. Just as she closed the door, her eyes landed on the restaurant window, and there sat Liam. He was looking through a file, making notes and drinking coffee. He was wearing khaki pants and a light blue, button-down shirt, which she knew would make his eyes look even more dreamy. She also noticed he was wearing glasses. Liam could pull off the Clark Kent look for sure. Hmm, she wondered if he looked like Superman under the button-down. No! She would not think about it. She needed to get her mind on her work, not on what was under Liam's shirt.

Maggie was about to look away when he looked up and saw her watching him. He pulled the glasses off and waved. She waved back and smiled; she was right about the shirt. He waved at her to come in. She gave him a shake of her hand and motioned to her wrist, saying she had to go. Pouting out his bottom lip, he looked so adorable her heart melted into a puddle. Feeling bad, she held up her hand to tell him he could have five minutes. The smile he flashed her was devastating, and she almost changed her mind. This was not helping her resolve to steer clear of him.

Maggie came right into the restaurant. As she walked up to Liam's table, a sense of déjà vu came over her, like she'd done this before. Shaking her head, she said, "Morning Liam. How was your first night?"

His smile turned into a slight grimace, and that worried her. She hoped whatever went wrong with his night wasn't a problem with his room.

"The room was great, and the bed was like a dream. But... Suzanna paid me a visit. I couldn't sleep after that. However, I got to have breakfast with Urbain, and the omelet was amazing."

"I'm so sorry about Suzanna. I can move you to another floor if you wish?" Maggie said.

Liam just laughed. "No, it's fine. Say, do you want to stay and have a coffee with me?"

"Wish I could, but I have to get to a meeting this morning. Sorry."

"No worries, I know you're busy. Maybe later?"

He looked hopeful, but she had work to do. "We'll see. I'll finish pulling the documents you requested and have them dropped off later." she said.

"That would be great. Thanks," Liam said.

She turned to walk away, but looked back over her shoulder and gave him a little wave. Yep, she needed to keep her distance from him. It was for the best. He wasn't someone she would get over easily. She had enough scars on her heart and there was just something about him, she knew, that would leave a hole in it.

After dropping off her things in her office, she went to see Nelson. She knocked and walked right in, knowing he'd seen her coming down the hall.

"Morning, Nelson. What's going on?" she asked.

Nelson was sitting in front of what Maggie liked to refer to as the command center. She always felt like she was in a war bunker with all the monitors. "Morning, Maggie. Thanks for coming to see me. I thought you'd want to see this." He pointed to a screen, and as he tapped a few keys, the scene changed to a timestamp of one thirty this morning.

As she watched, a car pulled up, but it kept to the shadows. A figure exited the car and then disappeared. Nelson tapped a few more keys, and the camera switched to the one at the back of the hotel. The figure crept along the far wall until it reached the set of back doors. Then, the person jammed what looked like a crowbar into a seam of the door. Dressed in dark clothing and a face mask, they kept their face away from the camera. Maggie wondered if the person was familiar with the hotel.

Nelson turned to her. "Maxon went right out when he saw the guy. No one was there when he stepped out. He checked the door. It has a few marks on it, but nothing too bad. Once he came back in, he checked the footage. The guy must have heard him and run. There was no sign of the car and the camera didn't capture the plate number either. He called the precinct and reported it. Officer Beauregard said he'd follow up. Speaking of the officer, he told Maxon to tell you not to be a hero. If anything comes of this, they'll handle it. Sounds like he was none too pleased with your help the other night."

Maggie rolled her eyes. "Sometimes treating people with kid gloves doesn't get the job done. Plus, that woman had her poor husband bleeding all over the lobby floor."

"I would appreciate you staying safe, Maggie. Leave the law enforcing to those who get paid to do so." Nelson gave her that 'I know what's best,' look.

"Yes, I know, and that's what Kenny said too," she grudgingly replied.

Nelson raised an eyebrow. "You know, I think he still fancies you."

Maggie laughed and shook her head. "That ship has sailed and will never come back to port, Nelson."

He held his hands up. "I know, I know. Just keeping you informed. Seems like maybe you have eyes for someone else now?" he hinted.

With an incredulous look on her face, she said, "Nelson, please tell me you aren't gossiping about me! It was *one* dinner. That's it. No story."

"That might well be Maggie, but I don't mind tellin' ya that his eyes light up at the mention of your name... every time. And that's not gossip; its fact."

"OK, but the fact remains, it was *one* dinner." Maggie turned to head towards the door. "Keep me informed if the police find anything."

"Will do, Maggie. And if that dinner turns into two... I won't say another word about it." Nelson waved and Maggie went back to her office. Geez, they were all just a bunch of gossiping hens.

Thinking back to the events at the hotel last night, she wondered what the individual was trying to do. They had some attempted break-ins before, but this one bothered her. Crossing the lobby, she heard her name being called and turned around to see none other than Officer Beauregard striding across to her. She faked a smile as he approached. This was not what she wanted to deal with right now.

"Hey Kenny, I just finished talking to Nelson. It looks like there was no real harm done, but do you have any updates?" she asked.

"I'm just finishing my shift and I thought I would come over and check in. No updates yet, but I'll keep you posted." He smiled at her and stood just a little too close for her liking.

"I just left Nelson in the security office, so if you..." she started.

Moving his arm, he brushed his palm along the side of Maggie's hand. "Yeah, I'll go back in a minute. I was wondering if maybe you might be free for dinner this week? After tomorrow, I'm off for the next three days. I'd love to get together with you."

"Oh, ahh..." Her mind whirled for any excuse.

She felt a hand on her lower back, as Liam said, "Sorry Officer, I'm pretty sure she has plans, right, Mags?" Maggie didn't know if she wanted to punch him or kiss him for interfering, but at this moment, she was leaning towards a kiss.

"That's right. We have plans. Oh sorry, let me introduce you. Officer Kenneth Beauregard, this is Liam Kavanagh. Liam's a structural engineer doing some work for Mr. Guidry. He's here from New York."

"New York? So what, Maggie, New Orleans doesn't have enough guys for you to date so you have to go out with Yankee strangers?" Kenny's smile disappeared and frown lines creased his forehead.

Before she could tell Kenny to mind his own Goddamn business, Liam piped in, "I was born and raised here. Mags and I go way back. Our families go to the same church. And Maggie's grandmother and my aunt are on several church committees together. Yeah, we've known each other for years." Maggie hoped that Kenny bought the bunch of bullshit that Liam had just laid out.

Kenny cleared his throat and moved back two steps. "Oh, I see. Sorry Maggie, I didn't know you were seeing someone. I'll talk to Nelson and keep him informed. See you later."

She could see the hurt in his eyes as he moved away. Guilt stabbed her in the heart, but she knew they could never be a couple. He just didn't make her heart sing. Turning to Liam, she said in a low voice, "Thanks for saving me. He's my ex-boyfriend, and I'm not looking to rekindle anything." Liam smiled, and her heart melted again. *This* guy was someone who made her heart sing. Too bad he wasn't staying.

"Anytime. I'm always available to ward off unwanted suitors. That way it keeps the field open for me." He winked and turned toward the elevators.

Maggie stood there as her mouth fell open. He turned back and said, "Maggie, I'll be in my room when you're ready with those reports." The elevator doors opened, and he disappeared inside.

What had just happened? He just hit on her again, right in the middle of her hotel! Turning, she huffed out a breath and went back to her office. She needed to stay away from him. Her new plan was to pull out the reports and have Rosie or Gen take them to him. With those eyes and that smile, she knew it was dangerous for her to be anywhere *near* him alone. She was on a mission, and nothing would stop her!

* * *

Saying and doing were two very different things. By the time Maggie got the reports pulled, it was six-thirty and her day had gone by in a whirlwind of phone calls, emails, and meetings. Now, as she printed the last of the reports, there was no one she could ask to deliver them. She would have to go up there and do it herself. OK, Plan B; she would just do a quick drop off and get out of there as fast as possible.

Knocking on the door, she was ready with her plan of dropping and bolting before he could ask her in. It took a minute for him to answer the door, and when he did, she couldn't believe what she saw. Liam was wearing a pair of black track pants, which hung low on his hips. That was it, except for the towel wrapped around his shoulders. All the exposed skin and tight abs drew her eyes, and she struggled to look away. This guy worked out, and boy, did it show.

"Hey Maggie, come on in, I just got out of the shower. I tried out your fitness center again. It's got great equipment. Let me slip on a shirt. Be right back," he called, on his way to the washroom.

So much for my plan. The naughty girl in her wanted to yell out, 'don't put on a shirt on my account', but it was for the best if she wanted to stick to her plan.

She walked into the living room and strategically sat in the armchair. This way he couldn't sit beside her, tempting her. Yeah, this was a good plan.

"Thanks for bringing these up for me. I'll look at them tonight and figure out if I need anything else. How was the rest of your day?" Liam walked out of the bedroom in a blue T-shirt that showed off his impressive physique. She had an urge to run her hands all over his chest so she could memorize it.

"Oh, ah, fine, you know... busy day. Sorry I didn't get these to you sooner," she said.

"No problem at all. I had some follow-up reports to do

from another job. Hey, I was just about to order something to eat. You want to stay and have dinner?"

Looking at him now, all relaxed and laid back, her heart was yelling at her to stay, but her head was telling her she couldn't risk being here with him. "Wish I could, but I've got a few things to do tonight," she explained.

He looked at her, and she could see the heat in his eyes. Yeah, she needed to leave before he ended up talking her into staying.

Clearing her throat, Maggie said, "Well, I'd better go. I'll see you tomorrow. Maybe I'll come early and we can have that coffee?"

She stood up and so did he. Moving around to the back of the chair to keep it between them, she said, a little too enthusiastically, "Yeah, coffee would work for me tomorrow."

He didn't say a word as he watched her move and followed her around the chair. She backed up, keeping the couch between them.

Liam tilted his head to the side and smirked. A knowing look came into his eyes, as if he realized she was keeping them a part on purpose. "I still have a f-few things to wrap up before I-I go." She stuttered as she beelined for the door as fast as she could, without making it too obvious.

Just as she was about to grab the handle, she felt him right behind her. She stood still and closed her eyes. The heat from his body was seeping through her silk blouse. The need to lean back and press against his chest was almost overpowering. But she knew she couldn't. Hanging her head, she said in a whisper, "We can't do this, Liam."

"Why not, Maggie? It's not like I'm working for you. We're like colleagues," he murmured.

"Still. There's something about you." She felt Liam sweep her hair away from her neck and her skin tingled from the touch.

"What is it about me, Maggie?" His breath caressed her nape and she could feel his lips soft upon her neck.

Groaning, she tried to concentrate on what she was saying, "You... you overwhelm m-me."

She shuttered again as she felt his hands run up and down her sides. "You overwhelm me too. The difference is... I'm not fighting it." He kissed her neck and rubbed his lips back and forth over the sensitive spot behind her ear. Then he whispered, "Don't fight it, Maggie."

His one hand wrapped around to her stomach and his fingers caressed her rib cage.

"You don't..." she gasped as his thumb rubbed along the underside of her breast, "... understand. I can't get attached to you."

"I think..." Another soft kiss along her neck, "it might be too late for me." Liam's words came out in a low growl.

He spun her around, pressing her back to the door as he claimed her mouth. Pulling her in close, he surrounded her. She could taste mint on his tongue as she pushed her fingers into his hair. Her breasts pressed against him, and her nipples pebbled from the contact. All she could hear was their heavy breathing. His cologne and the undertone of the soap he used drew her in; Maggie started thinking about touching her lips on all the spots where the scent clung.

She wore a flowing skirt and she could feel Liam gather

it in his hands. His fingers brushed over the bare skin of her thigh, and she felt almost drugged. He pulled her leg up and pressed his hard cock against her sex. Kissing him deeper, she pulled his hair, and she felt more than heard him growl. Breaking the kiss, his lips traveled down her neck.

As if coming out of a dream, she struggled to think straight. Realizing this was the exact opposite of her plan, she knew she needed to take back control.

"Liam, stop, please!" She drew in a deep breath, trying to calm herself.

He stopped right away, but still held her. Placing his forehead against hers, he was also panting.

Taking a deep breath, she said in a frustrated tone, "Why do you have to be so damn irresistible?"

He grinned. "You find me irresistible? That's good to know. Maybe I should try to persuade you with my irresistible charm to stay."

Laughing, she said, "No, I don't think that's a good idea."

He looked deep into her eyes and she felt like he was reading all of her emotions. Then, he gave her his panty-melting smile. "Fine, but come out with me tomorrow night. We can see your friend, Bobby Joe. It'll be fun."

"Liam, I can't." She was available, but that would go against her plan.

"Yes, you can. All work and no play will turn you into a boring old lady," he countered. She laughed again and looked into his eyes. He rubbed his thumb along her jaw as he whispered, "Come on, Maggie, you know you want to." He stuck his bottom lip out in a pout and looked even more adorable.

She could feel herself caving. Reluctantly, she said, "Fine. But, just to see Bobby Joe."

"Yes! You won't be sorry. I'll come and pick you up."

Frowning, she said, "We can go from here. Plus, you don't have a car.

He raised an eyebrow. "Don't worry about my lack of transportation. I've got it covered. And, I want to walk you to your door again."

"I don't think that's a good idea." Shaking her head, she knew that was a bad idea.

"Why? Don't you trust me?" His look was intense, and she almost wanted to cave.

"I trust you," Then quieter, she said, "I don't know if I trust myself."

Looking up into his eyes, she could see the heat simmering just under the surface. "Maggie, don't say stuff like that or I might not let you leave." Laying her hand on his chest, she pushed him away, and he let her. "I'll see you tomorrow."

She stroked his cheek with her hand, and he held it to his face. The move had her unnerved as it felt familiar and very intimate.

He reached over and opened the door for her. She walked out without another word. As she reached the elevator doors, she heard a faint giggle behind her. She turned around but saw no one there. Smiling to herself, she said out loud, "Well, Suzanna, hope you liked the show."

8

Liam tossed and turned. He should just take himself in hand and help relieve some sexual tension, but knowing Suzanna might show up, he decided not to. Thinking about Maggie and how good she felt was *not* helping matters. Remembering the warmth of her core through the thin skirt, he was lucky she'd stopped him as he might have embarrassed himself. He couldn't remember wanting anyone this much.

Just as he drifted off, he heard something. At first, he thought maybe Suzanna had come back. But looking around, he couldn't see anything strange in his room. Then a noise came from outside, and he got up to look out the window.

Down below in the alley, all he could see was darkness. Maybe someone was just parking down there. But there were no lights, and it hadn't sounded like a car. He waited, but heard nothing else, so he crawled back in bed. Lying back down, he drifted off to sleep again.

* * *

He was standing waist deep in the middle of a muddy, coffee-colored pond, bugs buzzing round his head. The sun beat down, scorching his skin, and he was thankful for the lukewarm water cooling him. Looking towards the bank, he saw a young blond girl wearing a pair of white pantalettes and a matching strapped chemise. The thin cotton was not much cover, and he could see the outline of her breast and the hard tips of her nipples.

She jumped into the water and swam across the small pond. Her blond hair pooled around her shoulders, the ends soaking up water like a wick. As she came closer, he pulled her to him and she wrapped her legs around his waist. She'd been unable to sneak away to see him the last couple of weeks, and he'd missed her. Pressing her body into his, he held her tight, loving the way they fit together. His member pushed against her, and she kissed his neck. The sensation felt amazing.

This was his Josephine, and he loved her more than anything. They'd been secretly seeing each other for over two months now. She was in her nineteenth year, while he was in his twenty-third. She was the most beautiful girl he'd ever met, with her sparkling grey-green eyes and a musical laugh.

As he kissed her cheek, he continued to press himself against her sex. He wanted to marry her, but her father forbid it. However, he refused to let go of his Josephine. She leaned into his ear and he could feel her warm lips as she whispered, "If he catches us, we'll be in trouble."

He didn't want to stop; it felt too good. Nuzzling her neck, he said, "Don't go yet. Just stay a little longer."

Looking down at her body, he could see the chemise clinging to her wet skin and the now almost transparent fabric outline of her breasts. He grew even harder. Reaching up, he cupped her breast and ran his thumb over the nipple, and it hardened further under his touch. What he wouldn't give to have her like he did the last time they snuck out.

She grinned at him mischievously as she said, "I can feel why you want me to stay, but he'll come lookin' for me." As he watched, she bit down on her bottom lip, and his heart melted. She lowered her hand between them as she said, "But a few more minutes shouldn't hurt?"

Before he realized her plan, she reached into his pants and took him into her hand. "Josephine, wait..., what... oh yes... that feels... good."

As she continued to stroke him, she kissed his neck and said, "Lucien, when can we sneak away for good? I want to leave this place and never come back. I want to be with you."

He could hardly think as she grasped him. She kissed his ear and sucked his earlobe into her mouth. With her breath in his ear, the warmth of her tongue and the way she would swipe her thumb over the head of his cock, she made it impossible to hold back. He groaned out as his orgasm hit and felt all his energy drain away. Drawing her closer, he kissed her deeper. She pulled away and gave him the sweetest smile.

All he wanted was to take her away from here. She should be his wife. Instead, her father would make her marry some banker's son. He couldn't bear to think about it. They would get away. All he needed to figure out was how. "I'm working on a plan. Just give me a few more days," he said. He kissed her and looked into her eyes. "I love you."

She nodded, and taking his hand in hers, she pressed a kiss to his palm. "I've got to get back before..."

Just then he could hear a man yelling. "Josephine Elizabeth, where you at?!"

The look of fear that entered her eyes made him want to grab her and run. She pushed him away and hissed, "Run up to the trees. Don't let him see you!"

Hating to leave her, but knowing he had to, he high-tailed it out of the water and crouched behind a large cypress tree. Josephine called out, "I'm over here, Father! I'm sorry. It was so hot I felt faint. I thought I would take a quick dip in the pond to cool off."

Lucien watched as Josephine's father broke through the trees. "You should know better than to go swimming here. There are snakes in these waters."

"I know father, but it's just too hot to wear all these layers. Just give me a few minutes and I'll head back up to the house. I just need to dry off." She smiled at him and then headed towards the tree where she had laid her dress.

"Don't be long. Your mother was asking after you. Hurry and get dressed now. You don't want to be late for tea."

"I won't. Be right there," she replied.

Lucien saw her father leave, walking back through the woods. He watched as Josephine went beside a tree and stripped off the pantalettes and chemise, then picked up a small piece of cloth. She dried herself off as best she could. He could see her breasts shift back and forth with the motion, and he wished they could have spent more time together.

She grabbed her dress and did her best to tie it up, then turned to look right at him. In a loud whisper that carried across the water, she said, "Meet me here, day after next. Twelve o'clock."

He watched her disappear into the trees and he resolved to figure out how they could run away. She was his, and he would let no one take her away from him.

Walking back over to where he dropped his shoes, he was slipping them on when he heard a sound behind him. As he turned, he saw Josephine's father, a rifle in his hands pointed straight at him. "Boy, I told you to stay away from my daughter. Are you some kinda idjit?

I can't have you comin' round here messing with her heart. I need this deal to happen. Now, I'm gonna make sure you never become a problem again."

Lucien felt the bullet as it slammed into his body, the force spinning him in place and knocking him to his knees. Gasping for breath, he could taste the metallic fluid as blood bubbled up his throat. He dropped to the ground, feeling the hard, packed earth and dried grass bite into his skin. Far off he could hear someone screaming his name over and over. It was Josephine. His Josephine.

"No! Father! No. Please, no!"

His eyelids grew heavy and his limbs felt like iron. He couldn't speak, and he could still hear her screaming. "Why Father? I love him. I love him. Lucien!!!" Then she was sobbing his name.

His body was so cold, his fingers and toes feeling brittle and prickly. He focused on the ground as blood pooled from his open mouth. At least he heard her say she loved him one last time. She loved him... she loved him...

* * *

Gasping, Liam sat up in bed, his body covered in sweat. Looking around, he found the covers piled on the floor. Touching the front of his boxers, he found they were cold and sticky, the result of having cum in his dream. Shaken, he went to the bathroom and climbed into the shower to wash the mess and sweat off his skin.

Rubbing his hand over the middle of his chest, he could still feel a lingering ache from the bullet. The dream was so real he'd felt pain. He hung his head; the hot water beating down his back. Breathing deep, the water helped ease his tense muscles. The feelings he had for the girl in the dream,

Josephine, they felt genuine. His emotions were so strong that he'd felt love for her, and how could that be? He didn't know her, but the way she touched and felt, it was as if he'd known her forever.

Shaking his head, he stood in the shower for a little longer, then turned it off. After drying off, he got dressed. Checking the clock, he saw it was seven-fifteen. The room still felt heavy with emotion from the dream, so he decided he didn't want to stay here right now.

He grabbed his tablet and files and made his way down to the restaurant. Maggie said she would come and have coffee with him this morning. If anything could pull him out of this mood, she could.

Sitting by the window like he did yesterday, he set himself up to work. A waitress brought over coffee and took his order for breakfast. He'd just started on his reports when he saw Maggie pull in. Watching her get out of her car, his breath caught in his lungs. Today she was wearing a sleeveless dark-blue dress, a small jacket draped over her arm. The dress fit her perfectly and, paired with the three-inch heels she wore, he could stare at her all day. After grabbing her bag out of the passenger side, she held up her finger, letting him know she was coming in. Smiling like a goofball, he motioned for the waitress to bring another coffee. He had caught on to Maggie's obsession with the life-giving elixir.

About ten minutes later, Maggie walked into the restaurant a file in her hand. God, she was sexy! He wanted to scoop her into his arms and devour her plump lips. The surprising need threw him, and he took a few deep breaths to get himself under control.

"Good Morning, Liam. Sleep OK?" she asked. Her genuine smile made his stomach do a flip.

"Oh, fine." His mind flipped back to the morbid dream, and he couldn't help the flinch.

She frowned. "That didn't sound very convincing. Is there anything wrong with the room? Did Suzanna bother you again?"

"No, no, she didn't bother me and the room is great, I just didn't sleep well. I woke up through the night and thought I heard something outside my window, but I saw nothing," he explained.

Maggie leaned forward and said in a serious tone, "At what time?"

He wondered why she seemed so concerned. "I think it was around two thirty. I got out of bed and looked out the window. It's hard to see down into the alley due to the windowsill, and it was pitch black. Why? Is there an issue?"

"We had an attempted break in the other night. I'll want Nelson to check out the cameras. If Maxon had seen anything, he would have notified me. He might have been on rounds. I'm just going to send Nelson a text about this," she said as she pulled out her phone.

Liam watched her complete a quick text, then she doctored her coffee before taking a sip. She closed her eyes as she swallowed, a happy humming noise coming from her throat. Liam swore he'd never found that action sexier than in that moment. She was so beautiful. Opening her eyes, she smiled, and Liam pulled himself together.

She took another sip before she said, "I was thinking about

tonight. I don't want you to have to go out of your way, so we can just leave from here."

He saw where this was going, and there was no way he was budging on his plan. "Oh no, I've already got this planned out. Are you trying to change this because you're scared to be alone with me?" he asked.

"No, I'm not afraid to be alone with you. I just didn't want you to have to come and get me."

"Maybe I want to come and see Margaret again." He tried to pull off an innocent look.

She laughed and smirked. "Oh, I get it. It's not me you're interested in, it's my grandmother. Well, I hate to break it to you, Liam, but with the number of suitors she has on the go, you'll have to get in line. Her social calendar rivals anything I've ever had."

Pouting, he tried to look sad. "That's disappointing. Guess I'll just have to settle for you then."

She gasped and leaned forward and smacked his arm. "I'd watch it if I were you. We'll see Bobby Joe tonight and if you're not careful, I'll tell him we aren't in a relationship. If you think he flirted before, that was only a sampling of what it would be like if he knew the truth," she mock-threatened.

Liam smiled at that. "OK, Miss Maggie, but just remember that if forced into a situation, I won't hesitate to prove my sexuality. After the kiss yesterday, I'm sure you know where I'm going with this."

Heat simmered in her eyes, and Liam wanted to grab her by the hand and drag her upstairs. He was glad to see he wasn't alone in his desire. "Touché, Mr. Kavanagh," she said.

They chatted for a few more minutes before she went back

to work. Looking down at the table where she'd been sitting, Liam realized she left her file. Standing up, he followed her when he heard a squeal from the front door.

"Auntie Maggie!" A little girl in dark brunette pigtails ran towards Maggie, her arms in the air wearing the cutest pink sundress. Maggie turned, and her whole face lit up. She scooped the little girl into her arms and gave her a kiss on the cheek. Liam looked back where the little girl had entered to find a woman and a small boy coming in. The little guy couldn't have been over two years old. He looked about the same age as his nephew, Jonathan. Watching, he saw him mimic the little girl and put his arms in the air and yelled, "Ana Ma!"

Maggie set the little girl down and crouched to the floor as the little boy ran into her arms. She held him as the boy put his tiny hands on her cheeks and kissed her. She kissed his cheeks, and neck and he giggled.

As Liam stood watching, he felt his entire world tilt. Watching Maggie hold the little boy, he felt something change. He wanted to be with her and have her face light up when she looked at their children. Just thinking about it, he could picture her with a swollen belly, pregnant with his baby. It was strange, but in his mind it was almost as if it had already been, like it had already happened. But the thought was ridiculous. Christ, he'd only shared a few kisses with her. Mind you, they were the most mind-blowing kisses he'd ever experienced, but still.

Closing the distance, he stopped and looked at the lady who stood beside Maggie. She had the same coloring and facial structure, but the lady had blue eyes instead of Maggie's grey-green. The lady looked over at Liam and raised her eyebrows. "Maggie, looks like someone is looking for you. And if a guy looking like that comes looking for me, I wouldn't keep him waiting."

Yes, she had to be related to Maggie's grandmother.

Maggie stood up with the little guy in her arms. "Oh hey, Liam, this is my cousin Delilah. The little girl is her daughter Maggie, or Little Mags as she's often called. And this little guy is Spencer. They're my Godchildren."

Putting his hand out to Delilah, he shook her hand and then got down on one knee to speak to Little Maggie, "Well hello Little Mags. How old are you?"

She looked him right in the eyes and said, "I'm five. I gots to go to kindersgarden this year."

"That's great. Do you like it?"

She shuffled her feet and shrugged. "It's otay. It's awful lots a work. And I have Logan Macey in my class. He's not too nice. He picks his boogers and tries to wipe them on my dress. Yuck."

Liam could hardly hold back the laugh, as he heard Delilah sigh. He looked at the little girl and in a serious tone said, "That sounds awful. Boys are gross, aren't they?"

She nodded enthusiastically. "The boys in my class sure are. But you seem otay. And you don't smell like they do. You smell nice. I think I'd like to be your friend," she said.

"I think I'd like to be your friend, too. How about a high five?"

He put up his hand, and she hit it. Then he stood up and held up his hand to the little boy. "How about you, little man, you want to give me a high five?"

The smile that spread across his face had Liam's heart melting. He held up his chubby little hand and hit it on Liam's, pleased with himself.

Maggie looked at him and smiled. Then, he heard Delilah clear her throat as she said, "Sorry to drop in on you this way, but I needed to talk to you. I was hoping to do it when there weren't little ears around, but I don't think this can wait."

Just then, Little Mags tugged on Liam's pant leg. When he bent down, she whispered, "That means it's big people stuff and I can't listen."

Liam smiled at her and turned to Delilah. "I was just sitting in the restaurant doing work. I could take them with me and then you can talk to Maggie."

Maggie looked shocked that he would offer. Delilah's face lit up as she said, "That would be great! I only need Maggie for a few minutes. Spencer has a doctor's appointment this morning."

"Sure, no problem. Take your time. He's the same age as my nephew. Come on, buddy, let's see if Urbain can get us a snack while we wait." Maggie set Spencer on the ground and he reached up and took Liam's hand. Little Maggie took his other one, and they walked into the restaurant. He'd always love kids with their unpredictable nature and curiosity.

Little Maggie looked up at him and said, "Do you think we could have scones, like a tea party?"

"Well, I think you might be in luck. I heard they have the best scones in the whole city here. If not, we'll get something just as yummy."

9

Maggie watched Liam and the kids as they walked into the restaurant. Seeing him hold Spencer's hand and talk to Little Mags, her heart swooned. How the hell was she supposed to stay away from this guy when he kept on doing things which made her want to jump his bones? Yeah, this was not good.

"Maggie, can I just say, coming home to a man who looks like that would not be a hardship. With looks like that, I wouldn't care if he left his dirty socks on the floor or left the toilet seat up. OK, maybe *not* the toilet seat part, but hey, I do have hard limits," said her cousin.

"Don't go reading into anything, Del. He's just here doing work for Damon and then he'll leave," Maggie said with a frown.

"And you're playing possum with your heart because you don't want to get it broken again. I've heard all about it. But Mags, look at him! Oh my, it would be worth the risk. He is the kind of guy that gives summer its sizzle."

They watched as he got Spenser seated in a booster seat as Little Mags sat down and talked Liam's ear off. He didn't even look frazzled. He listened to her with total concentration as he fastened Spenser in the seat. Wow, he was a natural. And wasn't that just her luck? She'd dated how many guys in her own city and never once been interested in pursuing anything long term with them. Now here comes this amazing guy who makes her heart melt, and he lives thousands of miles away.

Letting out a sigh, she turned and said to Delilah, "Let's go to my office while he has the kids distracted. My next meeting starts in about thirty minutes."

Once inside, she turned to Delilah and said, "Spill it. You never come to my work and want to talk in private."

She watched as Delilah bit her bottom lip and seemed on the verge of tears. "Oh God, Mags, I'm pregnant!"

Maggie let out a small happy scream and pulled her into a hug. "Why do you make it sound like a bad thing? You make beautiful babies. There's something more isn't there?"

Delilah nodded, still looking miserable. "Eric and I talked about another, but he just got laid off and we're not sure when he'll go back. And even if he went back, how the hell are we supposed to afford another baby? My job isn't stable, and this will add a lot of stress. I haven't even told him yet. What am I going to do?"

Maggie took Delilah's face in her hands. "First, you take a deep breath. That's it. Second, you will go home tonight, make your husband a nice dinner, and sit him down and tell him. I've known the man for almost ten years and I'm telling you he will be over-the-moon happy. He loves you more than anything. Actually, it's kind of sickening to watch. Third, you can't worry about this alone, that's why marriages are partnerships. And last, you have a wonderful family who will help you through this. We're here for support, and you know if you need any kind of help, we are there. How far along are you?"

Delilah tried to smile and said, "About twelve weeks. I had

this appointment for Spencer anyway and I called the office and they said they can confirm it today." Then, looking up at Maggie she said, "You're right, Mags. I'm sorry, I just panicked."

"No apology necessary, Del. I'm always here for you, whatever you need and so is the family, especially Grandma," she said reassuringly.

Delilah was Maggie's second cousin, but her own grandparents were gone. Her parents divorced and moved out of state when she'd turned twenty. They had more family, but she was closest to Maggie and her grandmother, and they would do anything for her.

"Don't breathe a word to her, please. I need to tell Eric first." Delilah squeezed her hands.

"I won't say anything. It's your news to tell." Maggie felt happy for her cousin, but part of her heart broke thinking she may never find someone to have children with. It was the one thing that would fulfill her life, but she wasn't sure if it would ever happen.

"Mags, you're no poker player, babe. You'll find someone, and someday you'll have news of your own to tell. We're Rivards; we come from great breeding stock. Your Mr. Right just hasn't shown up yet. Or maybe he has, and you're playing hard to get. Sorry to tell you, but the whole family knows about this guy. Grams was talking about him and word has spread. We even know about the date tonight," Delilah said excitedly.

Maggie rolled her eyes. "That's the last time I tell that woman anything."

"Oh, so you *admit* there is something to talk about then?" Delilah looked smug.

"Stop putting words in my mouth, Del. I don't know what this is. All I know is that if something happens with Liam, I think the heartache would be too much. You know my batting average is low, right?" she said sadly.

It was Delilah's turn to take Maggie's face in her hands. "With the way he looked at you just now, I'd say he's not like the others, Mags. He looks stable, kind, mature and super, crazy hot."

Maggie laughed at the last part. "He is crazy hot, nice, kind, interesting, funny and a bunch of other things I haven't discovered yet. If I chance it, what will I do if he breaks my heart?" she asked.

"Then I'll be here for you, and the rest of the family will be, too. You deserve so much more, Mags. No one deserves happiness more than you. Take a chance."

She shrugged and nodded. Maybe Delilah was right. If you didn't take chances in life, it would pass you by. But, she would take this slow, like, glacier slow. And if all that happened was a fantastic few days, she would find some way to live with it.

Walking back toward the restaurant, they saw at least a dozen ladies surrounding the table where the kids and Liam were sitting. It looked like she might have to beat off the locals if she wanted him. As they reached the table, they watched as Liam and Spenser fist bumped and, as expected, all the ladies swooned over the cuteness that was Spenser, and obviously Liam, too.

Delilah cleared her throat. "Liam, I see you've realized

what a chic magnet my son is. He has them coming in droves when my husband has him out. But twelve in fifteen minutes, it must be a record."

Maggie watched as Liam's cheeks flushed and she wanted to grab his face and kiss him.

"They've been great, Delilah. Hope you don't mind, but we had pancakes. They might be sticky." Looking at the kids she could see Little Maggie wasn't too bad, but Spencer looked like someone had dipped him in maple syrup.

"It's all good, Liam. I keep extra clothes in the car. I'll grab an outfit and a washcloth. He'll be good as new." Delilah left to get the extra clothes as the kids finished their pancakes. Maggie took the seat between Liam and Little Maggie. She leaned over and swiped an orange slice off her goddaughter's plate.

"Hey, are you hungry? I can get Nina over here." Liam's smooth, deep voice seeped into her and she wanted to curl up in his lap and listen to him all day. *Mmm*, Little Mags was right, he did smell good.

"No, I'll just share with Little Mags. You're good at sharing, aren't you, sunshine?" Maggie said.

Little Mags watched the two of them, curiosity clear in her eyes. Tilting her head to the side, she blurted out, "Yep, he's a keeper, Auntie Maggie. You look good togethers. Bet yous would have beautiful babies. At least dat's what great Grammy said. She also said that there was some ting special 'bout him, and if you turned down da chance to have sexes with him you were crazy. What is sexes anyway?"

Beside her, Liam choked on his coffee and Maggie's whole face turned beet red. "Oh well, it means... um, hmm how to explain it. It means... oh, look here comes your mom. Tell me, does Mommy know you heard her conversation with Grammy?" Maggie said, relieved to change the subject.

"Oh no, they was having tea on the front porch and I was colorin' in the sittin' room. They was talkin' low, but I still heard," the little girl replied, oblivious to the embarrassment she'd just caused.

Maggie nodded as Delilah walked up to the table. Noticing both Maggie's beet red face and Liam's smirk, her eyes went wide. "Oh God, what did she say?"

"I'll let her tell you. Just as a side note, she listens to whispers while she colors in her books."

Delilah gasped and put her hands over her mouth. Maggie watched as the color crept into her cousin's face as she realized exactly what Little Maggie told them. She dropped her hands and said, "I'm just going to take Spencer to the bathroom and get him cleaned up. Come on, Little Mags, you need a wipe too. We don't want to be all sticky when we go to the doctors."

Little Mags crossed her arms, sulking. "I don't need a wipe, I'm not a baby."

Liam piped up at that moment. "You are definitely not a baby, but we did have a lot of syrup on those pancakes. Plus, if you get cleaned up, I'll give you something special to take home with you."

"You will?" Little Maggie's eyes grew wide.

"Yep, but don't keep your mom waiting. Hurry along now." Liam's eyes sparkled as they watched them head for the bathroom across the lobby.

Maggie looked at him, curious. "If she comes back here and

you have nothing, she'll be very disappointed," she pointed out.

Liam *tsked*, "If it's one thing I know, it's kids. I'll be right back."

As she watched, he got up and walked out to the gift shop in the lobby. She lost sight of him for about ten minutes. Then he walked out with a little bag and looked pleased with himself.

"Well, what is it?" She glanced down to see after he sat and placed the bag under the table.

"No peeking. Since we have two minutes alone, I think we should talk about the interesting information Little Mags told us. Sounds like I've made quite an impression on your grandmother," he said slyly.

Maggie could feel the heat in her face again. Closing her eyes, she could feel his warmth as he leaned closer to her and whispered, "I'm just hoping you might think she's right and you're not crazy."

She opened her eyes to find him close. His one eyebrow rose, and he licked his bottom lip, looking like he might want to kiss her. Clearing her throat, she leaned back just as Little Maggie appeared ahead of her mother.

With a big smile on her face, she held up both hands. "See, Liam, I'm all clean!"

"Come here and let me check." She walked over and held out her hands. He took her small hands between his and rubbed them. He pulled his hand back and checked if they came away sticky. "Good job. Guess I better give you your surprise." He pulled out the bag and took out a little stuffed kitty and a little stuffed dinosaur. Little Maggie's eyes lit up as she accepted the kitty and held it up to her nose.

"Mmm, it smells like stwaberries. Tank you Liam!" She leapt into his arms and gave him a hug.

"You're very welcome. Here, give this to your brother," he said.

Spencer looked thrilled, too. Delilah looked at Liam and said, "You didn't have to do that."

"I know, but I wanted to." Liam smiled as he watched the kids.

"Thank you very much. We'd better get going. I'll talk to you later, Maggie."

Everyone came over to Maggie to exchange hugs and kisses. She loved seeing them; it always made her feel good. Looking over at Liam she said, "OK, I've got to go, I'm late for my meeting with Nelson."

"Wait, I have one more thing in the bag." He pulled out a dreamcatcher. It was a light tan suede heart with beautiful beaded webbing. A small little silver *fleur di lis* hung in its center. Larger beads hung in three separate tassels with small purple feathers at the end. "I hope it helps you sleep."

The gift touched Maggie. If he only knew what she was going through with her dreams, he would know how much it meant to her. "Liam, I love it. It's perfect." She reached over and gave his hand a squeeze.

"You're very welcome. If I don't see you the rest of the day, I'll see you at seven-thirty." He rubbed his thumb over her fingers and she stood up to go to her meeting.

Nelson was sitting at his desk and didn't look over at her until she closed the door and sat by his station. "Looks like you've had a busy morning. Those kids sure are gettin' big." He smiled at her, and she couldn't help but smile back.

"I know, they're growing like weeds."

"Looks like Liam was enjoyin' himself too. Did I see him give you a present just now?" he said.

Shaking her head, she replied, "Wow, you don't miss a thing here at your mega command center, do you?"

"No, I don't. That was awfully nice of him."

She smiled, still glowing with the happiness of their encounter. "Yes, it was."

Nelson turned and looked her in the eyes, as if searching for something. Huffing out a breath, he said, "I *knew* it. He's made you fall for him, hasn't he? *Damn.* I knew he was trouble when he walked in here the other day. He was too nice, and way too good lookin'. I just knew you wouldn't be able to resist him. Just promise me you won't do anything rash and run off with him," he pleaded.

Maggie laughed. "What are you talking about? I haven't fallen for him and I'm not running away from here. I love this place, you know that. My whole life is here in New Orleans."

He shook his head, "Oh Lord, she doesn't even see how far gone she is. I knew it would happen one day. A woman as beautiful as you wouldn't stay single foreva'."

"Nelson, I don't know what you're going on about, but I'm not going anywhere. Now let's get on with the reason I'm here," she said.

They chatted about her text and he'd reviewed the footage from last night, but there was nothing showing on the cameras. He was expecting a call back from the police department about the report he requested concerning burglaries and break-ins in the area. They also chatted about needing further security depending on what the report said. She would need to discuss this with Damon when she had the chance.

* * *

Leaving work at six, she stopped and got her items at the cleaners and picked up a few things at the little market. Back in the car, she made it home by quarter-to-seven. She jumped in the shower, washed up and did a quick shave; not that she thought he would touch her legs, but why chance it? A quick blow dry and she pulled her hair up in a clip. Applying some makeup and a few dabs of her favorite perfume, she was good to go. Looking at the clock, she saw that it was seven thirty-five. Damn, she was late!

Grabbing her little shawl, she did a quick check in the mirror. She hadn't gone to fancy. She was wearing a beautiful floral watercolor print skirt and a light-blue sleeveless top. It was just dressy enough for an evening out.

She put on her strappy sandals and opened the door that lead to her grandmother's apartment. Listening, she heard Liam's deep voice, and knew the visit would please her grandmother. She took her time just waiting to see if she could hear any conversation. Maggie should have known better.

"Come on down, Magpie. Don't be pulling a Little Mags stunt." At the mention of her goddaughter, she remembered everything the little girl had told them and she blushed all over again.

Walking into her grandma's kitchen had always made her happy. It was her favorite room in the whole house. With its white cabinets and old Elmira range, it always felt cozy and inviting. She remembered growing up, her and her grandma baking together and laughing over dinner. They were some of her most cherished memories. After her parents died, her grandmother had shouldered the responsibility of caring for her. Maggie could never repay her for all she'd done, but she would never stop trying either.

Looking over at the table, she saw Liam with a mug in his hand and some of her grandma's homemade beignets. He had icing sugar all over his bottom lip, and her first thought was that she wanted to lick it off. Liam looked good enough to eat. Dressed in jeans and a Hunter green golf shirt, he looked so handsome.

"This one definitely has a good appetite. He's downed five beignets in less than five minutes," Margaret said.

Both Maggie and her grandmother looked at him, and he just shrugged. He licked all the sugar off his fingers and Maggie looked away because even though the act was innocent; she knew her face would heat again if she watched. "What can I say? Those are the best beignets I've ever had. And they're still warm. Sorry Maggie, I might slip into a hot sugar coma before we make it to the bar." He smiled and winked at her.

Wow, he was charming the pants off her grandmother! He was smooth all right. Trouble, trouble, and more trouble!

"Magpie, are you and Liam going out for dinner again?" Her grandmother was smiling at Liam as she asked.

"No, just to see Bobby Joe and Stan at the Spotted Cat," Maggie replied.

"When was you planning on having supper? I bet you haven't eaten since lunch."

Her grandmother was always after her about eating. It

wasn't unusual to find dinners wrapped in foil in her fridge with notes stating, 'Eat This Now'. The best one was, 'Men don't like women with boney asses'. Yep, her grandmother had a way with words.

Before she could answer, Liam jumped in and said, "Not to worry, I haven't eaten either."

Her grandmother smiled at him. "All right then, as long as you take care a my girl. Don't wanna see her with no meat on her bones."

Well, that was great. Now she felt like a prized beef cow. She rolled her eyes, and Liam smirked at the gesture. "I'll make sure. Besides, I think she looks fantastic."

Her heart fluttered. Oh God, she was in so much trouble.

"Liam, if you're done gobbling down the beignets, let's go. I know a little place on the way," Maggie said.

"Oh Maggie, don't you dare take him to that greasy spoon. Good Lord, it's like a heart attack on a plate and enough grease to float a bayou boat on!" Her grandmother gave her a disapproving frown.

Maggie huffed out a breath. "Fine, we'll stop for pizza. You like pizza, right?"

"Is the Pope Catholic? I love pizza." Liam gave her a big smile.

She walked over to her grandmother and kissed her on the cheek. "Have a nice night and give Bobby Joe my love. I'm going out with Gladys. Don't know when I'll be home, or if I'll be home. Who knows, maybe she and I'll get lucky... at the casino," Margaret said grinning wildly.

"OK, be safe. Text if you need me."

Her grandmother cupped her cheek. "Just have a good time."

The evening had lost its heat, and the breeze felt good on her face as they stepped outside. She stopped short on the top step. "Oh. My. God! Where did that come from?"

In front of her house was a black Corvette Stingray C3 convertible. It was gorgeous, all shiny, sleek, and in pristine condition. She couldn't wait to go for a ride. Maggie looked at Liam and he seemed just as enamored with the car as she was. "My cousin Walker is a collector of old cars. He restores and sells them. This is on loan for the evening. She's a beauty, isn't she?"

"She sure is! Come on, let's go for a drive." She laughed and practically ran to the car. Running her hand along the side, being careful not to scratch it, she had a moment of pure automotive joy. She loved old classic cars.

Liam walked up behind her and placed his hand on her hip. He put his other hand on the handle but didn't open it. He leaned in and said, "I don't think I've ever seen a woman get this excited about a car. It is a very sexy quality."

She moved her head to look into his eyes. Yep, lots of heat in that look. Before she could stop the flirty comment, it just slipped out, "I'm full of all kinds of sexy qualities."

Moving closer, she heard him breathe in deep and brush his lips over her temple. "That almost sounded like an invitation, Maggie. If you keep talking like that, we won't make it to the Spotted Cat."

He was leaning down to kiss her, when she spotted her grandmother at the window. "Um, Liam, we have an audience."

"Oh, I know. Might as well give her something to tell Gladys." Then he gave her a slow, sweet kiss. The kind that made her toes curl and heated her body to the core. It was a kiss that promised more.

He pulled away and smirked at her. Once she was in, he looked back at the house and waved. She could see her grandmother smiling and waving back. Oh man, he was such a flirt, and it looked like her own flesh and blood was on his side.

Liam walked around and got in. Starting the car, she could feel that engine roar to life. Oh yeah, she loved fast cars. Watching him, he looked good behind the wheel. She looked around the interior and felt the supple leather under her hand. The bucket seats were in great condition, and she could tell that a lot of love had gone into this restoration. Rubbing her hand over the wood inlay on the door, she admired the details. "This car is amazing. Your cousin must be so proud of her. He will get some great offers, too," she said.

"Yeah, he said it would be hard to part with it, but that's part of the business. But she's ours for the moment. Let's take her for a spin."

10

Once on the Pontchartrain Expressway, Liam let the car eat up the road. Maggie laughed as her hair whipped around and she tilted her head back. It was wonderful to feel the wind and sun on her face. She hadn't felt this carefree in a long time. She looked back at the road and saw Liam look away from her. With her hair all windblown, she must look a fright. After a while, they got off the expressway and made their way back into the French Quarter. Liam parked the car in one of the premium lots just off Toulouse Street and put the top up.

Walking along Decatur Street, they turned and went into Louisiana Pizza Kitchen. Liam mentioned he'd been here many times as a kid. They ordered pizza and shared it while talking about people they knew. Liam found out he knew some of her relatives and friends. They were four years apart in age, but in all the time he'd lived there they'd never met.

Walking out into the warm evening, they enjoyed the sights and sounds that made New Orleans unique the world over. The sharp blast of a trumpet and the gritty growl of a saxophone accompanied them along the sidewalk. People hungry for good food and amazing music piled into restaurants along Frenchmen Street. The sun had long since set and she enjoyed being out among the crowds.

Liam slid his hand into hers, and she liked the warmth on her palm. It felt good, and she had the strange sensation that she'd held his hand before. Things felt easy with him. It was like every time they were together; it was effortless and familiar. She never felt like she had to say certain things or be a certain way. He seemed happy just being with her, and she enjoyed being with him.

They arrived at the Spotted Cat Music Club and made their way inside. It had always been a favorite place of hers. She'd seen many bands play and enjoyed coming here. Seating themselves by the bar, they could see Bobby Joe and the rest of their band. Now, watching them get ready, she was glad she came.

They got their drinks, and Liam shuffled her chair closer to him. He draped his arms over the back of her chair and rubbed his fingers along her arm. Leaning in, he kissed her temple. She was both moved and curious about what had brought on the wave of affection.

"OK, Mr. Kavanagh, what's with the manhandling again?" she said lightly.

Liam frowned. "I told you before, you'll know when I'm manhandling you. But if you must know, I'm doing us both a favor. They're watching us, and I am confirming our relationship," he said.

Maggie looked over at the band and noticed Bobby Joe and Stan watching them with curious stares and open interest. She also noticed that two of the other members of the band seemed to watch her. Deciding not to point out the obvious caveman move, she showed the whole band that they need not be interested. Looking up into Liam's face, she took in the dreamy eyes and full bottom lip and let herself go with the need she felt. Allowing, just for a moment, to take what she wanted and not worry about the consequences. "Here's one healthy dose of confirmation."

Reaching up, she rubbed her thumb along his bottom lip, then kissed him. Maggie tasted the beer he'd just taken a sip of and enjoyed the malty flavor. He was a great kisser, with the right amount of pressure and the perfect twirl of his tongue. Shifting towards her, he moved from her lips to kiss along her jaw until he reached her ear.

"Wow, anytime you want to confirm again, I'm all in," he murmured.

Laughing, she tucked herself against him and looked back to the small stage in front of the window. The band must be convinced, as they were all busy with the remaining set up.

The band started, and Maggie watched with rapt attention. They were superb. You could tell when a band worked well together because they played off each other and had fun. From where they were sitting, she could watch people come in the door, drawn in by the amazing musical talent.

Beside her, she could tell Liam was enjoying it too. He tapped his foot to the music and swayed along, holding her close. He ordered her another drink and got a soda for himself. During the band's break, Bobby Joe came over and pulled her into a big hug.

"Bobby, that was fantastic! You've really got something here," she said.

"Hey, thanks. Yeah, I think we've found who we need to make it just right."

Just as she was about to sit back down, Stan came up to her and gave her a bear hug. To say that the man was big was an understatement. He was like a giant, all six-feet six-inches of him. But, he was the biggest marshmallow on the planet.

"Hey Maggie girl, how you been doing? Not staying outta trouble, I hope." She noticed the definite twinkle in his eye as he looked at Liam.

"What fun would that be?" Turning she said, "Stan, this is my boyfriend Liam. Liam this is the best sax player in Louisiana, Stan Umbridge."

Leaning over, he accepted Liam's outstretched hand. "Hey, Liam. So how long have you and Maggie been together?"

Oh shit, this could blow their little lie right out of the water. Clearing her throat, she was about to jump in, but Liam had it handled.

"About a year. Our families have known each other for years. First time we ever met, she fell head over heels for me. And I wasn't far behind her." Maggie smiled and blushed.

Bobby Joe stepped in. "I told you Stan. He is too gorgeous to be straight, but I guess we can't have all the handsome ones for ourselves." He winked at her as he and Stan went to the bar to get drinks.

Maggie sat back down, and Liam leaned in and kissed behind her ear. "So, when can we take our leave?"

"Have you had enough?" Maggie looked up into the face that made her feel like she'd seen it a million times in her dreams.

"The band is great, but I'd like to spend some time with just you." He took her hand in his and kissed her palm.

Smiling, she said, "Let's go." They said their goodbyes to Bobby Joe and sent Stan a wave.

The evening was a little cooler, but it felt nice. They walked in silence for a few minutes, just enjoying the night and the feel of her hand in his. Hearing music as they turned down another street, they could see a guy sitting on a set of steps with his guitar, his case open at his feet ready for tips. He was great, singing a popular radio song, and the two of them slowed as they came close to him. The guy finished, and she and Liam applauded.

The guy was young with dirty blond hair and a skeleton tattoo on his forearm. He smiled at them and said, "Have any requests?"

She watched as Liam moved closer to the guy and said something she couldn't hear. Pulling something out of his pocket, he handed it over. The singer smiled, slipped whatever Liam just handed him into his shirt pocket and started strumming. Liam turned to her and pulled her into his arms. They danced right there on the sidewalk. As the guy started singing, she recognized the song as, 'Hold You In My Arms, by Ray Lamontagne. She remembered the song from a concert she, Delilah and Lola had gone to in Austin, Texas.

He held her close, tucking her head under his chin as they swayed to the music. The streetlight illuminated them, making her feel like they were on a stage. She knew she would remember this moment forever.

Liam pulled her tighter and brushed his lips along the side of her neck. "Mmm, you smell so good." He whispered into her ear and she felt the simmer of heat in her belly. She didn't think she could hold herself back if he pursued her harder. He was defeating her defenses.

They danced until the song ended and when he stared down into her face, she could see how much he wanted her. He ran his thumb across her bottom lip, then turning to the singer he said, "Thanks, man. Have a good night."

Making their way back to her place, she got nervous. Maybe she shouldn't take the next step. She must be crazy to even consider this. He was the guy who would get under her skin and when he left, it would ache like an abscess. Hell, he already was under her skin. Delilah was right; he wasn't a loser like the usual guys she dated. Well, they hadn't *all* been losers, but the ones who weren't didn't hold any appeal. But with Liam, she could feel something more, and it scared her.

They drove onto her street and pulled into the driveway. He turned off the car, and they sat in silence. Taking a deep breath, she waited for Liam to make the next move.

"Maggie, I can see you're struggling with your feelings. If you're unsure, then I can just go. The way things went tonight, I thought you might have changed your mind. But it's OK, I get it. I'm only here for a short time. Perhaps getting involved with me isn't the best idea. But, I can't say I'm not disappointed. I like you a lot," he said.

Hearing Liam say those things, she panicked. What if she was giving up her last opportunity to be with him? What if he really was 'the one' and she was about to ruin everything? Damn it. It was time for her to listen to her heart and turn off her brain. If she didn't take this chance, she knew she would regret it forever. Turning to him, she smiled. "Come on, let's go upstairs."

Before he could say anything, she was out and making her way to the backstairs. She just needed a moment to compose herself before she opened the door to her apartment. Climbing the stairs, she took out her keys with trembling fingers. She could hear Liam following her up. Reaching the top, she was just putting her key in the lock when Liam reached for her hand.

"Wait. Look at me, Maggie. I don't want to stress you out. I've loved spending time with you, and I don't want to damage the friendship we have. If you don't want this to go farther, just know that I'm thrilled to have had the chance to get to know you. I won't lie and say I don't want you, because you know I do. I think you're an incredible woman and I'm just as scared as you."

His honest words had her heart bursting. They were sincere, and the tightness in her chest loosened, making her anxiety disappear. Grabbing his hand, she said, "Thank you for being honest. Come in. Let's start with a drink and see what happens."

The look on his face was priceless as he grinned at her. Yeah, there was no way she was backing out of this now.

Once inside, she slipped out of her sandals and turned on some music. Heading over to the fridge, she wondered what she could offer him. Looking back over her shoulder, she watched as he checked out her place. He looked at the pictures on her table then picked up the book she'd just started, flipping it over to read the back cover. He wandered to the windows overlooking the driveway and then went to her bookshelf to read all the titles. She saw him grab a picture off the shelf.

It was a picture taken on a school trip in the fifth grade, when her class went to the Cabildo Museum. The picture was of her teacher, Miss Rodriquez, and her classmates in front of the General Andrew Jackson statue in Jackson Square. It had almost been a tragic day.

She'd trailed behind as her class was crossing the street. A car came screeching around the corner and hadn't noticed her. Fear froze her in place, but arms surrounded her and carried her off the street. He was an older boy she didn't know. No one from her school had seen it happen, it was just the two of them. He wore a dark blue hoodie and blue jeans with red running shoes. He frowned at her as she looked up into his face, and beautiful dark-blue eyes. Bending over, so they were face to face he said, "Be careful OK." Then he'd walked away.

"Maggie, how long ago was this picture taken?" His voice sounded strange, but she answered, "I was ten, in the fifth grade. We were on a field trip."

She grabbed a beer and a bottle of wine. Just as she was pouring some wine in a glass, she heard him whisper, "I don't believe it."

Turning, she saw him still staring at the picture. "What's the matter? You can't believe how dorky I looked as a ten-year-old?" She laughed, but he didn't smile.

Leaving the beer and wine on the counter, she made her way to where he was. He pointed to someone in the background. It was the boy with the red shoes. She'd looked at the picture many times and knew the boy who'd saved her was in the picture. It always reminded her there was good in the world.

"That's me, Maggie. My class went to The Presbytere Museum that day. I pulled you off the street when that car almost hit you. Your class crossed the street, and I saw you fall behind. You were playing with something in your hands, and you slowed down. I heard the car squeal its tires, and you froze. I raced over and picked you up. You looked so frightened. Part of me wanted to yell at you for not moving, but then you just stared at me, so all I could say was be careful."

Maggie took the picture and stared at the boy with the red shoes. Yes, she could see it now. She couldn't believe it. What were the odds that in a city this large he would be the one to save her? Almost twenty years had passed, and she'd always wished she could have thanked the boy who saved her. Now she finally had her chance. Finding her voice, she said, "I never told you thank you, Liam. I could have died. You just walked away, and I didn't even say anything. I can't believe it was you."

Liam looked stunned too. "I saw you getting your picture taken, and I wanted to walk over to you and find out your name. But then our teacher told us it was time to go."

Still in shock, she turned back to the counter and grabbed the beer and wine. Liam set down the picture and made his way to the sofa. He sat close and took his beer from her. Maggie held up her wineglass, and he tipped his bottle so they could clink them together.

"Here's to fate." Liam tipped back his bottle and drank as she froze.

Fate... Destiny? Oh no, that hit far too close to home. If

Emeline ever heard him, she'd laugh her ass off. No, she would not let her thoughts go down that road.

"Here's to finally being able to say thank you." She sipped her wine as they settled beside one another. He put his arm around her, and she eased into his side.

He smelled amazing, like soap and cologne, with a hint of man. The heat of his body made her melt into him. The slow saxophone in the background felt right for the mood. He set his beer bottle on the coffee table and took her hand in one of his. Rubbing his thumb over the top of her hand, she loved the feel of his skin on hers. His other hand caressed her shoulder, and goosebumps formed.

Liam stared down at her, a look of concern on his face. "Are you cold?"

God, he was so handsome it almost was too much. Those dreamy denim-blue eyes, the hint of a beard, not to mention the full bottom lip that she knew felt fantastic. He was so thoughtful, and that was what finally pushed her over the edge. Yeah, she wanted him and she wasn't about to wait one more second.

Setting down her wine, she maneuvered her body to straddle his lap. He seemed surprised by the move, but ran his hand along her sides. Moving her face in close, she said, "No Liam, I'm not cold, and if I were, I can think of some great ways to warm up."

Then her lips were on his, and she didn't hold back. She pushed her hands into his hair while he ran his hands all over her back, pulling her tighter against him. Kissing down her neck, he reached the top of her collar. The next thing she knew, he was pulling her top up over her head. He stopped, looking at her and her light-blue lace bra. His hands moved to cup her breast as he groaned, "My God, you are so beautiful."

Leaning in, he kissed the tops of each breast and caressed each nipple through the material. She tipped her head back, enjoying the sensation. Reaching behind her back, he unclasped her bra and pulled the straps off her shoulders. Breasts bare, his lips grazed, then sucked a nipple into his mouth, which pulled a moan from deep inside her. The pressure made her pulse pound and a flood of moisture coated her sex. His hands cupped her ass as he pulled her tighter against his rock-hard cock. Oh God, it felt so good.

She reached for the buttons on his golf shirt. He stopped kissing her and reached back with one hand and pulled his shirt over his head. As soon as it was off, it was like a feast for her eyes. She remembered his cut muscles from the hotel, but now she could finally run her hands over the taut smoothness. The patch of hair in the center of his chest felt course under her fingertips.

Liam pushed himself forward on the couch, grasping her hips as he stood up. He took them across to the bed. Kissing her, Liam almost tripped over an end table and she heard a thump on the floor.

Laying her on the edge of the bed, he stood before her. As she watched, he popped open the button on his jeans and pushed them down his legs, leaving his underwear in place. Maggie could see the full outline of his cock, and she was more than impressed with what lay covered. Her hand itched to touch him.

Before she had a chance to, he was peeling off her skirt to

expose the matching light-blue lace panties she was wearing. Liam knelt on the floor and leaned over so he could kiss along her stomach. The sensation felt so good. He dipped his tongue into her belly button, and the ticklish sensation almost made her giggle. When he reached the elastic of her panties, he ran his lips along the edge and she could feel the wetness between her legs increase.

Liam reached over and rubbed his thumb over her panties, right on top of her clit, and she rocked her hips up to feel more pressure. Looking down, she saw him rub his lips over the same area.

He looked into her eyes with a dirty, sexy grin on his face. "I gotta have a taste."

With that, he dragged her underwear off and spread her legs. The sudden cool air on her swollen sex made her gasp. A moment later she was gasping for another reason entirely. He kissed and licked until she was writhing on the bed. The tingle of her orgasm started low in her belly when Liam dipped his fingers inside. Working his fingers slowly in and out, he sucked her clit into his mouth, and that was it. The spiraling tingle went through her like wave after wave of hot release. When she finally came down, her body felt boneless.

Liam appeared over her. He lifted her arms, wrapping them around his neck so he could reposition their bodies in the middle of the bed. Once settled, he kissed her and she could taste herself on his tongue. Feeling the slickness of his skin made her want to touch him everywhere.

He sat up and leaned back on his heels, and she could see he was naked. She couldn't help but stare; he was magnificent. She watched as he opened a condom wrapper and rolled it down his hard length. Liam spread her legs wider, than grabbing a small pillow, he slid it under her hips. His voice sounded husky with desire as he shifted into position. "I want to watch your face as you come for me again."

The sound of his dirty talk sent a shiver through her. He entered her slowly, pulling back then entering a little further still. The feeling was incredible. By the time he was deep inside her, she felt like every part of her was being touched.

Liam moved his hips, and all she could do was feel. He was so sexy. Rubbing over her clit, he swiveled his pelvis, hitting her spot over and over. Every muscle in her body felt tight as a bowstring. She knew when it snapped it would be epic. "Baby, I can feel you squeezing my cock. I want to watch you soar, Maggie. God, you are so perfect. Come for me." And then, she was flying again. Crying out as every muscle quivered, she could feel the grip she had on Liam's cock and the pulsing shocks trembled throughout her body.

Liam grunted, and she heard him mutter a tense curse between erratic breaths. She watched as he threw his head back and called out her name as he came. Feeling the warmth of his orgasm as it filled the condom, she had the strangest thought. For one crazy moment she wanted to feel him fill her. To know that nothing separated them. But she'd never gone bare with anyone, and there was no way she would.

Liam pulled the pillow out from under her hips and lay over top over her, trying to catch his breath. Their skin was damp as she rubbed her hands over his back. That had been the best sex of her life. She wondered if it was as good for him, or if he had epically good sex like this all the time. And if he did, why hadn't someone scooped him up already?

As his breathing calmed, he kissed along her shoulder and neck, nipping her earlobe and nuzzling his nose into her hair. Liam kissed her lips and her heart both swelled and broke at the same time. Why did he have to live over thirteen-hundred miles away? He was everything she'd ever wanted, and they had, like, twelve states between them.

As if sensing her mood, Liam stopped and looked down into her eyes. She could see the same emotions in his eyes. She'd never moved this fast with anyone before; she'd never felt so attached this fast. If she were honest, she never allowed herself these kinds of feelings.

He gave her one last tender kiss and pulled out of her. She felt like he took a piece of her when he moved away. As he went to the bathroom, she watched the muscles move along his shoulders, down his back to his well-toned gluts. The marble statue of David had *nothing* on this guy.

Liam disappeared into the washroom and she knew she had only a few minutes to talk herself out of falling for him. Maybe she should suggest he leave, but the thought of sending him away made her heart ache. Oh God, what if he came out and told her he needed to go? Maybe he was in there trying to figure out a way to tell her he had to leave. Ok, if he came out and said he had to go, she would just have to be strong. Once he left, it wouldn't matter if she cried. She'd just deal with it.

Preparing for the worst, she sat there, waiting. She would handle this like she did everything in her life. Maggie just hoped the ache wouldn't last forever.

11

Staring at his face in the mirror, Liam's mind was a jumble of emotions. Being with her, touching her, tasting her, feeling every part of Maggie's body was incredible. No other woman had ever made him feel this way. Maggie was the most sensual person he'd ever met. Being with her was like a dream, and everything he'd ever wanted in a lover. But how would a relationship work when they lived almost twenty hours apart?

Liam knew he could live anywhere. His job only required him to come to the office once a month. He video conferenced most of the time due to his travel schedule. Staying in New York after graduation just seemed the best choice. However, the travelling took him away for weeks at a time and that would be the hard part. But having New Orleans as his home base could be a start.

Shaking his head, he couldn't believe he was even considering this! He'd only known her for a few days. Was he ready to uproot his life to be with her? He'd never forgotten the little girl he'd saved, and now she was right here. It had to be a sign. And damn it, he wanted her like he'd wanted no one else.

Glancing at the door, he was sure she was laying there wondering what he was doing. He hoped she wasn't thinking this was a one-night stand. In his mind, there was no way it could be. However, if she thought it was... it was just too much to think about. He would just have to convince her he knew she was worth more than just one night.

Walking out of the washroom, he could see Maggie sitting in the middle of her bed with the blankets wrapped around her. She looked gorgeous. Lips swollen from their kisses, hair all messed up and sexy from having his hands in it. And the pink flush of her skin, the same skin that he'd tasted. Just thinking about the sounds she'd made was making his cock spring back to life.

Before going back to bed to pounce on her again, he went to the kitchen. Filling two glasses with water, he walked towards her. She was watching his every move, and he realized she thought he would leave. To put her at ease, he turned off the lights as he passed the light switch. There was enough light coming in from the street that he could still see. Stopping beside the bed, he handed her a glass, and watched a small smile cross her face. Finishing his water, he climbed back into bed and pulled up the light blanket to cover the lower half of him.

Maggie set her glass aside and lay down facing him. He pulled her in close and stared down at her. The shadows played across her face, but he could see the look of relief. She smiled at him, and his heart melted. His relief matched hers, knowing that she didn't want this to be over. In that moment, he knew he had to figure out a way to keep her.

Maggie yawned, and a little giggle followed. "Sorry about that. Good sex makes me sleepy."

Glancing down he said, "So it was only good then?"

"Are you fishing for compliments, Mr. Kavanagh?" He could hear the laughter in her voice.

"Ah, we're back to being formal, I see. Well, Miss Rivard, I'll be the first one to give compliments. It was amazing, and I can't wait for round two."

"That's presumptuous, but I will confess that two orgasms in a night has never happened to me before. You have some serious skills, Mr. Kavanagh." Pulling her closer and kissing the top of her head, he said, "It was my pleasure. And if you play your cards right, I'll give you another two before you leave for work in the morning."

"Now you're just trying to show off. How about we get some sleep?" He could see her eyelids drooping.

Maggie kissed him one last time, turning so her back was to his front. He wrapped his arm around her and she wiggled back so he could spoon her. It felt perfect. He lay there holding her, hearing the steady rhythm of her breathing. Tucking his face into her hair, he breathed her in. She smelled like citrus and magnolias. He could get used to this. Climbing into bed every night, falling asleep after making love to her. Yeah, he could see it. He just hoped she could see it too.

* * *

It took Liam a while to figure out what had pulled him from such a deep sleep. Then he felt Maggie moving. Her whole body shook. He thought maybe she was laughing or crying, but then her whole body went rigid. Her panting breaths became labored and Liam pulled away to turn on the light so he could see her face. Once he did, he could see her eyes roll up into her head.

Kneeling over, he brushed the hair away from her face and held her, as he called her name over and over. "Maggie, Maggie, it's me, it's Liam, wake up, baby! It's me. I'm here," panic lacing his voice.

He was just about to grab his phone to dial nine one one, when she gasped and struggled against his hold. Pulling his arms away, she stopped struggling and looked at him as if surprised to see him there. Maggie took in deep, gulping breaths. Just as Liam was about to ask if she was all right, her lips trembled and tears streamed down her face. He recognized they weren't sad tears; they were tears of relief.

Liam lay back down and pulled her into his arms. She returned the hug and held on tight. He rubbed her back, murmuring words of comfort, and was glad he was here for her. Maggie calmed down after a while. Looking down at her, she tried to hide her face.

"Hey, look at me. Why are you hiding?" He pushed a lock of hair out of her eyes.

Staring at his chest, she said, "I'm just embarrassed. I've never had one of my nightmares with anyone around before, except Grandma."

Pulling away, she sat up and grabbed a few tissues off the bedside table to blow her nose and dry her face. She drank some water from the glass he'd brought her earlier. Lying back down with her back to him, she made no move to get close to him. He thought maybe he should leave her be, but he couldn't.

"Maggie, come here." She was slow to turn to him, but when she did, he pulled her to his chest. He rubbed her back again and pulled the blanket up as she shivered. "Do you want to talk about your dream?" Liam felt the shake of her head as she said, "I don't want to talk about it."

"It might make you feel better. They're just dreams, Maggie, it's not real." Kissing the top of her head, he waited.

He felt her huff out a breath. "Not according to some, but I don't want to talk about that either."

Liam thought that was a strange comment, but didn't question it. "What was the dream about, Maggie?" There was a long pause, and he thought maybe she had shut him out.

When she spoke, her voice sounded strained, and it almost broke his heart. "I was in a hospital, or I think it was a hospital. There were people lying on stretchers, all bleeding and bandaged. It felt like a dangerous place to be. There was someone yelling, so I ran down into a basement, but a man with dark skin followed me. He told me I would never see Mikael again. He said I belonged to him, and if I didn't agree, then no one could have me. I cried as I told him I would never choose him. Then he wrapped his hands around my neck and was strangling me. I couldn't breathe and he kept saying that I'd brought this on myself. I felt devastated that I would never get to see Mikael again. The weird thing was he kept calling me Celina."

She stopped talking and he could feel her fingers running over his chest, loving the way it felt. Pulling her closer, he said, "That is strange. But it's over now. You OK?"

"Yeah. Thank you." Maggie leaned her cheek against his chest.

"It was my pleasure. Looks like the sun is coming up. Do you want to get up now? Maybe a shower will help."

He watched as she looked over at her nightstand and nodded. "Yeah, I think that's a good idea. It's early, but a shower would feel good."

She pushed back the blanket and walked to the washroom. Liam followed, pulling a condom from his pants pocket.

"What are you doing?" Frowning, she cocked her eyebrow and stopped walking.

"I'm coming with you. You didn't think I was going to just lay there while you showered, did you? Someone has to come in and wash your back." He tried to look innocent, but she didn't look like she was buying it.

"I'm not sure that's a good idea, plus I'm a big girl and I've been washing my back alone for a long time."

"Ah yes, but you see I'm a fantastic back washer. I think you need to see my skills in action. I'll even throw in a back massage. And I don't like to brag, but I'm pretty good." Liam wagged his eyebrows.

Maggie looked skeptical. "I don't know. I think it might be faster if I go alone," she said.

He knew what he had to do. Looking into her eyes, he popped his bottom lip out into a pout and used his sad eyes. No one could resist it.

"Oh my God, are you serious with that face now? Jesus, you must have been a brat as a child! You must have driven your mother crazy with that pouty face. Come on then." Maggie rolled her eyes.

She walked into the washroom and turned on the shower. Liam trailed behind, pleased with himself. He closed the door and waited for her to get the water to her liking. Stepping in, he was right behind her. His eyes hadn't strayed far from her naked body. Holy hell, she was sexy as sin. All tanned skin, outrageous curves and those soul-searching eyes. Mmm, he couldn't wait to get in and help her forget all about her bad dream.

Leaning into the spray, Liam watched as she let the water pour over her hair and body. He grabbed her shampoo and put some in his hand, and when her back was to him, he lathered it into her hair. It was thick and beautiful and being able to have his hands in it was amazing. He scrubbed her scalp and heard a moan escape her lips. The sound had his already hard cock throbbing. He turned her and leaned her head back to rinse out all the suds. He pumped a few squirts of her conditioner into his palm and worked it through her hair before rinsing again.

Having completed her hair, he grabbed what looked like a sponge and put body wash on it. Rubbing in slow circles, he washed her back, hips and tantalizing ass. Moving to her legs, he washed both front and back. Moving up, he cleaned her neck and arms and then grazed the sponge over each breast. She kept her eyes closed through this whole process, and he liked that she trusted him. Rubbing the sponge over the tips of her breasts again, she let her head fall back and he decided he needed to use his hands for the next part of the job.

Kneading each breast, he watched the pleasure on her face. Leaning forward after he rinsed them off, he pulled one rose colored nipple into his mouth and she gasped. Soon he was pinching her other nipple and had her arching into his mouth. He knelt on the tub floor and, pulling one leg over his shoulder, pleasured her again. Before long she was crying out his name, her fingers tangled in his hair. Liam knew he'd never tire of hearing his name on her lips.

She slumped against the shower wall and he gathered her in his arms and kissed her. Deciding he couldn't wait another minute, he turned her around and placed her hands on the shower wall. Grabbing the condom he'd brought, he rolled it on. Placing one leg on the edge of the tub, he slid into her. He leaned over her back, kissing her neck and shoulders. He pumped his hips, and soon she was pushing back onto him. Maggie was panting as he moved his hand to her clit and stroked.

Liam couldn't believe how good she felt, he almost didn't want it to end. But too soon he could feel his balls tighten. When she moaned out her second release, her body milked his cock and pushed him over the edge. Riding it out, he felt every pulsing grip.

Then she looked over her shoulder at him and grinned. His entire world shifted in that moment, and he knew he could never live without her. There was no going back for him.

He removed himself, and she turned to kiss him. Tilting her head, she scowled at him. "Hey, wait a minute. I hope that didn't count as a back rub because I think I might have gotten ripped off."

"Sorry, I got a little distracted. But how about I make it up to you tonight?" Liam prayed she'd say yes.

A knowing smile spread across her face. "Oh, I see, so the lack of a back rub was just a ploy to get me to agree to yet another date. Very tricky, Mr. Kavanagh."

"A date? What makes you think I want to go out on a date? No way! Now that I know what pleasures await me in the bedroom, I think we should come straight here after work and not leave your bed all weekend." Liam then dove in and kissed her whole neck until she squealed.

* * *

It thrilled Liam that Maggie hadn't turned him down for getting together tonight. He needed to be with her again, but first, he had a car to return and work to do. He was meeting Damon just before lunch. He was looking forward to giving him an update on the progress and outlining the items which still needed completing. Liam also wanted to tell him about a few ideas for reconstruction which could enhance the look of the building.

Liam drove over to his cousin Walker's shop to drop off the car. He loved driving this car. It was a magnificent machine, and it had impressed Maggie for sure. And who would have guessed she'd be into cars. *Damn*, that was hot.

Pulling in front of the shop, he could see Walker at the front counter. He owned a little auto shop just off Rampart Street, and you could tell he loved what he did. Walker had started the business a little over seven years ago, and it had been flourishing ever since.

"Hey Bud," Walker said as Liam entered. "Guess your date went well, as you're still wearing the same clothes as yesterday." Walker wagged his eyebrows.

Liam smiled and laughed. "Yeah, it was great. Thanks again for the car. I was wondering if you have one a little more ordinary. I don't want to keep that one and park it in the underground parking. Just seems wrong, somehow."

Walker laughed. "Yes, it would be a shame to hide all that

beautiful raw power in the underground. Did your date like the car?"

"Are you kidding? Maggie stroked it like a long-lost lover. Gotta tell you, it was kinda' hot."

Walker's eyes went wide. "Sounds like I need to meet her. She might be my kind of woman."

Liam knew his cousin was joking, but the thought of her being with anyone else set him on edge and made him want to punch something.

"Whoa, Liam, I'm just joking man! I'd never steal your girl. She must really be something to put that kind of look on your face. Plus, I've been with Lynne for a long time. She'd castrate me if I tried to leave," Walker said.

Liam laughed at that because his cousin was right about Lynne. "Sorry. I don't know what it is about her, but every time I'm near her, I act like a total caveman. Maggie is smart, funny and beautiful. I know it's only been a few days, but damn, the thought of leaving her to go back to New York is not sitting well. Christ, do you think I'm crazy?" Liam pushed his fingers into his hair.

"I'm not the best one to ask for romance advice, but I've never heard you say anything about anyone you've dated. Plus, I haven't heard you talk about your job much either. You used to love talking about your work and all the places you've traveled. Maybe it's time to figure out your next step. In the meantime, you could book some vacation and see what comes of this thing with Maggie." Walker raised his dark eyebrows.

Liam grinned in agreement. "You know what? That sounds like a great idea. I could use some vacation. When did you get so smart?"

"I've always been smart, you just never noticed," Walker replied.

"Oh, I noticed things about you. You were always the best at armpit farts." They both laughed as Walker took the keys back. He loaned Liam another car, and they parted ways, saying they'd get together soon.

Liam spotted a flower shop as he drove back to the hotel, and on impulse he stopped. If Maggie had any lingering doubts about how he felt, he wanted to ease them. He ordered a gorgeous bouquet of purple and red roses and white lilacs. Filling out the card, he asked to have them delivered to her at the hotel that morning.

Walking out of the flower shop, he noticed Damon Guidry sitting outside a coffee shop with two men just across the street. The man with his back to the window was in a suit similar to the one that Damon was wearing. The other guy didn't look like someone who would associate with Damon. His blond hair and scruffy beard looking unkempt, and his button-up plaid shirt looked worn. Damon was leaning forward, waving his arms and looked angry. The other suited man held his hand up and started pointing at Damon. Liam thought about walking over, but the situation looked intense. Instead, he got into his car and drove away.

Getting back to the hotel, the ladies at the counter noticed him and waved. He wondered if Maggie told them about her date or the fact that he'd stayed over. If he was to guess, everyone knew he hadn't come back to the hotel and the gossip mill would work overtime today. It didn't matter to him, but he knew it would matter to Maggie.

Once in his room, he changed into fresh clothes and

printed the report he needed for this meeting with Damon. Heading back down to the lobby, he waited in the lounge. He couldn't help himself. He wanted to be there when the flowers came and hoped she'd have to come out to get them.

In the lounge, he got a coffee and checked his email. After half an hour, a man with a flower delivery walked up to the ladies at the desk. As the man left, Rosie checked the receipt, then picked up the phone. Perfect, Maggie would come out to get them.

A few minutes went by before Maggie walked out. She looked just as beautiful as she had this morning in her linen coral dress. However, now he knew what was under all those well-pressed, professional clothes. All he wanted to do was strip her bare and take her again. Geez, he better calm down or he'd be sitting there with a bulge in his pants when Damon arrived.

She walked over to the flowers and undid the paper wrapping, uncovering the stunning bouquet. The ladies at the counter *ooh'd* and *ahh'd* while Maggie pulled one flower forward and smelled its delicate petals. She closed her eyes, and he knew she was enjoying the fragrant roses. She reached up and took the card from the bouquet. Opening it, the sweetest smile appeared on her face as she read. It was worth every penny he'd spent.

As Liam watched, Maggie spoke to Rosie, who pointed to the lounge. She turned towards him and the smile widened as she gave him a little wave. He knew she wouldn't want to give the gossip mill any more to talk about.

Picking up the large bouquet, she started carrying them back to her office, but turned and gave him a quick wink. He wondered what she thought of the note, and he couldn't wait to ask her when she got off work.

Liam finished his coffee just as Damon walked through the door. He wasn't alone. Trailing behind him was a blond woman in a tight black dress which struggled to contain her ample cleavage. She couldn't have weighed more than ninety pounds and half of that was because of her breasts. To Liam's eyes she looked almost skeletal, but her face was pretty. As Damon walked towards him, he stopped and pointed to the lobby sitting area and she pouted but sat by herself.

Damon walked the rest of the way to Liam and said, "Hey, Liam, hope Maggie's been treating you well. She didn't skimp on the service once I left, did she? I told her to give you the best we had?"

Liam almost choked on this last part. Smiling, he responded, "No, she didn't skimp."

"Good to hear it. I can't take too long today. As you can see, Candice is waiting on me. Told her we'd go to my place in Baton Rouge until Tuesday. I hope to get in a game or two of golf. So, what's the bad news?"

Liam frowned at that. Why would he assume that Liam would give him bad news? Maybe he was just preparing himself in case there were issues.

"Actually, there is no bad news. I have it all outlined in the report. It details the repairs which need addressing, starting with the plumbing issue. But other than that, it's good. I am still waiting for some reports from the city, but I am confident in the report. I also prepared a reconstruction report to give you some ideas to consider for the future."

Liam watched as Damon flipped through the report, his

face remaining neutral as he read. In all the years he'd been in this business, clients loved finding out this kind of information about their business. Damon seemed almost *blasé* about it. But then again, he didn't seem to get excited over much.

Damon flipped to the end and said, "Thanks for being so thorough in your report, Liam, and good work. I'll give this a proper read through this weekend. Do you have questions for me?"

"No. Once I have this finished and all the details worked out, I'll let Edith at our main office know the work is complete and she'll send your secretary the invoice. If you have time on Tuesday, we can meet again and go over the final report in more detail," he explained.

Damon nodded and looked distracted. "Yeah, that sounds like a plan. Not sure when you wanted to head back North, but Tuesday afternoon works for me. Stay here until you head home. It's the least I can do for you. You've been able to put this together sooner than I realized. We'll talk soon."

Liam watched as Damon made a beeline for the front exit, almost forgetting to call Candice over to go with him. He couldn't figure Damon out. If he was honest, Damon seemed disappointed that Liam didn't find some major problems with the place. Maybe he'd be better once he read through the whole report. The guy didn't strike him as a snap-decision kind of person.

He picked up his few things and decided to go back to his room to work while he waited for Maggie to get off. Thinking of her, he sent her a quick text as he waited for the elevator.

> **Hey Gorgeous, hope you liked the flowers. Can't wait for tonight.**

Liam got to his room and was just opening his laptop when his phone signaled a text.

> **Hello, Handsome. I love the flowers, they're beautiful. You didn't need to do that, but I'm glad u did. I should finish up here around six. See ya soon. XO.**

Setting his phone down, he wanted to fist pump the air. He could hardly wait until they could be together tonight. He'd better get his own work done so he would be ready to go when she called.

12

Maggie sat at her desk and looked at the little note which had come with the bouquet. Running her finger over the writing on the card, she read it over and over in her head.

Maggie,
Long ago I saved an angel,
And she stole a piece of my heart.
It might be fate, or maybe destiny,
But I call it unbelievable luck.
Yours, Liam.

She let her eyes skim over the reference to fate or destiny, because she refused to think about it. But it was a sweet little poem, and the flowers were beautiful. Maggie had been floating on air the whole morning. She saw a few people look at her curiously, but she didn't care. This was the happiest she'd been in a long time. Not even the pithy email she got from Damon a few minutes ago could bring her down. He'd denied her request to put on additional security over the next couple of weeks. It should not surprise her and in that moment it didn't matter; she was walking on a cloud.

She worked away on her email and met with a few of the

staff to go over some scheduling conflicts. Once resolved, she moved on to making some calls. She scratched several things off her list this morning. Feeling good, she turned to her coffee maker and made herself a cup of her favorite chai tea. The mug's printing read, '*You don't have to be crazy to work here, we will train you*'.

Just as she was about to take a sip, Rosie popped her head in. "Hey, Boss, just wanted to know if you wanted a tea, but I see you're already ahead of me. Can I come in and chat for a few minutes while I'm on break?"

Maggie nodded and waved her in. Rosie was one of her favorites because she was a hard worker, never complained and was always willing to cover any additional shifts she could. Rosie lived with her mother in an old house close to Maggie.

"Well, are you going to spill it or what? Or do I have to pretend that I'm not *dying* for you to tell me how your date went, and why the very handsome engineer sent you flowers?" Rosie said.

Maggie continued to sip her tea and waited to see what else Rosie would say. She thought for a moment that she should keep it to herself. But who was she kidding; she was busting at the seams to tell someone, and she knew she could confide in Rosie.

"Come on Maggie, don't leave me hanging!" Rosie clutched her hands together.

"Fine. The date was very nice. We shared a pizza and then walked to the Spotted Cat to see Bobby Joe's band. They were great, you've got to see the new band. Then, as we were walking back to the car, he paid some guy to play a song for us and we danced on the sidewalk. We went back to my place.

I found out he saved my life twenty years ago when I almost got run over by a car. It's a long story and I'll tell you another time."

Rosie leaned forward in her seat and stared at Maggie. "Um, there had better be a second part to the story because there's no way he dished out that much money for flowers because of a goodnight kiss."

"If you must know, nosy pants, he stayed over. I will not get into the specifics with you because a lady doesn't kiss and tell. But I will say that I will never look at my shower the same way again." She looked at Rosie with a shy smile.

Rosie laughed and covered her face. "Oh my God! The two of you together are like this hot, sexy model couple. Tell me you'll see him again," she begged.

"Yes, tonight. Not sure what we'll do, but he wants to spend some time together."

Rosie looked at her and winced. "Wants to spend time before he goes back? What will you do when he leaves, Maggie? Do you think he'll move here and get a job? Then you guys can get married and have babies. Oh, the babies would be beautiful, with your complexion and his dreamy eyes."

Maggie held up her hand. "Slow down there Rosie, geez. It was one night. Let's not get carried away. I don't expect him to give up his life, and I don't want to give up mine. I've worked hard to get to where I am. So, I'm just going to enjoy this right now and we'll see what happens."

Sensing that Maggie didn't want to dwell on the hard questions, Rosie said, "OK, I won't bring it up again. But just tell me one thing. Does he have a twin?" They both laughed and sipped their tea.

After Rosie went back to work, Nelson dropped by her office. "Afternoon, Maggie. I wanted to let you know we found some homeless guy wandering around out back. He said he was just looking for a place in the shade to sleep, but there is no shade back there. I called the police station, and an officer came over. They took him to the precinct to ask him some questions. He's clean so they let him go. I just wanted to keep you in the loop."

"Thanks, Nelson. I'm reachable by cell all weekend if the guys need me. Aren't you going to see that beautiful granddaughter this weekend? She started high school this year, right?"

Nelson smiled his proud grandpa smile. "Oh yes, my baby's baby is officially a freshman. It seems like only yesterday she was running around our backyard calling me DamPa. Now she's all into clothes, hair and makeup. But, she's so smart." He looked at Maggie with a twinkle in his eye. "I saw Liam watching Delilah's kids yesterday. The man looks like a natural."

Maggie rolled her eyes. "Nelson, don't go putting something together that's not there. He just did Delilah a favor. His sister has a little boy, and he's watched him before."

Nelson smiled at her and nodded. "Oh, I see. So watching him with your godchildren didn't make your heart pitter-patter?"

She hung her head and put her hands over her face. "How bad is the gossip, Nelson?" she asked.

"I'm not gonna lie, Maggie, the staff were a-buzz with it. I don't think there was a single employee who hasn't heard about the scene with the kids. They were all wondering what was going on between you two. But I covered for you. Told everyone Maxon saw Liam come back at around twelve. I didn't think you'd want to have everyone knowing your business."

Maggie's shoulders sagged in relief. "Thanks for that, Nelson, I appreciate it."

"You're welcome. I better get back. We'll update you on any issues, but I told them to vet them through me first. You and your grandmother are going to the cemetery on Sunday?" he asked.

Maggie and her grandmother would go to visit her parents' graves. They made a special trip every year on the anniversary of their deaths. She couldn't believe it had been twenty-four years since they'd died. "Yeah. Well, have a good weekend, and have fun with Rachel."

Once Nelson left, she checked the clock, and it was almost four. Turning back to the pile of mail on her desk, one envelope caught her eye. The logo was that of the hotel's insurance company, Allicot Insurance. It seemed strange, as all correspondence from them went to the head office of Guidry Corp. Maybe this had to do with the claim they put in a few months ago for water damage in the basement. She decided to call over to the head office and let them know it had come here. Dialing, she waited until the line picked up and a professional voice said, "Good Afternoon, Guidry Corp. how may I help you?"

Maggie smiled and said, "Hey, girl, it's just me. You can knock off that fancy talk." She and Leticia had worked together forever.

"Hello, Ms. Sassy Pants. I hear you've been driving the boss man kinda crazy?" Leticia replaced her professional tone with her usual smart ass, sarcastic one. She loved that about her.

Maggie laughed. "Well, someone has to keep him off his pedestal. And besides, if he'd listen to me and allow me to get things done then I wouldn't have to drive him crazy."

They both laughed until Maggie got down to business. "I'm calling, not just to hear your sexy voice, but to let you know that an envelope from Allicot Insurance came here. Do you think they would send that claim from a few months ago directly here?"

She could hear Leticia typing on her keyboard. "No, I put the head office address on it. How about this, just open it up, scan it over and I'll look at it? But it'll have to be on Monday. I'm leaving in a few minutes. I need to take James to the doctors." Leticia said.

"Sure, no problem. I'll talk to you later. And give that baby boy a kiss for me." They said their goodbyes and hung up.

Grabbing her letter opener, she sliced opened the envelope. Scanning the initial page, it looked like insurance renewal documents for The Colonial. Strange that renewal papers would come here. She flipped a few more pages and her eye caught on a section of the document about policy beneficiaries and the name listed there was Mr. Damon Guidry. That was also strange. It should say Guidry Corp. Rolling her chair over to the filing cabinet, she pulled out her copy of the insurance papers Leticia had sent a while ago. Flipping to the beneficiaries page, she could see that it stated Guidry Corp.

Looking back at the document she just opened, she could see that the date of renewal was early last week. Maggie reviewed the paperwork one more time and scanned it over to Leticia. She'd let the people at head office work this out. Once she finished, she put the whole document in a folder and put it in her desk drawer. Leticia would get back to her on Monday.

Maggie continued through the stack of mail when her cell rang. Glancing at the screen, she saw it was Damon. Odd, she thought he was meeting with Liam. She answered on the third ring.

"Afternoon Damon, everything OK?" she asked.

"Hey, Maggie, just wanted to let you know that I'll be out of town over the weekend. I should be back by Tuesday. I'm reachable by cell. Anything I need to know before I leave?"

Maggie glanced over at the papers from the insurance company. Did she tell him about those? Maybe a half truth.

"No, everything is fine here. I added some extra hours to the cleaning staff schedule for this weekend. They will need the extra help with the weddings happening tomorrow. I have Gen working extra, too."

Damon huffed but didn't say too much, so she continued. "I have some mail that needs to go to head office, but I'll get one of the guys to run it over on Monday, there's no rush on it."

There was silence on the other end then Damon said, "Is it important? I haven't left the city yet. I can drop by and get it?"

He'd never offered to do that before. "No, it's nothing but bills and junk. René can run it over on Monday once the checkout rush is over."

"Anything in there that I should know about?"

His voice sounded weird, but she just wanted to get the call over with, "Oh no. You just have a great weekend. Is Candy going with you?"

Maggie had seen Candy a few times. She always seemed to trail behind Damon like a lost puppy. Well, a puppy with breasts the size of basketballs, and the waist size of a six-year-old child.

Damon sounded bored as he responded, "Yes, *Candice* will be with me. She wants to do some shopping and needs a break from New Orleans." He never called her Candy; it was always Candice, like he was trying to make her sound classier than she was. But they both knew she was just arm candy.

Maggie rolled her eyes. Like Candy would need a break. As far as she knew, Damon kept her in a lovely condo somewhere and the hardest thing she had to do was hang off Damon's arm at all those high-class parties.

"Well, you two have fun and I'll see you next week. I'm around all weekend."

Damon laughed. "Maggie, you need to get out more. How are you ever going to get barefoot and pregnant if you never leave work? Oh, that's right, you didn't have to leave work to meet someone. I delivered you the perfect man, didn't I?"

Annoyance flared as Maggie said, "I don't know what you're talking about."

This time Damon's laugh lacked humor. "Come on, Maggie. You think I don't have eyes? Liam drooled when he saw you. I know you went out on a date and he didn't come back to the hotel last night. I didn't hire him to provide you with a plaything, Maggie. Let's keep it professional, OK? I'm trying to run a respectable business."

Shocked, she didn't know how to respond. How had he heard about that? As far as she knew he never spoke to any of the staff.

"Anyway, Maggie, I've got to go." Then the line went dead, leaving her gaping at the phone.

Sitting there, she could feel her anger spike. Did he think she was being unprofessional? It's not like she was hooking up with Liam at the hotel. Her mind flicked briefly to the scene inside Liam's room. Her back pressed against the door and his hard... body pressed against her. But she'd put a stop to it, and since then she had done nothing at work. And what business of it was Damon's if she found Liam attractive? God, he could be such an asshole.

Shaking her head, she decided that his opinion didn't matter to her. He might be her boss, but he didn't deserve the respect that should go with the title. He belittled her at every turn and she worked damn hard. No, she wouldn't give him the satisfaction of pissing her off. She liked Liam, a lot, and if she wanted to spend her free time with him, she would.

Getting back to work she finished her last couple of emails for the day. Grabbing her purse and briefcase, she was about to head for the door when her phone rang. She looked at it and saw that it was the front desk.

"What's up, Gen? Is there a problem?" Maggie was slipping her shoes back on her feet.

She could hear Genevieve whisper into the phone, "You better get out here before he gets arrested."

"Who's getting arrested?" Maggie asked with concern.

"Liam. I mean not yet, but he might. Hurry up and get out here." Genevieve hung up.

Maggie quickly locked her office door and hurried to the lobby. As she came around the corner, she saw Liam and Kenny standing close, staring each other down. Nelson was watching off to the side. If she wasn't mistaken, Nelson almost looked please the two were facing off. Geez, that's all she needed was a fist fight to break out. Walking up to the three men, she said, "What's going on here?"

No one spoke or moved and that just made her angry. "Somebody better start talking or I'm going to get really annoyed!"

Liam was the first one to speak, his tone laced with anger. "It's nothing Maggie, just a misunderstanding."

Nelson chuckled, and she looked at him for answers. "It seems Officer Kenny here has been asking around about Liam. He saw your grandmother today, and he was asking her some questions. Ones she couldn't answer, which the Officer thought was strange because he thought you and Liam had known each other a long time."

Oh Christ, like she needed this right now. "And why is *this* happening?" She waved her hands between Liam and Kenny.

Liam stared at Kenny as he said, "He thinks I'm hurting his chances at getting back together with you."

Great, that's not what she wanted to hear at all. "Well, boys, how about we back away from each other and discuss this like adults?"

Liam stepped back and walked right over to her side, wrapping his arm around her waist. In a whisper to him, she said, "Not helping."

To that, Liam whispered back, "Don't care."

OK, so this was fun... not. "Kenny, what are your issues?" she asked.

Kenny looked at her and she could see the hurt there, but she was not about to own any of it. They'd been over for a long time. "Maggie, my concern is that this guy comes to town and you're spending time with him and you don't even know him. Your grandmother seems to like him, but she doesn't know him either. I'm just worried that maybe he might not be the right guy for you."

That excuse was so thin she could see right through it. "So, what you're saying is, that even though I'm a grown woman with a mind of my own, you decided I wouldn't know a good man when I see him? Is that right? And that if my grandmother, who has always been as sharp as a gator's tooth in picking out the assholes in my life, says that he is a good guy, you think she doesn't know what she's talking about? Is that correct? And, because the person I'm choosing is not you, that means it is the wrong decision?"

Kenny stood there and stared at her. He knew his reasoning was selfish, and she'd called him out on it. "Maggie, if I could just speak to you alone for a minute."

Liam's hand gripped her waist tighter, and she knew he'd be upset if she spoke to Kenny alone. She didn't want to risk upsetting him, however, she also needed to make it clear the choice was hers. She needed to move the conversation so she could say what she needed to say.

"I will speak to you alone, but just over there. Trust me, this won't take long," her voice came out clipped.

She tried to move away from Liam, who still hadn't let go of her. She looked into his face and squeezed his hand. Knowing he didn't want to, but showing her he trusted her, he let go.

Kenny walked away from the other men and out of earshot. He stopped and leaned his shoulder against the wall, his back facing Liam and Nelson. Maggie walked over and faced him.

"All right, you have me alone. What's going on here Kenny?" she demanded.

He shuffled his feet and said, "Damn it, Maggie. Ever since I saw you the other night, I haven't stopped thinking about you. I want to see if we could try being together again. And now this guy shows up and you don't even know him."

Maggie shook her head. "Kenny, I like you, I do, but just as a friend. You were fun to hang out with, but I don't feel that way about you. I hoped when you saw Liam and I together the other day that would be the end, but now you're here and you're going to make me say it. I don't want to go out with you, Kenny. Even if Liam wasn't in the picture, my answer would still be no, so don't blame him. You'll meet someone else someday and you'll know I wasn't the girl for you. I'm sorry. Now, *please* don't start something with Liam."

Kenny looked at her and a sad smile appeared on his face. "Fine, I won't start anything. I can't say I'm not disappointed, but at least I know. But I still think given time, you'd choose me."

He reached up and touched her cheek, and from the corner of her eye she saw Liam move towards them. She grabbed Kenny's hand and moved it away. Geez, that's all she needed, was for Liam to get arrested for assaulting an officer.

"I think you better go, Kenny." She hoped it didn't sound

rude, but she didn't want to push her luck. Liam had stopped, but no sense poking a rattler, so to speak.

Kenny turned and walked to the exit, only sparing Liam a glance. As he passed Nelson, he said, "We'll be in touch."

Looking down at her shoes, she took a big breath. Wow, that was extra stress she didn't need. All she wanted now was to go home and have a glass of wine and order in some Chinese.

She looked up and Liam was standing right in front of her. His face held a slew of emotions. She knew she needed to reassure him. Taking his hand in hers, she smiled up at him.

"You ready to go? I thought a quiet evening at my place with a bottle of wine or beer and Chinese takeout was in order. What do you say?" She could see the relief on his face and he gave her a huge smile.

"That sounds great. I was coming down to get you when... all that happened. Sorry, Maggie, but he just started in on me. He was just jealous, but it was hard not to take offense. Anyway, that's all I will say about that.

"Ok, let's go," she said, tugging on his hand.

They made their way out to her car and Liam took her keys. Driving along they chatted about general stuff like favorite bands and movies they liked. They argued over whether comedy was better than action; Maggie liked romantic comedies and Liam rolled his eyes. Deciding that it would be best, they settled on a funny action movie for tonight. It was nice to just leave work behind and have someone to take her mind off everything.

Pulling into the driveway, Maggie could see her grandmother sitting on the porch swing. Her usual sidekick,

Gladys, was missing. They got out and walked up the front porch stairs and her grandmother said, "Ah, there's my girl." Maggie could hear the fatigue in her voice.

Once Maggie reached her, she gave her a kiss on the cheek. She noticed her grandmother looked tired, and she got worried. It must have showed on her face, because the older woman said, "Oh now, don't go frettin', Magpie. I'm feeling fine, just tired is all. Thought I'd come out here and watch the neighbors and enjoy some of the evenin'. Stop worrying." Her grandmother looked at Liam and said, "Hey there, handsome. How was your day?"

"Fine, Margaret. You sure you're feeling all right? I can fetch you something to drink?" Maggie fell for him a little more with the show of concern for her grandmother.

"Well now that you mention it, I would love some lemonade. I made a pitcher earlier, it's in the fridge. Thank you so much, Liam, that's awful nice of ya."

Liam gave her a sweet smile and went into the house. As soon as the screen door closed, her grandmother turned on her with a deep frown on her face. "Margaret Grace Elizabeth Rivard, why didn't you tell me you lied to Kenny? I didn't know what to say this morning when he cornered me at the coffee shop. He was acting all Mr. Investigator and interrogated me like a criminal. It's none of his damn business who you spend your time with. I never liked that boy." She scowled and shook her head.

"I'm sorry, Grandma. We only lied because I didn't want to deal with telling him I wasn't interested. But, he knows now. He stopped by the hotel to speak to Nelson and then he and Liam got into an argument."

Her grandmother smirked at her. "It's nice to have two men fightin' over ya. I know I've always enjoyed it."

Maggie rolled her eyes, as she'd seen a few men almost come to blows over her grandmother's affections. It had been quite the spectacle. "I tried to let him down easy, but I'm not sure he sees it that way."

"Oh, my sweet Magpie, it's never an easy thing. He'll get over it. But you're home now. What are your plans this evening? You goin' out somewhere romantic?" she asked.

Maggie sat down beside her and said, "We're just staying in tonight. It's been a busy week and I just want to relax. We're ordering in Chinese and watching a movie. You want to join us?"

Frowning, her grandmother said, "Now, why would I want to do that and ruin your evening? No Baby Girl, I'm takin' it easy tonight. I've got to be over at the church for eight tomorrow morning to help with the bazaar. I need to get there before Moira does. If not, she'll just throw stuff on the tables all willy-nilly and you know it drives me crazy."

Just then, Liam came out with a glass of lemonade and a napkin. He set it down on the table and took a seat just opposite them. Maggie was sure she saw her grandmother's eyes flutter. She was such a flirt.

"I'm just going to drink my lemonade, then I'm goin' to head in. You two enjoy your dinner and a movie. I put some cookies on your counter. Hope you like oatmeal, Liam."

"I will sample some when we go up." Liam gave her grandmother his sweetest smile, and Maggie heard the older woman sigh.

She and Liam left her on the porch and went upstairs.

Once there, she went to get changed while Liam made his way to the kitchen in search of her grandmother's cookies. The next thing she heard was Liam moaning in the kitchen. "Oh my God, these are delicious! Between the beignets and the cookies, I think I might have to marry your grandmother. If she cooks as good as she bakes, then I'm in."

Maggie walked out of the washroom to see Liam stick a whole cookie in his mouth. He closed his eyes, a look of absolute bliss on his face. Watching him lick his fingers had her thinking some inappropriate thoughts.

She shook her head at him and said, "Oh, I see how it is. Suddenly it's all clear to me. You're one of those guys who scout out elderly woman to keep them stocked with baked goods and meals. Well, I dare you to say that louder, because I think my grandmother fancies you and she may take you up on the offer."

Watching Liam stare at her, crumbs still stuck to his lips, she winked at him. A slow, sexy smile spread across his face and he began stalking towards her, as though she were prey. Maggie started backing up and then turned to dash back into the washroom. She didn't make it two steps before he wrapped his arms around her waist. Slipping his lips along her neck, he said, "No, my actual nefarious plan is to charm your grandmother into making me delicious confections, while keeping her granddaughter so I can do all manner of naughty, tantalizing things to her." He flicked his tongue along the outer shell of her ear making her shiver.

Breathlessly, she said, "So you're saying all I have to do to make you stay here for good, is pimp out my Grandma's baked goods?" Shit, why had she said that? Damn it, she was trying to avoid talking about him leaving, and now she'd turned it into an even bigger elephant in the room.

Liam turned her to face him. She could see he wasn't sure how to answer. Maggie didn't want to make tonight awkward. She looked down at his chest and let him hold her. All she wished for was to take back what she'd said and go back to their playful mood.

"Maggie, look at me." Liam's delicious bourbon voice seemed to soak into her skin and make her think of hot summer nights and mint juleps. She lifted her face to look into those dark denim eyes. Deep blue pools, so soulful and breath taking, she was powerless to look away. Liam took his time looking at her face. It was unnerving to have him study her so closely.

She was just about to pull away, when he said, "My God, you are the most beautiful woman I've ever seen. I don't know what it is, but everything about you feels... I don't know... familiar. Like when I touched you for the first time, it felt like I'd touched you before. And looking into your eyes it's like I've seen them many times. I think I've been dreaming of your eyes forever. The day you fell at my feet in your office you looked up at me, and it was like... I wanted to say, 'Hey, there you are.' Wow, that sounds crazy, doesn't it?"

He then dipped his head and took her lips in the sweetest, most tender kiss. Pushing her hands into his hair and deepening the kiss, she knew what Liam meant, because she felt it too. The only thing was she wouldn't allow herself to dwell on it. She could taste the cookies he'd just eaten and heard his breathing take on a distinct panting quality. Her own breaths joined his, and as he pulled her closer, her breasts rubbed over his hard, chiseled chest. Thoughts about how much she'd love to kiss every inch of that magnificent chest came to an abrupt halt when Liam's stomach growled so loudly, she thought it would reach out and grab her.

"Sounds like the beast is hungry. Why don't I call in our order before we get too carried away?" she asked.

Liam smirked and looked a little embarrassed. "Yeah sorry, my stomach has a mind of its own sometimes."

Maggie kissed him and went to grab her phone. She was glad to have a few minutes to sort out her feelings. She could feel herself falling deeper and deeper, and damn, if she didn't love the feeling. It had been a long time and even back then it was nothing like it was now. Maggie realized if she didn't keep her head on her shoulders, this would crush her when he left. But, if she were honest, she didn't know how to stop it.

13

Once they'd eaten, they settled on a movie. Curled up together on her couch, which was too small for Liam to get comfortable, Maggie started to nod off. Her eyes grew heavy and the warmth of Liam's body was seeping into her like a drug. He moved his hand over her shoulders and then down, kneading her lower back and it felt fantastic and she moaned. Whatever he was doing felt magical.

"Mmm, do you like that? How about we move over to the bed and I'll give you a real massage? This couch is way too small for me to give you a quality rub down. I believe I still owe you one."

Maggie looked over her shoulder at him, and said, "That sounds like a very convenient excuse to get me in bed. I better keep my eyes on you, Mr. Kavanagh. But, if you think I'll turn you down, you're wrong. Come on, city boy, show me your skills."

Liam laughed as they made their way over to the bed. Before Maggie could lie down, Liam stopped her. "Massages are best done with bare skin." Before she could protest, he was pulling her top up and over her head and unclasping her bra. Both the shirt and bra landed in a pile at her feet, and then

Liam was turning her so she could lie down on top of the comforter.

She stretched out on her stomach, getting comfortable. Looking towards the washroom, she watched him walk out with a tube of her lotion. Looking up at her with a sexy smile spread across his face, he said. "Can't do a proper massage without lotion." Then he winked.

Liam climbed on the bed and moved her hair to one side, exposing the back of her neck. He kissed her there a few times, and she loved the feel of his warm lips. Before long she heard the pop of the cap on the lotion tube. Liam was taking his time squirting some on his hands, then rubbing them together to get the lotion warm. The bed dipped on either side of her hips as Liam positioned himself to hover over top of her.

The smell of citrus filled the air as his big, warm hands rubbed her skin. It was heavenly. He coated her whole back with the lotion and kneaded it into her skin. He hit all her pressure points and worked out every kink. Trying to hold back, she kept her moans and sighs to a minimum, but sometimes it just felt so good she couldn't help herself.

Finished with her back, Liam pushed his fingers into her hair and massaged her scalp. It was superb, and her toes curled. Removing his fingers from her hair, he ran his fingertips over her skin. Running his hands along her sides, his fingers caressed the exposed slope of each breast and her nipples hardened from the contact. Liam shifted, and she felt his lips on her shoulder blade. He licked her skin, then kissed where his tongue had been. He repeated this action over and over, as if tasting her, and in some ways consuming her. The move was so intimate and reverent it brought tears to her eyes; she couldn't remember a time when anyone had treated her with such tenderness and adoration.

Liam continued until he reached the waistband of her yoga pants. She could feel his breath on her back, running little circles around the birthmark on her lower back. It was in the shape of a ragged star. Two branches of the star were shorter than the other three. Feeling Liam's lips on her birthmark, the long, sweet kiss he placed there almost made her sob. It was as if he was trying to memorize everything about her. Her heart broke at the thought.

He shifted again and hovered over her, inhaling her scent and the warmth of his body circled her like a cocoon. She wanted to look at him, but knew the moment she did, the tears would spill. She didn't want to wreck this moment, even if it was breaking her heart.

"I'll be right back." Liam whispered and his voice sounded strained.

Maggie looked over her shoulder and glimpsed his face, just before he closed the washroom door. In that expression she saw all her own emotions reflected. The longing, sadness, and everything in between. It was awful of her to think, but it relieved her to know she wasn't alone in her torment. But what did that solve? If he was feeling the same way, how did that help either of them?

She knew in her heart she couldn't up and leave her life. Everything she loved in the world was here. Her family, friends, coworkers, and all the connections she'd worked so hard to make. Not to mention the job she'd put her whole heart into. New Orleans was her home and if she left to follow her heart, part of it would always be here and she would regret it forever.

She didn't know enough about Liam to know what his plans were. Maybe his plans had nothing to do with settling down. He'd spoken of a few things when they went out, but she couldn't base much on that. He might have aspirations for something that took him away from here, and she couldn't be the one to take away his dreams. And she refused to think about Emeline and the things she kept saying.

Her grandmother mentioned several times that Emeline said that Maggie's true love would walk into her life and knock her sideways. Gladys said just over a month ago that Emeline stated Maggie needed to be ready because when 'he' walked into her life, he would shake her foundation. She wouldn't allow herself to believe in any of it, let alone that Liam was her true love.

She moved off the bed and grabbed a short nightgown out of her drawer and slipped it over her head. Her body still felt like jelly from the massage as she made her way to the kitchen for some water. She filled two glasses and brought them back to bed. Shutting off the lights, she decided to crawl under the covers and wait for Liam. She didn't want to talk or think about anything; she only wanted him to hold her.

* * *

And here he was again, sequestering himself in her bathroom as his emotions spiraled. Sitting down on the edge of the tub, he held his head in his hands as he took a deep breath. Maggie pushed every button for him and damn it if that wasn't amazing. It was almost as if she was custom made to fit everything he loved and desired in a woman. Right down to the grey-green eyes which had been part of his dreams forever. Telling her about how he felt the first time they met had felt right, and even though she said nothing, Liam knew she felt the same.

Touching her, tasting her and just being with her was messing with his head. He knew there was no way he could ever leave her. Everything about her called to him. Taking the time as he had the last hour, getting to know her this way had his mind in a tailspin. Hearing her breath, feeling her skin and the response she gave to his touch was one of the most intimate things he'd done with a woman. He wasn't sure, but he felt she was just as caught up as he was. Either way, the emotions were real, and he would have to give serious thought about his next move.

Opening the door, the room was in total darkness. Making his way to the bed, he saw a glass of water and smiled thinking about how thoughtful she was. He took a drink, and then crawled in under the covers. Once he was in, he moved in behind Maggie, spooning their bodies together. He could tell she had drifted off to sleep. She shifted and looked over her shoulder. "Sorry, I must have dozed off. Um, if you want to..."

Liam shushed her. "Maggie, you've had a busy week and I don't want you doing things just because you think it's what I want. Let's just get some sleep." With that, he kissed her on the shoulder and pulled her close.

Sometime later, when her breathing had evened out and her body was lax against his, he whispered, "I think I've fallen for you." He drifted off then, the smell of her skin pulling him under.

* * *

Looking around the room, he remembered when he'd first arrived here. Kolton was a midshipman on Gunboat 156. Having served three years in the US navy, it had thrilled him to get orders for active duty to protect the waters of the Gulf against the British.

On that horrible night over a month ago, when the call sounded that long boats were in the water, everyone flew into action. Cannons fired, but before long the British were crawling all over the ship. Panic among his fellow mates set in, and the fear in their eyes was unsettling.

He had done little hand-to-hand combat, but as the enemy surrounded them, he held his own. That was until one of the British soldiers slashed his knee, cutting deep, leaving a nasty wound. But Kolton stabbed the man in the heart. He stood frozen, watching the life leave the man's eyes as he fell onto the blood-soaked deck. A few moments later, a shot rang out, and it threw Kolton back. The bullet tore through his shoulder, and the pain was excruciating. The impact had thrown him against the low railing and he was free-falling, arms and legs pinwheeling over the side of the ship.

Rising to the surface and struggling to keep himself afloat, the searing pain in his arm made him vomit. Looking around at the debris floating in the murky water, he found a length of wood and pulled himself on top of it. Stealing a few minutes, he lay clinging to the board, catching his breath until he could move. Paddling with one arm and one leg, it was slow going. The sound of gunfire and the crackling of flames were everywhere. The acrid smell of gunpowder and salt water mixed in his nostrils. He heard screams as his own ship was now facing the others in the flotilla, and cannon fire shook the air. The British were using their own ships against them!

Kolton was losing blood fast. His mind was feeling boggy, and fatigue was seeping into his limbs. He needed to get somewhere to hide. Glancing around at the terrifying chaos, he knew he would be as good as dead if the British got him. He would rather die than be a prisoner.

After what seemed like hours, he reached the shore. Rolling on to his back and gulping in air, he prayed to God the pain in his shoulder and leg would disappear, but he was also grateful to be alive to feel it. Stumbling along the water's edge, he moved away from the melee. He watched as the last of the destroyed ships shuttered and creaked as they were pulled below the water's inky surface. Kolton followed the curve of the bank and saw a ship some distance away from the fighting. It was ablaze, even though it was nowhere near the attack. He could see men in boats paddling away from the wreck and he limped faster, hoping they would take him to safety. Just when he thought they would leave him behind, a crew member saw him and one boat headed in his direction. They pulled him into the already cramped space and set off away from the fighting.

The trip through the swamps had almost done him in. Between the mosquitoes and flies, lack of clean water and the constant threat from alligators and snakes, he was delirious by the time they got to where they were going. His wounds reeked of infection, and he'd convinced himself that the remaining men in his boat were just keeping him around in case they needed to distract the gators. It had been two weeks before he was coherent enough to know what had happened.

The remains of the group had found a little house west of Waveland. The house was an isolated summer property, but a few of the locals helped when they found out soldiers needed shelter, food and medical aid. Several of the sailors succumbed to swamp fever, and others had died due to blood poisoning. Still others had gotten separated or lost in the maze of the swamps. Out of the thirty-five men that had made the trip through the swamp, only sixteen survived.

If he was honest, the only thing that kept him going once he had regained consciousness... was her. Lord, if the only thing that came out of this whole war was meeting her then it was all worth it. The moment he'd opened his eyes to look into that angel face, he thought he'd died and gone to heaven. Luckily, it wasn't heaven and that sweet girl had moved him like none other. Her name was Ava, and she was the most beautiful woman he'd ever seen.

She took care of him, nursing him back to health as best she could. Now, as he looked around at the few remaining men still recovering, he waited to find out what was happening with the war and wondered how he would ever leave her. He knew it was absurd, but there was something about her, and he knew she felt it too.

He went downstairs to where he knew she would be. Kolton stopped in the doorway and watched as she washed her hands and arms. She had her light brown hair pulled up in a loose bun, as it always was, and he wondered how it would look hanging down her back in lovely waves. Her face was delicate, with high cheekbones, long lashes and porcelain skin. She was wearing a light blue dress with a scoop neckline, allowing Kolton just a glimpse of the top crest of her breasts. Her cheeks were flushed, and Kolton could tell she had been working hard. Her face looked serious as she continued to scrub, lost in her thoughts. She looked beautiful today, and Kolton's whole body sang with need for her. Clearing his throat, she looked over at him, and her whole face lit up. He knew for a fact that she didn't give everyone that look, and it made him solidify his resolve to make her his.

"Kolton! It's good to see you up and moving. How you feelin'?"

Her sweet southern twang filled his heart, and he smiled as he watched her dry her hands. Looking at those gentle hands made him think about all the times she'd touched him, caring for him.

As she moved towards him, he said, "Doing much better, Miss Ava. I think you done fixed me up right good." She smiled and looked deep into his eyes. Realizing that she may have stared too long, she glanced away and fussed over the wound on his shoulder. She uncovered the area and took a good long look to make sure it was healing as it should. Then, motioning to the chair by the door, she asked him to sit down. "Let me take a quick look at that leg since you've come all the way down here. And I don't want you over-exertin' yourself. You need plenty of rest, ya hear?"

He smiled down into her face as she knelt and unraveled the bandage. Just above his right knee was the nasty gash. Kolton looked on as Ava went over to get some water to clean the wound. She rinsed the cloth as she cleaned, her cool, gentle fingers holding his leg as she re-bandaged it. God, he wanted to touch her. Staring at her, he felt the overwhelming need to feel her in his arms.

Ava was getting up from the floor when she fell forward and landed against his good arm. Kolton wrapped his arm around her and looked into her grey-green eyes. Leaning forward, he brushed his lips against hers and heard her gasp, but she didn't move away. Pulling her closer, he kissed her deeper, and she parted her lips and he took the invitation to continue.

A noise coming down the stairs made her pull away. He continued to look at her as she took the bowl she'd been using over to the pail against the wall. Kolton sat there thinking about the kiss, and every bone in his body pulsed with need. His heart burst knowing she'd kissed him back. Maybe she wanted to be his. The sound from out in the hall grew louder and Major Temple appeared in the door-

way. He was a good man and Kolton owed him a debt of gratitude for pulling him into the boat which brought him here.

"Son, how you feelin' today? You're looking better than you did a fortnight ago," the major said.

"I'm feeling much better, Sir, thank you. Any news?" The major had traveled to get information about who was winning the war and what the next move should be.

The major moved further into the room. "I heard they're moving across the river in two days. We best pray hard. We'll need all the help we can get. I know you're not ready, but we need all the able bodies we have. Rest up, we'll be moving out at sunrise tomorrow."

Kolton nodded as he said, "Yes, Sir." He may have agreed, but his heart sank. He wasn't ready to leave Ava yet.

As the major moved off to tell the other soldiers the news, Kolton watched as Ava stood staring out the window. He couldn't see her face, but the stiffness in her back betrayed her feelings. Moving over to stand behind her, he could see her shift as he got close. Just as he was about to touch her, she spun and kissed him hard. Circling her waist, he pulled her close. She pulled away just as quickly. Looking deep into his eyes, she said, "I'm sorry. That's twice now you made me lose my head. It's just... I'm sad to see you leave is all. I don't think you're healed enough for this journey, and I'd hate to see you get injured again."

Seeing the pain in her eyes, he pulled her close and whispered in her ear, "Meet me at the long barn at the edge of the woods tonight. Don't let anyone know you're coming. I have things I need to say before I leave." And with that, he left the room.

Later, during the twilight hour, Kolton stumbled through the long grass making his way to the barn at the edge of the woods. He slipped out right as everyone was coming and going from dinner. He considered it a small miracle he'd gotten away unnoticed. On his way passed the house, he found a lantern sitting on a stump and grabbed it. He pushed himself through a doorway at the back of the old barn. He lit the lantern and set it on an old wooden crate. The space was dirty, and full of spider webs, but at least it was private. He found some hay bundles, and though it took way more energy than it should have, he moved a few together so they would have something to sit on. There was a moth-eaten blanket hanging on the one wall and he placed it over the hay.

He sat on the hay and lay back. Moving those bales took a lot of his strength. He closed his eyes until Ava appeared at the door. She'd changed into a thin white cotton dress. By the light of the lantern she was breathtaking, almost glowing. Moving further into the room, she didn't approach him right away. She looked around the space and stood in the middle of the floor.

"I was kinda hoping I wouldn't have to yell, but with you being way over there, I might have to." Kolton smiled as he watched her blush, her cheeks and chest flushing pink. His tiredness forgotten, all he wanted to do was hold her.

She walked closer and sat on the bale beside him. He stared at her hands as she nervously gripped them, not looking at him. The cotton of her dress looked soft and tight over her breasts, and Kolton had to concentrate on his breathing.

"Now that's better. No sense wasting precious breath." He shifted closer and was glad when she didn't move away. She looked at him and could see the mix of emotions in her eyes.

"I've never been with a man alone before. But I couldn't stay away. I wanted to see you before you left. I... I will miss you. It's only been a short while, but I feel like I've known you forever. Doesn't that seem strange?" she said softly.

Kolton spoke, "No, not at all. I feel the same way."

Ava smiled up into his face, and his heart swelled. It took all his willpower not to lean in and kiss her. But he had things he still needed to say. "Ava, I know I'm not going about this the right way, but I already know I want to be with you. You've said you have no one else except your aunt. I would love to take you back to my home, you'd love it there. And your aunt could come too. But I need to go with Major Temple to fight this battle. When it's over, I'll come back for you."

He watched tears fill her eyes as she nodded. Kolton cleared his throat and pulled a cord from around his neck. He'd put it on before he left home some four years ago, and he'd been saving it for someone special.

"I have something for you, Ava. I know this is not the proper way of such things, but seeing as I'm short on time, I must ignore the expected formality. With your permission, I would like to give you this ring. It's my promise to you. I will come back for you, no matter what, unless death takes me. I want to make you my wife, Ava. You saved my life and now I want to build a life with you."

Taking her hand in his, he pushed the ring onto her finger and it fit perfectly, as if it were meant to be. He pulled her hand to his lips and kissed it, then looked at her face. She was smiling and tears spilled down her cheeks. He took her face in his hands and brushed them away. "Ava, don't cry. You've made me the happiest man. I will make you happy, too."

Kolton leaned in and kissed her. It was tender and her lips were so soft and warm. She smelled like gardenias, like the ones in his mother's garden. Ava's hands gripped the front of his shirt and the kiss became deeper, more urgent. Before he could think better of it, he was pulling her onto his good leg so he could feel her body closer to him. His thin cotton trousers could not hide the evidence of how much he wanted her, nor block the heat of her body from his skin. Running his hand down her neck, he could feel how soft her skin was and her breaths were coming faster. Dragging his hands down her sides and back up, he cupped the underside of her breast.

Breaking the kiss, his lips traveled to her neck. She didn't resist and he could feel her hands travel up his back and into his hair, gripping it and him tighter. Everything about her urged him to hold her and feel every part of her body. Kissing her just above her breast, Kolton heard a soft moan leave her lips and his trousers tightened further.

Stopping to look into her face, he could see her kiss-swollen lips. Her eyes were half-lidded, almost as if she had too many sips of bourbon. He waited for her to focus on him and said, "I want to be with you Ava, and I know that's not proper, but everything about you makes me want you. I won't push you. We can stop this now, if you wish." It had almost killed him to say the last part, but he would respect her wishes.

She looked deep into his eyes and smiled. "Kolton, you just promised to marry me. And now you're goin' back to the war, and I don't know when I'll see you again. I know it is not proper, just as you said, but I want to be with you too. We only have this one night to hold us until your return. I want as many memories of you as I can hold in my heart. This might not be right, but you are who I want. Make me yours, Kolton."

They kissed again, and he didn't hold back. Untying her dress, he pulled it over her head to find she had a white camisole slip underneath. Ava removed it herself, along with her undergarments. She undid the string on his shirt and pulled it over his head, being careful to not tug his shoulder. She moved off the hay and helped him swing his leg over so he was lying down. Ava's fingers undid the laces of his pants. He watched as she pulled them off, fascinated as he watched her. Her smooth skin and rounded hips and breasts were more beautiful than he imagined.

Once he was naked, she stood before him. Breathtaking was all he could think. She lay beside him, and he felt overwhelmed by what they were about to do. Ava reached for him, and they kissed. He ran his hands all over her body, enjoying the feel and sounds Ava made. Her hand slipped along his stomach and hesitated before she gripped his cock. He touched her, slipping his fingers inside to feel her wetness. She gasped at the contact, but instead of moving away, she pushed herself against his hand. This was as far as he'd ever been with a woman, and although he had heard stories, he was nervous. It also worried him that he couldn't do things the way he'd been told because of his injuries.

As if realizing his concerns, Ava stopped and looked him in the eyes. She ran her hands over his chest, and then pushed him onto his back. Before he could ask, she straddled his hips, and he felt the tip of his cock rest at the entrance of her sex. The moisture coated his length and he struggled to hold back.

Watching her, he could see she was nervous too. Pulling her down, he kissed her, telling her it was her choice. Then she shifted her hips, and he was inside her. Every muscle in his body contracted and relaxed at the same time. It was the most incredible feeling he'd ever experienced.

As he watched Ava's face, he could see how she concentrated, not enjoying it, but not giving up. She moved, pushing him deeper, and he felt something inside her tear. Her face contorted with pain and he sat up as best he could and held her. She clung to him, and he kissed her, trying to help her through the pain. He whispered and consoled her, telling her how much he loved her for giving herself to him, and if she wanted to stop, they could. After a few minutes she moved again, and he looked into her face for assurance. She smiled and nodded and he lay back down, overwhelmed by the sensation.

Moving deeper into her, she gasped and tightened her fingers against his chest. He pulled her forward, and they lay chest to chest, her hair falling around them like a silken curtain. Strangely, he didn't remember when she'd taken her hair down, but he pushed his fingers into it, feeling the thick locks with his hands. Pushing his face into her neck, he breathed her in, but she didn't smell like gardenias anymore; she smelled like magnolias.

* * *

Liam slowed his hip thrusts and realized he was awake, and Maggie was straddling him, his cock buried deep inside her and she was making small sounds of pleasure as she slid up and down his length. Pulling her back down against his chest, he held her tight and pushed in deep. She gasped, and a moan escaped her lips.

Keeping up the rhythm, he couldn't help but think back to the dream. It was strange to know he'd started this rendezvous in a dream only to wake up, his cock hard inside Maggie.

"Baby, you feel so good." Maggie stilled and pushed back to look into Liam's eyes, surprise on her face. "Hey there beautiful, didn't you think I might wake up once you started doing this to me?" Then he kissed her deep, and she was right there with him.

Wanting more control, he flipped them over to her back and pulled her hips up, getting the angle he knew she liked.

He pumped into her faster, hitting her pleasure spot and feeling her passage tightening around him.

"That's it, Baby, I can feel you on the edge. Ah, fuck, I'm there too... don't hold back. Come for me!"

And with that they both slipped into the abyss. He didn't stop pumping until he felt her relax underneath him. As he stared down into her face, he saw the contented smile and kissed along her shoulder, tasting the lotion he'd put on her earlier. He wanted to stay inside her, but his body had other ideas. It was then he realized he wore no condom and his eyes flashed up to Maggie's face.

"Um, Maggie? I'm not wearing a condom. Don't, um, there's no need to panic. I was tested not too long ago and can show you my test results. I never have sex without a condom. Well, except this time."

Maggie was watching him, and she bit her lip. "I'm so sorry, I don't even remember... I guess I was distracted. I'm clean too and I'm on the pill."

Dipping his head down, he kissed along her jaw. "Sweetheart, you can take advantage of me like that anytime. It was like a dream come true. Anyway, I better get us a cloth, before we make a complete mess."

Giving her one last kiss, he slipped out of her and went to the washroom. He hadn't been kidding about the dream come true part. As much as he joked with her, he was a little unsettled about how real the two events were. His dreams recently had felt real, and this one left him with a sensation of pain in his shoulder and leg from the injuries. How strange to experience a dream so real, there seemed to be no line between it and reality.

14

Waking up from a fitful night sleep, Maggie's head felt foggy. She and Liam had curled up after their midnight sexcapade and he'd fallen right back to sleep. Meanwhile she lay there staring at the ceiling wondering what the hell had happened. One minute she was with an injured soldier named Kolton in her dream, and next she was having amazing sex with Liam. In the dream, her feelings toward Kolton felt genuine. Her heart was breaking knowing that he had to go back to the war. Then, with talk of the future, she could feel hope and love.

Then she heard Liam speak, and the dream was real. Or at least that's how it felt with their bodies together. The bridge between dream and reality had been... seamless, like there had been no difference between Kolton and Liam. And the situation unnerved Maggie.

Not to mention the fact that she'd been so deep in her dream it didn't occur to her that there was no condom. Guess safe sex was not on the top of Kolton and Ava's mind considering he'd just proposed. Never in her life had she taken such risks. That dream was beyond real, and along with all the other dreams she'd been experiencing, she knew what she had to do. No matter how much she dreaded it. She needed to get some answers.

Glancing at the clock, she could see that it was almost seven. She knew she wouldn't sleep anymore, so she dragged herself out of Liam's hold. She tiptoed into the washroom, grabbing a sleep shirt and pajama shorts along the way. Once finished, she went straight to her coffee maker and started a pot. Coffee would be her best friend today, as it was most days.

Checking out her fridge, she realized the pickings were slim. To be honest, she didn't keep much here anyway, since her grandmother was a fantastic cook and fed her most of the time. She would just sneak downstairs and see if there was something she could 'borrow' for breakfast.

Making her way down the stairs to her grandmother's apartment, it always reminded Maggie of how much she loved this house. It held her grandmother's scent of Chanel No. 5 and an underlying smell of sugary confections. It was a wonder Maggie could keep her figure trim with the amount of baked goods available.

As Maggie strolled into the kitchen, there was a note on the table in her grandmother's flowing script.

Morning, Magpie,

There are two plates in the oven. I knew you would need something to feed to your very handsome house guest, and since you didn't get groceries, I made extra this morning. You can thank me later by taking my garbage out and getting some groceries. I attached a shopping list since you're going.

Love Gram xo

Maggie's stomach grumbled knowing that her grandmother had cooked them breakfast. She opened the oven door, and the smell of waffles surrounded her. Grabbing the oven mitts, she used the tray on the counter and loaded the two plates. Maggie also grabbed syrup and some creamer she pilfered out of the fridge for coffee and made off up the stairs like a bandit. God, she loved that woman!

As she stepped back into her apartment with her treasures, she glanced at the bed to find it empty. Liam must be in the washroom. She placed the tray on the kitchen table and went to get utensils and mugs. Just as she was reaching into the cupboard, Liam slipped his arms around her and kissed her neck. His hands drifted over her breasts and tweaked her nipple and she almost dropped the mug in her hand.

"Good morning, Babe. Sorry, didn't mean to distract you, but watching you in these tiny, fitted shorts has me thinking about ways I would like to remove them from your body." He continued kissing her neck for a few more seconds, then his sense of smell caught up with his brain and he pulled away to eye up the table. "Do I smell... waffles?"

"Wow, it took you a whole twenty seconds to notice. Guess I'm not losing my touch," she said with a laugh in her tone.

Liam gave her a final kiss and took a seat at the table. She filled their mugs and followed him, noticing how good he looked all rumpled from sleep. Even waking up with bed head, this guy looked like he could pull off a cover shoot for Esquire. He uncovered his plate, and Maggie watched his eyes widen. Licking his lips, he looked over at her and smiled. "It's official. Your grandmother loves me, and I'm falling hard for her too."

Maggie rolled her eyes and took a sip of her coffee. Liam dug right in and had devoured half his plate before she'd even started. She took the first couple of bites and let the flavor take her back to her childhood. Back then she would have put whipped cream, chocolate chips and all kinds of stuff on them. Now she would stick with just a little syrup.

Looking back over at Liam, she could see that his plate was empty, and he seemed to eye up her breakfast. Frowning, she pulled her plate closer. Liam's eyes went from her plate to her eyes and she watched as his lip popped out. "Are you kidding me right now? You had, like, four waffles! I only have two! Besides, you actually want me to give you some of my precious waffles, after you just said you were falling in love with my grandmother? Think again, Mr. Kavanagh." She huffed out her breath and looked down at her plate.

Taking her fork and cutting off a piece of waffle, she slipped it between her lips and chewed. Maggie licked the syrup off her bottom lip as she ate, and Liam's eyes darkened as she did so. She went through the motions again, and he watched every move she made. Cutting off another piece, she dipped it in syrup and held it out for him to eat. He hesitated for only a moment, then put it in his mouth. Swallowing, he licked his bottom lip and smirked at her, but looking eager for the next bite.

This went on until Maggie's plate was clean. She set her utensils down and cleared her throat, "I have to say, this has been the most fun I've ever had with waffles. We should do it again... sometime." She kept it light as she didn't want to have another awkward situation like yesterday.

Before she could make a move, Liam was out of his seat and moving her chair. Maggie watched as he knelt on his knees between her legs. Without a word, he dipped his finger into the leftover syrup on her plate and ran it across her bottom lip. He then laid that same finger on her lip until she opened her mouth. Inserting his finger, she licked off the syrup and watched his eyes heat with desire. He dipped his finger back in the syrup, repeating the motion.

Liam leaned in and licked her bottom lip and sucked it into his warm mouth. She gasped and moved into the kiss. He pulled away and dipped his finger into the syrup again, this time dabbing it onto her neck. He moved his head down and licked it off. She could feel the swirl of his tongue on her skin and she became wet. He repeated this on the other side of her neck and the motion of his tongue had her squirming in her chair.

The next thing she knew, Liam was pulling her sleep top over her head and he swirled syrup coated fingers around her nipple. His eyes were on hers, pupils dilated with need, as he moved his lips, covering her erect nipple and sucking it into his mouth. Maggie's head fell back, and a moan escaped her lips. Liam released that nipple and was coating the next one, pulling it into his mouth and sending tingles straight between her legs.

Liam swirled a line of syrup around her belly button and she watched as he licked it all away. While he did that, he peeled her pajama shorts over her hips. She shifted her body so he could drag them down her legs. She knew where this was going, and she was greedy enough to let it happen. Opening her legs, Liam dipped his two fingers in what remained of the syrup and swirled it on her clit. She half gasped, half panted as she watched him take his time. His lips followed the syrup trail, and then it was all sensations. He had the most incredible mouth, and she was reaping the benefits of his skill.

Her hands buried in that messy hair, she directed him as she sought her pleasure. But soon that wasn't enough. She needed him inside her. "Need you." Maggie's voice was strained with arousal.

Liam didn't need to be told twice. Shuffling his pants off, he picked her up as if she weighed nothing at all and buried himself inside her. Standing and moving away from the table, he leaned her against the wall and rocked into her nice and slow. She'd been on the verge of orgasm before, and with this motion it launched her into a complete tidal wave of ecstasy. His movements became erratic and she knew he was close. Hanging on tight, she felt him go over the edge, calling out her name. It was the sweetest sound, and she swore she would forever remember this moment.

Once Liam stopped moving, she could feel his slicked skin beneath her hands and continued to feel him pulsing deep within her. Holding on, she waited for it to stop. She never realized before what an intimate moment that was. The feeling as his climax continued to roll through him. She kissed his neck and waited for him to make the next move.

Instead of putting her down, he pulled her tighter and walked them both into the bathroom. Holding her with one arm, he turned on the taps and started the shower. Before stepping in, he kissed her again. Maggie loved the way she felt every ounce of his desire in his kiss.

Stepping under the spray, he placed her feet on the tub bottom and in doing so, his now flaccid cock slipped from her. The emptiness she felt made her feel overcome with emotion. As if reading her thoughts, Liam tipped her chin up and kissed her again. She let him take care of her, washing first her hair, then her body. He took special care of all the places he'd put syrup on her skin. As he took care of her, she did her best not to think about how things would be when he left.

* * *

After they showered and got dressed, Liam's phone signaled an incoming text. He walked over to the bedside table to retrieve his phone and read the text as he walked back towards her.

"My aunt's having a BBQ this evening at her place. My uncle Lukas and aunt Lilian are down from Baton Rouge. Sounds like a lot of my cousins will be there. She said that since I'm here they would love to see me."

Maggie's heart sank a little. She'd decided in the wee hours to do something she'd been putting off for years. Having woken up in Liam's arms, but thinking she was with Kolton, she knew she needed to find out what was going on. And that meant she needed to finally go and see Emeline. But, it would mean she would need to give up most of the day with him, and now he needed to spend time with his family tonight.

She decided she couldn't be selfish and keep him all for herself. She'd seen that too many times, and she would not do that to Liam or herself. He had a family to see, and they wanted to spend some time with him too. Maybe it was for the best. She was no stranger to spending time by herself. She didn't need anyone's help to find entertaining ways to spend her evening.

Even thinking it made her heart ache knowing that their time was slipping away. And knowing she was getting too close to him was making her feel anxious and needy. Geez, she knew this was a bad idea. Why had she listened to her heart! Stupid heart. Maggie knew she needed to start pulling away.

Liam didn't look up from his phone, as he said, "So what should we bring to this shindig?"

"Oh, um, I think it would be a nice idea if you spent some time with your family. They don't get to see you much and I wouldn't want to intrude. After all you're not here for... you must get back soon and it's not fair to them if they have to..." Maggie let her statement trail off as Liam stared at her, his brow furrowed.

"What are you talking about? I don't want to go without you. I thought it would be nice for you to meet some of my family." Liam rolled his eyes and continued, "Wait, was I supposed to *ask* if you want to come? Because, with all the time we've spent together this week, I thought we were passed that."

For whatever reason, that got Maggie's back up. "Passed what, exactly? I didn't want to bring this up, and I still don't want too, but what is this Liam? For all I know, you're leaving to go back to New York in a few days. Once your work is finished, you'll be going back to your life and I'll get back to mine. I'm not asking for promises, which will undoubtedly be broken once you go back to your big city life. I'm just saying that if my heart is about to get crushed, then I don't think I want to drag any more people into this scenario. No, you know what, forget I said anything. I have to be somewhere this morning and I don't have time to deal with this."

As she moved to head towards the washroom, Liam stepped in front of her, palms out as if trying to stop a charging horse. "Whoa! What just happened here? What'd I miss? I'm just talking about you and I going to a BBQ with my family. The next thing I know you're fuming about me leaving, breaking promises and crushing your heart. Then you say you don't want to talk about it and you're leaving? Where the hell are you going? You never said you were going anywhere until right this second," he said, expression perplexed.

Maggie couldn't seem to control her raging emotions. She wanted this conversation to end, or even better, for it to never have started. But she couldn't seem to stop the tangent.

"How dare you demand to know where I'm going? I'm a grown woman and I can do what I please. And yes, in fact, an invitation to go with you would have been nice. I don't know you well enough to read you. Meeting your family is many steps beyond some sleepovers and wild sex. I was only trying to respect your family's time with you. And I don't want to talk about whatever this is Liam. I didn't mean to infer that there was anything more than us just having a fun romp in the hay. I'm not a fool, Liam. People hook up and walk away all the time. We knew going into this that it would end. I'm not blind to the possibility. You know what? I'm done talking about this." She pushed passed him and walked into the washroom, but before she could close the door, Liam was standing there staring down at her. His eyes looked sad and hurt, and this was why Maggie hadn't wanted to have this conversation. She knew her emotions were a mess and anything she said about their 'relationship' would come out wrong.

Before she could say anything to fix the mess she just caused, Liam said, in an almost tortured tone, "Is that all this is to you? A fun romp in the hay?" He shook his head, staring deep into her eyes. "I refuse to believe you feel that way, because I've seen the way you look at me, and the way you touch me. Those are not the actions of someone who is just going through the motions. You feel something for me, Maggie, and I sure as hell feel something for you. Damn it, I've never felt like this before, so don't go thinking this is just some cheap fling. I won't lie and say it isn't scaring the shit out of me, but I have feelings for you. We might not have all the answers, but I know I haven't had this much fun being with someone ever. This is not a one-night stand, Maggie, I've done those."

He moved the door further open and cupped her face. Tears filled her eyes as a lump formed in her throat. He leaned in and kissed her, soft and very slow. It wasn't like the other kisses they'd shared. This kiss was conveying something much deeper.

Liam pulled back so he could look deep into her eyes. "How about we start over? I'll say, 'Hey, Maggie, I would love for you to come to this BBQ with me. It should be a blast'. Then you could say, 'Thanks Liam, that would be great and sounds like fun, I can't wait'. Then I would say, 'That's great. I wouldn't want to go without you because I want to spend all my time with you'. You'd reply, 'I want to spend all my time with you, but I have something to do this morning, so I will meet up with you later'. And I would say, 'That's just fine. You do what you need to do and we can meet up and get something to take to the BBQ'. Then you would say, 'And after the BBQ we can come back here and I can ravage your body for hours."

Maggie rolled her eyes, but grinned. She could see the tension easing from Liam's face. "I'm sorry I got upset. That was uncalled for. I was judging you against others I've been with, and that wasn't fair. I would love to come with you to the BBQ. And I have a great idea for what to bring," she said.

Liam hadn't let go of her face yet and he was studying her as he said, "When we have more time, and if you're willing to share, tell me about all the assholes that've hurt you. But they couldn't have been all bad. I recall a certain law enforcement officer who seems to be willing to give you another shot."

At the mention of Kenny, Maggie groaned. "Poor Kenny, he wasn't one of the bad ones. He's sweet and kind, but I didn't feel the same way. I never felt..."

"Passion, desire, butterflies?" Liam asked, brows raised in question.

Maggie raised an eyebrow. "Butterflies?"

Liam smirked. "Sorry, I was trying to think like a woman."

She shook her head. "I just never had feelings for him that way. He always felt like a friend. I never wanted him."

Liam grew serious and opened his mouth as if to say something further, but closed it. Instead, he placed his lips on her forehead, giving her a light kiss. Maggie was glad he asked nothing further, because she would have loved to add, 'Like I want you' to the end of her sentence.

15

Maggie dropped Liam off at the curb just outside the hotel. After he gave her a lingering kiss that made her heart swoon, he winked and waved as she pulled away. That guy gave her a case of the lower trembles with just a look.

Traffic wasn't bad as she made her way onto Highway 10 and before she knew it, she was moving across the Maestri Bridge to Slidell. The warm wind whipped through her open window and tugged at the loose strands of her hair. Looking out over the water, she watched the rippling waves of Lake Pontchartrain catch the sunlight, reminding her of dancing diamonds. Off to her right she could see the patches of green where the Bayou Sauvage National Wildlife Refuge began before it widened out to the lake.

Enjoying the moment and lost in her thoughts, Maggie let her mind drift back to Liam. How had it been less than a week since they'd met? She already couldn't imagine her life without him. This was utter madness. Sure he was handsome, smart, kind, funny, thoughtful, great with kids, super-hot and sexy and an incredible lover, but still she'd known him less than a week. However, when they were together, and she looked deep in his eyes, he felt familiar. He was right on the mark with his comments about feeling like they had known each other before. And not just like an acquaintance from somewhere, but intimately.

Shaking her head, she decided she would deal with her feelings about Liam later. Right now, she needed to prepare for her encounter with Emeline. She'd seen her fleetingly at parties and church gatherings, but had avoided her for the last several years. Not that she didn't like Emeline, but the woman made her feel uneasy. Maybe uneasy wasn't exactly what she felt. It was the prophetic air about her that was unsettling. As well as Emeline's way of looking at her with remorse and sorrow.

After she'd lost her parents, lots of adults looked at her that way. However, Emeline's eyes made her feel exposed. She had the most unusual light amber eyes, and while that alone was rare, paired with her dark complexion, they stood out even more. They made Maggie feel like Emeline was looking into her somehow; like she knew of ancient sorrows that would break souls and steal all the joy from the world.

As a mambo, Emeline saw many things. Perhaps it wasn't just Maggie she looked at that way. Maybe it was just her view of humanity that made her seem almost other-worldly. Geez, now she was getting carried away. The impending visit with Emeline was wigging her out.

Getting off the highway, she drove into Slidell. Maggie wove her way through the town to Cemetery Road where Emeline lived. It was a short dead-end road that led to an old cemetery. Her house backed right onto the Bayou Bonfouca. Pulling into the dirt driveway, she took her first real look at the house in seventeen years. It had changed very little in all that time. Built back in 1859, it had been in Emeline's husband's family from the beginning.

They made the house of cypress wood, which could withstand the regular downpours and constant humidity of Louisiana. The exterior was unpainted except for the red trim on the windows and the dark green hurricane shutters. They painted the tin roof a dark brown and there was a wide wraparound porch, which made you feel like you just stepped back in time. As with most homes in this area, they built it on risers, over three feet off the ground to guard against flooding.

She stepped out of the car and felt enveloped in the sounds and smells of the bayou. Laurel oak and bald cypress trees surrounded the house and Spanish moss dripped from their branches, draping the house like moth-eaten curtains. Flowering plants bloomed on either side of the front stairs, a tapestry of whites, pinks and reds. Birds chirped and swooped through the front yard, while the frogs croaked out a tune down by the water. Standing still for a few minutes, Maggie let herself enjoy the moment engulfed in her senses.

Jolted out of her thoughts by a high, ragged voice, Maggie spun around to the front step. "Took ya seventeen years to get back 'round to a visit, and now I find you, statue still on my front walk. I ain't got no hex on my property, so why are ya standing there?"

Maggie's cheeks pinked as she started towards the door. "Sorry about that. I was just enjoying the surroundings. Your house is just like I remembered it."

Emeline's amber eyes crinkled at the corners, her dark skin showing a few dark freckles across her nose. Maggie may have an issue with the amber eyes, but Emeline was stunning. She was tall and thin, with a regal posture. With a luminous tone to her skin and a sassy tilt to her chin, she was a sight to behold. Dressed in a light-blue embroidered top with bell sleeves and black capri pants with a purple scarf over her hair, she did not look like she was a practicing mambo. But then again, Maggie didn't know many voodoo priestesses, so how would she know what they wore.

"Come on up here. Oh my, child, look at ya. What a beautiful woman ya are now. I remember ya comin' here with little Lolita, all knobby knees and just starting to bud into womanhood. Those big grey-green eyes lookin' up at me." Emeline paused before she said, "I scared ya that day, I know I did, and I'm sorry for it. But having ya come here after having so many dreams about cha, I just couldn't believe ya was standin' in my house. But let's not get into that. I fixed us some sweet tea and baked some of my famous spice cookies. Let's sit a spell, then we can get down to business."

Pausing, Maggie looked at Emeline with a curious gaze. "How did you know I was coming? I didn't tell anyone."

Emeline gave Maggie a serious look and nodded her head. "Well now, that's a story, isn't it? But I've known ya were coming this morning. The elders, they tell me things, and I never question it. And here ya are, standing on my front porch, looking as pretty as a magnolia blossom. And since you're here, I'm guessing ya have some questions. So, let's have us some tea."

Walking into the house transported Maggie to another time. The hardwood floors were dark and polished to a glossy shine, the smell of lemon in the air. Glimpsing the front parlor, she could see a large black marble mantle with ornate furnishings.

The room opposite was a dining room with a long oak table, a hand-stitched runner down its center. Six chairs circled the table, and it all gleamed with a high shine. A beautiful chandelier hung over the table, its clear gems glinting in the muted light coming through the white shears on the windows. Pictures and paintings covered every wall in the house. Family photos, both current and generations past, and paintings of Christian saints and still others of different practitioners of voodoo, all hung in ornamental frames. As she moved further into the house, she saw a beautiful photo of Emeline and her husband Louis, with their three children, Aimee, Jules and Laurent hanging in the main hallway.

Maggie stopped to look at the picture as Emeline said from behind her, "Lookin' at that picture makes me remember when they was little. They would fill this house with the sound of their feet running up and down the stairs. Their friends would come and go. My sweet babies. They all grown up now.

Aimee and her husband live over in Biloxi. He's got that high-paying job at a law firm. She's at home right now with her two babies. She calls me just 'bout every day. That girl thought having babies would be easy, but she still needs her mama. Then there's Jules. Oh Lord, but that child has always been my trial! He's at Tulane trying to finish his master's degree in some biomedical engineering something or other. Never thought I'd see the day when that boy would sit still and learn, but then children are full of surprises, aren't they?"

Emeline reached over and pointed at the smallest boy in

the picture. “Then there is my baby of babies, my Laurent. He is my special love. Now I love all my children the same, but that one, he fills a space in my heart. Maybe it was because I almost lost him when he was born, but he was a gift to us. I just look at him and my heart swells. He’s so handsome in his N’Orlean’s police department uniform. Been with the force over two years now. My Laurent comes and sees me every chance he gets. He’s been datin’ Adela May now for a while. I suspect he’ll pop the question one of these days, but we’ll see.”

Looking over at Emeline, she could see the pride on her face and a glisten of tears in her amber eyes. Seeing the look of love and joy on Emeline’s face, Maggie felt a wave of shame for having not come sooner. Just being in the same room with this woman, feelings of love coming from her, she knew she’d been missing out on something special.

They made their way towards the back of the house, but as they did, Maggie spied another room. This room held the tools of Emeline’s trade. The light was low inside, but she could make out an altar of sorts. There was a statue made of wood, but Maggie did not understand who it was. Surrounding it were candles and dishes and what looked to be offerings of food, drink and other sundry items. In behind it, hanging on the wall, was a woven blanket with intricate patterns in red, black and white. She could see shelves filled with jars of medicinal herbs. A countertop was also visible, and it held crosses and bundles of herbs, a mortar and pestle, and many other items.

Maggie heard lots of stories over the years from her grandmother and Gladys. Emeline was always helping the sick and destitute. They said she could fix anything, from croup, hangovers, cold and flu, bad luck, broken hearts, and cheating husbands. People came from everywhere just to see her.

Seeing Maggie stare into her workroom, Emeline said, "Now child, we'll get to that soon enough, but let's have ourselves a drink. It's gonna to be a warm one today."

Looking away, she followed until they made it out to the back porch. Slow moving fans hung from the porch ceiling and they sat at a small table. The pitcher of sweet tea and a plate of cookies covered over with a piece of foil sat on the table.

The gardens were flourishing. Maggie could make out a vegetable garden off to the side where there was an opening in the trees to allow more sunlight. The other gardens were full of various plants that she couldn't identify, but she was certain every plant had a purpose. "Your gardens are amazing. It's beautiful back here and smells so good." Maggie closed her eyes and took in a deep breath.

"Probably the almond verbena or the confederate jasmine you smell. I love those, too. And thank you for the compliment. I spend a lot of time out here, tending and talking to my lovelies. They grow better when I talk to 'em. Plants are important to the things I do, so I give them all the attention they deserve."

Maggie could see the bees and butterflies hovering over the plants and could hear the water gurgle along the bayou. The whole scene was right out of a painting. "You must love sitting back here. It's so peaceful and relaxing."

Emeline smiled. "Yes, I enjoy my little slice of heaven. But I love to have visitors too. Now that my babies are off livin' their lives, it gets lonely some. People come seekin' my help and I do all I can to fix 'em, but nights can be lonely."

Watching, Emeline filled two glasses with tea and place one in front of her. Maggie smiled at her and said, "You're still young, why don't you find someone else?"

A high-pitched laugh came from Emeline. "Now you sound just like your grandmama. Oh my, that woman is somethin' else! She told me the same thing not too long ago. I know it's goin' on four years since Louis passed, but I loved him so. Ya know, he courted me for two years, and in the beginning I never gave him the time a day. Between you and me, I played hard to get. I mean, I wanted him to earn my affection. And boy, did he. He was *some* handsome. Oh Lord, but he could make my heart flutta' non-stop. The first time he kissed me, my whole world just up and tilted and I swear I floated on air for weeks."

Maggie remembered the first kiss from Liam and knew how Emeline felt.

"I was never so happy as when he asked me to marry him. I walked down the aisle, making him mine and promising our love and hearts to each other. Only thing better was looking into the faces of our babies when they was born. I don't know how I feel about lookin' for someone else. Some nice men in town have asked me out, but they're not for me. Maybe someday some nice man will come along, but until then I have my gardens and my babies and lots of good friends." Smiling, she looked over at Maggie. "I hear someone has caught your eye? Someone tall, dark and handsome. From New York, but born here, is that right?"

Maggie nodded, wondering where this conversation was

going. With Gladys and her grandmother on the top of Emeline's conversation list, she could only imagine what she had been told.

"That fits. He comes from far away, but his roots are here. His foundation always starts in the South, but he has him a sense of adventure. He's sharp too. Educated, with a big ol' heart a gold. They whisper to me, the elders do, and they tell me he's the one. They say your heart feels the pull. Are they right, child, do you feel somethin' for him like none before?"

Blowing out a breath, she didn't know how to answer. Did she feel that way? Yes, maybe, she wasn't sure. She could lie to herself and say no, but she didn't think this was the time to hold back on what she felt. "Yes, I haven't felt this way before, but it's been less than a week since I met him. There isn't much to say about this relationship... if you can call it that. I mean... who really knows anyone... much less say out loud..." She let the words die as she wasn't sure what she was saying.

Emeline's eyes sparkled. "Oh my, listen to her try to convince herself. Ya must have it bad. And the heart knows Maggie. Your heart will feel different from anythin' else you've have ever felt. He must really be somethin'."

To distract herself, Maggie grabbed a cookie and took a bite. Emeline wasn't kidding, these were amazing.

Clearing her throat, Emeline said, "I think it's time you hear a story, child." She took a drink of her tea and sat back in her chair.

"Now before I start, you need to understand religion. Did you know there are over forty-two hundred religions in the world? So many different faiths. Ya have Christianity, Islam, Hinduism, Buddhism, Judaism, and that's just the tip of the iceberg. But within some religions you have, what I like to call, a blend of traditions. For example, those practicin' Voduo, Santeria, Candomble, Umbanda, and others, well, these are different traditions brought together. Now in all things there are good people who worship and live by these rituals, and then there are those who seek the darker side. This story ain't about painting any faith with a dark brush. This here story is about love, life, jealousy, and vengeance and how it affects you." A hush seemed to sweep over the garden, as if even the birds and insects wanted to hear the story.

Maggie nodded, and Emeline leaned forward in her chair. "Hundreds of years ago, years after the Spanish had come to N'Orleans, there lived a woman, a Santero who practiced the traditions of Santeria. This woman's name was Delia. Her nature was one that ran to darker rituals.

Delia fell in love with a free man of color; Benoit was his name. But as much as she wanted him, he did not love her in return. Ya see, he fell in love with another. He'd met a young Acadian girl. She'd lost her family during the voyage to N'Orleans, and she was all alone. He took her in and fell desperately in love with her. Her name was Césarine.

When Delia heard that Benoit was in love with Césarine, she became angry. She was in love with him, and there was no way she would lose him to this poor waste of a girl. So, she asked him to come and see her. When he arrived, she poured out her heart. But he told her he loved Césarine and nothin' she said or did would ever change his mind.

This sent Delia into a rage, and before she thought 'bout her actions, she placed a powerful curse on Benoit and Césarine. The curse she placed on them bound their souls together, but along with that bond and the love they shared, came death. She cursed them to die because of their love. But even worse, she cursed their souls. So, in every lifetime they live, once their souls fall in love, they die.

Not long after she placed the curse, Benoit perished in the fires that burned down N'Orleans in 1788. Twelve hundred people died in those fires. You might be thinkin' he was just in the wrong place at the wrong time. However, Delia made sure he was there and that he suffered. Poor Césarine met her end not long after, by consumin' poison. Now, anyone who has knowledge of plants and a kitchen can make some deadly treats. Add a little hemlock to tea, or a poke berry jam, or even some yellow jasmine honey added to a favorite recipe. I think ya get my meanin'."

But what does this have to do with me? Maggie thought.

Emeline looked over, a serious look in her eyes. "I hear your dreams have been makin' ya lose sleep, is that right?"

Looking away and down at her hands in her lap, Maggie nodded.

"I tol' ya long ago that dreams would tell your story. Dreams can be glimpses through the back door of life, did ya know that? These dreams can show ya where you've been, and who ya were, and why you've lived. But, I believe these dreams are trying to tell ya somethin'. They're tryin' to tell ya to beware, that somethin' bad is comin'."

Maggie's eyes shifted back up to Emeline's amber eyes, and she felt mesmerized. Tilting her head, Emeline asked, "Tell me, child, who have ya seen in these dreams?"

Shifting in her seat, Maggie was silent, not sure she wanted to speak the names out loud. It would make them too real.

Emeline nodded. "I see. Well, hows 'bout I toss out a few names and see if it helps jog your memory. Does Josephine ring any bells for you? Poor girl died after she got bitten by a cottonmouth in the bayou. She was running away from her father after he shot and killed her love, Lucien."

Frowning, Maggie wasn't sure, but shook her head. Emeline continued, "What about Felice? Hmm, I see that's not ringing a bell either. Died during Mardi Gras in 1978. Lord, how that girl suffered. I hope you never dream of her." Emeline shuddered.

Maggie swallowed, hoping she never would either if the tortured look on Emeline's face meant anything.

"How about Celine?" Maggie's eyes widened and her hand went to her throat at the mention of the name from her dream in which she was being strangled. "Ah, I see. Yes, Celine was strangled by a man obsessed with her after she fell in love with Mikael. What about the name Lydy?"

Maggie gasped and placed her hand over her mouth. For as long as she lived, she would never get that dream out of her head.

Glancing up to the trees, Emeline said. "That was a horrible thin' that happened. So sad, and his death tormented Lydy until the day she died. Unfortunately, she died during childbirth that same year. The baby came early and complications made it hard for her to deliver. They was both lost."

Tears sprang to Maggie's eyes. She lost the baby after all that tragedy. It was unfair, and the sorrow welled up in her chest.

"Yes, it was tragic and my heart broke when I learned of it. It was such a senseless death, poor Tomas."

She heard Emeline take a ragged breath, and the silence between them grew. Maggie took a sip of her tea, trying to calm herself from the pain she felt.

Calming herself, Emeline continued, "What about Ava? Have ya heard of her?"

Nodding, Maggie said, "Yes, I dreamt about her last night."

Emeline's eyebrows rose, and she waited for Maggie to continue.

"Last night I was with... Liam, and we... we..."

Emeline huffed out a breath, "Oh, come now child, just tell me. I'm a grown woman who has had plenty a sex in my time, so if that's what ya need to say, just spit it out."

Maggie let out a nervous laugh. "OK, well we were sleeping together and when I woke up I was... I mean he was... inside me. In my dream I was with a soldier named Kolton. He'd been injured in a ship battle and I helped to heal him, but he was leaving to go back to the war. He asked me to marry him. We kissed and one thing led to another. When I woke up Liam was there, and we were kind of caught up in the moment. Afterwards, when we were falling back asleep, I thought about how real the dream was. I mean it was so *real*. Being in the dream, then finding myself with Liam, well it was like he and Kolton were the same person. I don't know how to explain it. My feelings were so intense in the dream, and I felt the same when I realized it was Liam. Doesn't that sound strange? God, I must sound crazy." She realized she was playing with a loose string on her blouse, and when she looked over at Emeline, she saw the woman staring at her. Maggie grabbed her glass and took a big drink, feeling parched.

"Maggie, are ya in love with Liam?"

Her head whipped over to look at Emeline. "In love? What are you talking about, I'm not in love? I hardly know him."

A smirk appeared on Emeline's face, but her eyes were still serious. "That may very well be, but watching ya right now makes me think your feelings are stronger than ya want to admit."

Shaking her head, Maggie said, "It was intense, but that doesn't mean I'm in love with him. And how do you know so much about these lives and these stories anyway?" She knew she sounded defensive, but she needed to deflect the questioning.

Emeline's smile looked sad, and Maggie wasn't sure she wanted to hear this. "I tol' ya I speak to the elders. They help me put together all the stories, the real facts of those lives. I've done some researching at the library and goin' online. I'm more tech savvy than anyone knows. Well, I've made a study of all the lives that have come before, you see. Now if this was someone else's story I don't think I'd have figured it out, but I have ties to your lives so that's made it easier.

I've been part of every one of those lives. I was Benoit's sister, Lydy's cousin, Ava's aunt and so on. In every life, I was someone in that life, too. The elders, they helped me search for myself and then we searched for ya. I've been at this a long time. And I refuse to let another lifetime pass and watch ya die for fallin' in love. It just ain't right. You shouldn't have to suffer because some bitter woman couldn't accept that a man didn't love her."

Maggie sat there, frozen from the revelation Emeline made. It seemed impossible, but how else would Emeline know about the people Maggie had been dreaming about. This was crazy, but it would explain the dreams and the feeling she had every time she awoke from them. But that would mean destiny was real, and she had a hard time coming to grips with the thought.

"I can tell you're strugglin' with this whole idea, so I'll let it sit awhile. What I need to tell ya now is, I've been studyin' how to remove this curse. There are spells and curses which can remove other spells and curses, but it's complicated. From what I've read and heard about this curse, Delia's powers created it to last an eternity. I've been gathering things, but the most important thing I need... are you and Liam. Actually, I need your blood."

Cringing, Maggie sat back in her chair, putting distance between her and Emeline. It wasn't so much about the fact she wanted blood, but more to the fact she wanted to have Liam's blood and have him here.

How in the hell was she going to explain this to him? *Oh hey, Liam, we need to take a drive to see my friend. She needs a blood sample to do some kind of ceremony to remove a curse that some bitter Santera put on us hundreds of years ago.* Yeah, because that wouldn't send him running.

Sitting up straighter and feeling slightly paniced, Maggie said, "Would it be possible to do this with just me? I mean, since I'm right here and you can cut my finger and drip it into a cup and say your spell and shake your rattle and make all these dreams just go away."

Emeline frowned, and she glared at Maggie. "I hope you're not insulting my faith and traditions by thinkin' all I do is shake some rattle, and that's it. I don't take kindly to being belittled or disrespected young lady."

Maggie's eyes grew wide. This is not what she meant at all. Fumbling, she said, "Oh Emeline, no! I'm sorry that came out the way it did. I don't understand what needs to happen, and I in no way meant any disrespect to you or your faith. I apologize if I made you feel that way. It's just… I'm worried about how I'll bring up this topic with Liam."

The tension eased out of Emeline's face. "I wish I had some words of wisdom on how to tell Liam about this, but I don't. The only thing I can say is tell him the truth. He may think it's crazy, but if he's fallin' for ya like you're fallin' for him, he'll follow ya anywhere."

Maggie looked at Emeline and said, "Give me two days. I need to figure out how I'll bring this up that won't send him bolting to the airport and hopping on the next flight to New York."

Emeline frowned. "I was hoping for sooner, but I don't want to send him scampering away either. If it makes it easier, we can do this at your place. I need to do some protection spells to make it safe, but we can remove the curse after that. I'll come early Monday afternoon and have everything set and ready. Your grandmama can let me in. The two of ya can just come in and I can explain the whole thin'."

Nodding, Maggie agreed. She did not understand what to make of this whole thing, but she would need to figure out a way to tell Liam and prepare him to meet Emeline. He'd been open to the ghost experience; maybe he would be just as flexible about voodoo.

Emeline was up and out of her chair. "I have something for

ya, I'll be right back." Maggie watched as Emeline hurried into the house. Taking a last sip of her tea, she contemplated how to bring this up with Liam. Before she could get too far in her musings, Emeline was back.

In her hand she held what looked like a piece of thin, black leather cord. When she opened her hand Maggie could see a round piece of silver. Emeline held it out to her, and she took it. On the silver were symbols. There were eight arrow-headed pitch forks, all pointing out from the center, with dots above some and lines across the pole line. It looked old and tarnished, but as Maggie held it in her hand, she ran her thumb over the symbols and it felt warm.

"This is a protection charm. Forged long ago, we have passed it down through the generations. As I knew ya were coming today, I cleansed it and re-established its power with a ritual and offerings to protect ya. I'd like ya to wear this Maggie. It will keep ya safe until we can remove the curse."

Maggie looked at the charm and lifted the cord to put it over her head. The charm rested between her breasts and she could feel its warm weight on her skin.

Emeline took Maggie's hand and said, "Don't forget to wear it all the time. It's very important ya keep it on, otherwise it won't help. Now come with me. I have a few other things for ya to take home."

Back in the house, they went into the room that Maggie had wanted to investigate earlier. Now she could see all the different items on the worktable and noticed several small cloth pouches and other items set out in bowls and dishes.

She watched as Emeline set about putting oil on three candles and the smell of rose, cinnamon and something spicy filled the air. Candles were lit, along with an incense cone. Emeline started chanting as she added a few items to one of the cloth bags. She put what looked to be some kind of grass, some dark powder, something that looked like a garlic clove, a root and a small piece of metal. Then she looked at Maggie and said, "Child, I need a few of your hairs, please."

Reaching up, Maggie pulled out a few hairs, wincing from the sting. She handed them to Emeline and watched as she added the hairs to the bag. The chanting started again as a piece of twine closed the bag tight. Placing the bag in the center of the candles, Emeline chanted louder,

"Gris Gris working strong,
All the day and night long.
Protect the home where you will lay,
Keep all harm and evil at bay.
A strong protection you will be,
To the home that does keep thee.
And thus no harm can penetrate,
The walls your energy permeates."

Emeline repeated this chant many times, and Maggie could tell all of Emeline's energy was going into this spell. She couldn't help but feel gratitude for this woman who would do so much for her after she had pushed her away. It made Maggie sad to think she could have had Emeline as part of her life if she hadn't been so stubborn.

Emeline picked up the bag and dragged it through the flames, then through the smoke from the incense. After extinguishing the flames, the ritual was complete, and Emeline handed her the bag. "When ya get home, put this over your door. I will complete the full ritual on Monday. Now that we're done, let's have us some more tea."

And that's what they did until it was time to go home. Maggie was glad she'd come, even if she still wasn't a true believer in all of this. But if Emeline could stop the crazy dreams, then Maggie would do it. She still wasn't sure how she would get Liam to be part of it, but she could figure it out. And with lots of luck he wouldn't think she was bat shit crazy and run screaming.

16

Liam filled his day with completing a few reports and doing some research on a location that his boss had asked him to check out. It was an old church in Savannah, Georgia, and the town wanted an evaluation. His boss hadn't said whether he wanted Liam to be the one to do the actual evaluation, but since Liam was already in the south, it might just be his next project.

Once he completed all he could, he went to the fitness center and did five miles on the treadmill. Arriving back at his room, he had a shower. As he lathered up, he wondered about whether he wanted to get serious with Maggie. His quick answer was yes. Never one to rush into things though, he needed to make sure before he said anything. Maggie was already thinking he would break any promises that he made to her, and he didn't want to hurt her. If he wanted to pursue this, then he also needed to wrap his head around what his next career move would be. Maybe he should talk to his boss and find out if there were options within the company that would allow him to stop the travelling and stay in New Orleans. If not, then he would have to think about what he wanted to do. Maybe it was time to consider a switch from just looking at buildings to getting his hands dirty.

Maggie texted to let him know she would swing by to pick him up. When she did, he slid into the passenger seat and smiled over at her. She wore a beautiful corn-blue sundress that highlighted her figure. Before she could pull away from the curb, he leaned in and gave her a sweet kiss. He pulled back and watched as her eyes were slow to open.

"Well, hello to you, too." She looked back at him with the most dazzling smile and he felt his heart bottom out.

Liam buckled up and Maggie pulled away from the curb. They chatted about random stuff and he sat back, enjoying his view of Maggie as she drove through the city. She said they would stop over at her favorite bakery for some desserts to take to the BBQ. He asked about her day and she said it was fine, but he could tell that she didn't want to talk about it. They drove in companionable silence for a while until she said, "Do you remember what you said to Damon when we were sitting in the tearoom the first day we met? You said something about how you wouldn't call voodoo any kind of hocus pocus. Were you serious or just pulling Damon's leg?"

Tilting his head to the side, he wondered where this was going. "I was serious. I mean, voodoo and other religious beliefs and rituals are important to those who practice them. I would never poke fun at any person's fundamental rights to worship and pray to whoever they wish."

She looked thoughtful for a moment. Clearing her throat, she said, "So then do you believe in such things as spells and curses? I mean, do you think people have the power to wield magic?"

Puzzled by the strange question, he answered honestly, "That's a hard question to answer. Do I believe there are those among us who could cast a spell or place a curse?" He thought about this, and Maggie didn't interrupt him. "I'd have to say I believe there are people who can make people believe they have power strong enough to cast a spell or a curse."

Maggie frowned and said, "So, then your answer is no. You don't believe."

Liam wondered why she seemed upset. "Do you believe?" he asked.

Frowning further, she didn't answer right away, she just concentrated on driving. She shook her head a moment later and said, "I'm not sure." Then in a whispered tone she muttered, "Guess we'll find out."

He was just about to ask what she meant when she stated, "We're here." She got out of the car and went into the bakery. Liam followed behind, still wondering what she'd meant.

* * *

Once they paid for their tray and drove to his aunt's place, the trip went fast and there was no time to continue their previous conversation. They found a place to park along the street and made their way up to the house.

It was an 1890s center hall Victorian home on a large lot. It had creamy beige siding and white trim. His aunt's gardens looked lush and creeping vines crawled up the railings. Opening the front gate, they took the small cobbled walkway around to the side of the house where he could hear voices. Looking behind him, he noticed Maggie trailing behind. Backing up, he took her hand in his and gave her an encouraging smile. She nodded and moved forward until they were both in view of everyone.

Aunt Nora was the first one to notice, and she came bustling over. "There you are Liam, come here and give me some sugar darlin'." She wrapped her arms around him and he gave her a one-armed hug as best he could while holding the tray. Aunt Nora was a tall, broad-shouldered woman, with short light brown hair, blue eyes and laugh lines that made her smile look warmer somehow.

Pulling back, she gave him a loud smacking kiss on his cheek, leaving a red lipstick mark. She then spotted Maggie, who looked like she wanted to flee the scene. "Oh my Lord, Maggie Rivard, you get more and more beautiful every time I see you!" Liam watched as Aunt Nora engulfed Maggie in a hug and worried that she'd crush her in her anaconda like grip.

Maggie stepped out of the hug and smiled at his aunt. "It's nice to see you again, Nora. Grandma said to say hi."

Aunt Nora laughed, "Oh, your grandmother is one of the sweetest women I know, and the cagiest. She don't take no guff from anyone on that committee and I love her for it." Turning her head, Aunt Nora said, "And what have you brought? You know you didn't need to bring anything sweetheart. Oh my, is that from the Gracious Bakery! I love their tarts! Thank you so much."

Liam allowed his aunt to take it and said, "Yeah, Maggie recommended them."

"Thank you both for bringing us a special treat. Why don't you take Maggie and introduce her to everyone? We have a few extras today too, but I always say the more the merrier!"

Aunt Nora turned and walked towards the house as Maggie reached up and tried to wipe off the smudge of lipstick from his cheek. "Let me just... there, I rubbed it in, but I still don't think it's your color." Her lips quirked up and Liam took her hand.

There were so many people as Liam did the rounds, introducing Maggie. He wasn't sure how to introduce her, so he left it loose and didn't label them. He wasn't sure if it would be an issue, but he made sure to never let go of her hand, so at least everyone would know she was here with him. His aunt Liliane and uncle Lucas were excited to see him. He introduced her to his cousin Sidonie and her boyfriend Justin and Jacqueline and her husband Leo. They were Liliane and Lucas's children.

Under the magnolia tree that Liam loved, were a bunch of other cousins; Larissa and her live-in boyfriend James, Nicolas and Nichole, who were twins and had no significant others. Ronan and his new wife Madison were there, and she was about six months pregnant with their first child. Vincent had come, and he hoped he didn't turn his charm on with Maggie. Liam held her closer when he introduced her to him. His other cousin Ethan was there with his girlfriend Ella. They made the rounds to where Walker and Lynne were sitting, and Owen was waiting for him.

Owen, whose baby face made him look five years younger than his actual age, came right over and bear-hugged him. "Dude, I'm glad you didn't leave yet, I was hoping you and I could have a few brews before you go back. I'm off on Monday, so how about tomorrow night? I'll take you out and show you the town."

Liam smiled. "Well, I'll check my schedule and text you in the morning to let you know." Pulling Maggie forward, he introduced her to Owen. "Owen, this is Maggie."

They shook hands, and Owen looked at her closer. "Hey, I think we've met before. Didn't you go out with Randal Bordelon? I think we met at a party a few years ago. Glad to see you dumped his ass, what a dick."

Maggie cringed. "Yeah, I remember meeting you. It was Bea Cormier's party. And yes, he was a dick. We broke up after that party. I found him in a bedroom with someone else."

Liam watched as Maggie looked sad, and he pulled her close. "Jesus, what an idiot. He didn't know what he had." He dropped a kiss on the top of her head and Owen gave him a weird look before excusing himself to go talk to some cousins.

They situated themselves in some lawn chairs and chatted with the group. Maggie knew more people than Liam thought she would. There were some extra girls at the party, and Liam didn't understand who they were. He didn't bother to find out as he was more interested in being with Maggie and talking with Walker, Owen and Ronan. Vincent only made one attempt at coming over to speak with Maggie, but one look from Liam and he nodded and moved along.

At one point he noticed a girl watching him, but he didn't return the look. Instead, he stared at Maggie while she was explaining to Lynne, how her charity work helped the homeless and the extra time she'd been putting in at the local soup kitchen. Lynne seemed interested and said she would love to help.

Liam noticed the girl again. She was pretty with blond hair and bright blue eyes, but she didn't hold a candle to Maggie. Sidonie came over at one point and whispered close to his ear, "I'm so sorry Liam. I didn't know you were coming here with someone. I brought some friends along, but I can see you only have eyes for Maggie."

Liam smiled at her. "Thanks for thinking of me, but consider me taken. However, I think Vincent is about to take at least one or two off your hands. Nicholas is always up for flirting with the girls, so he might help you out."

Sure enough Liam could see Vincent hone in on the blond and she looked to be blushing down to her toes from something he said. Good, that meant there would be no one looking at his girl. Did he just say his girl? Yes, yes, he did, and it felt so right. Maggie was his girl.

He watched as she flipped her hair, laughing at something Madison said, and just like the time he watched her pick up her God son Spencer, his world shifted. She looked perfect sitting here with his family, and everyone seemed to enjoy being with her. In that moment, he knew he had to be with her. Not just for today, or until he went home, but forever. Yeah, forever with her sounded amazing.

"Sweetheart, you keep staring at her like that and Uncle Lucas will have to bring out the hose and spray you down. Seems like you're a little more than smitten."

Looking over his shoulder, he could see Aunt Nora looking between him and Maggie. Her eyes sparkled as she said, "Makes me wonder if your wandering heart has finally come home."

Smiling, he didn't say a word as she cupped his one cheek. "She's a good girl, Liam. She's been through a lot, but she is a wonderful person. I'd love to see you settle with a good-hearted woman like that." Aunt Nora let go of his cheek and stood up. "Soup's on everybody. Come and get it."

Everyone got up and headed for the tables laden with food, except Liam. He lagged and grabbed Maggie's hand, pulling her into his arms. "You having a good time?"

She smiled up into his face. "Yeah. I wasn't sure in the beginning, but I'm having a wonderful time. How about you?"

Liam leaned down and gave her a slow kiss before saying, "Yes, this has been great."

Just then his stomach let out a growl and Maggie laughed, "Oh no, the beast has awoken. Let's get you some grub."

Before she could turn away, he cupped her face and gave her another kiss, this one a little longer than the last. From across the yard, his aunt yelled out, "Liam, I meant what I said about that hose! Now leave that poor girl alone so she can get her dinner."

The two of them laughed and heard everyone on the porch laugh too. He raised his hands in surrender, and Maggie grinned at him. Liam followed behind her, watching her smooth legs and curvy ass ascend the steps. He wished he could pull her into one of the spare rooms for a few minutes to finish their kiss. But he also knew they wouldn't be leaving that room until he had her breathless and panting his name.

Hours later they left, hugs and kisses exchanged and they discussed future visits. By the time they got back to Maggie's they were both yawning.

Maggie was about to head into the washroom when her phone vibrated on the table. She grabbed it and checked the number and answered right away. "Hey, Maxon, what's going on?"

Liam couldn't hear the whole conversation, but as he watched he saw a frown crease Maggie's brow. As she spoke, he sat on the sofa, not knowing whether they would have to go to the hotel.

"Did you contact Nelson? OK, that's good. Do you need me to come in?" Liam could hear a low voice come across the line and watched as Maggie nodded. "Fine, I'll wait to hear from Nelson in the morning. Thanks for keeping me in the loop. Make sure I get a copy of the report. I'll want to review it. Good job tonight, Maxon."

She hung up and placed her phone on the table. Liam waited and when she said nothing he asked, "I would ask if everything is OK, but if security is calling you this late at night maybe not."

Maggie moved over and sat beside Liam on the sofa. "There was another attempted break-in tonight. That makes three in the last week. I asked Damon about putting on extra security, but he thinks it's just vagrants and said we didn't need the extra expense. I only have three guys rotating through the schedule and they can't be everywhere all the time. Maxon said he reported the break-in to the police and an officer came by. He said there was nothing that I needed to be there for, so I'll get a call from Nelson in the morning and we can discuss our next steps."

Liam moved closer to her, putting his arm around her waist. "Then there is nothing you need to do tonight. Let's get some sleep," he yawned the last part and rubbed her back.

She nodded, but said, "I just don't understand Damon sometimes. Why wouldn't he just let me put on extra security? You'd think he'd want to protect his property." Shaking her head, she sighed. "Anyway, let's go to bed."

As Maggie went to get ready for bed, Liam thought about

what she'd said. He'd wondered about Damon too, but figured he viewed the hotel differently than Maggie did. For her, it had emotional attachment and workers that felt like family. For Damon, it was just another asset to buy and sell and make him money.

After locking up and switching off the lights, he stripped down to his underwear and waited to brush his teeth. Looking around her place in the soft light of the bedside lamp, it seemed strange how at home he felt in such a short time. It felt right being with her, and doing things that couples did.

She came out wearing a white cotton nightie with little blue flowers and spaghetti straps. Face scrubbed clean of makeup, and hair braided, Liam thought she looked even more beautiful than she did earlier. Something about her all natural skin and the delicate nightgown pulled at his heart.

He was in and out of the washroom in no time. Snuggling up behind her, he spooned around her warm body and her magnolia perfume surrounded him. He kissed along her shoulder and the back of her neck, letting his lips rub against her soft skin. Maggie sighed and the feel of her skin and warm body had him wanting her. Running his hand down over her curvy hip, he pulled her back against his hard cock and felt her push back. Slipping his hand under the thin cotton, he ran his fingers along her abdomen and cupped her breast. He could feel the hardened nipple. Kissing the back of her neck and playing with her nipple, he heard her say, in a sexy, breathless voice, "Liam." That was all the go ahead he needed. Moving so she could roll to her back and sit up, he pulled her nightie up over her head. He placed himself between her legs and kissed her, tongues tangling and teeth nipping lips. She pushed her hand into his hair and gripped it and held him close to continue the kiss.

Before long they were grinding their hips together and Liam was wishing he hadn't left his underwear on. Shifting, he tried to pull them down, but he felt Maggie's hands helping him and within a few seconds they vanished and then he stripped Maggie of hers. He was thinking about where he'd put his pants to get a condom, when before his eyes, Maggie held one up. As he stared down at her heavy-lidded eyes, puffed lips and moon lit skin, she looked exquisite.

Her smile was sexy as she said, "Let me help you out, handsome." Before opening the package, she closed her fist around his length and he felt a rush of lust spread through his body. Watching her, she pumped his cock then dipped her head. Warm, wet heat enveloped his erection and it was excruciatingly amazing. Maggie must have known that he was on the edge because she didn't linger on the blow job. Instead she gave it a final teasing lick before opening the package as Liam sat back on his heels. Her light touch as she rolled it on made his already throbbing shaft pulse. Trembling, he worried he might not make it inside her before he came. Liam concentrated on keeping his orgasm at bay by closing his eyes, taking deep breaths and trying not to think about the feel of her soft hand. She seemed to take a long time, so he opened his eyes to find her looking at him. He couldn't decipher the look on Maggie's face, and he worried that maybe she'd changed her mind.

She took one hand and cupped his cheek. He pressed her hand to his face and closed his eyes. He felt her reassurance as he looked into her eyes again. She muttered something which sounded like, "So many lives".

Before he could ask her to repeat it, she lay back down and tugged him forward. He entered her with more force than he would have liked. Her head pushed back into the pillow and a soft moan left her lips and all he wanted in that moment was to mark her as his. Feeling her fingernails scraping along his back scoring his skin had his blood pumping into overdrive. The sound of their bodies moving and breaths coming fast filled the room.

Liam tilted her hips and after a few more strokes she slipped over the edge. Watching her body as she claimed her release was the most incredible sight. But he didn't get to stare too long. As her body milked his already sensitive cock, he began pounding into her, feeling the rush of his orgasm as it pulsed out. The feeling was beyond incredible.

He slumped down on his elbows, trying not to crush her with his body. Her hand rubbed along his back as their breathing leveled out. Liam didn't want to move. He wanted to stay in this exact spot forever, feeling their skin slide and their breath mingle while utter contentment coursed through his body. Liam couldn't leave her. All he'd ever wanted was right here in his arms.

Wrapping those arms around her, he kissed along her jaw and then moved to her shoulder and neck. Looking down to the center of her collarbone, he saw a pendant laying there. The tarnished metal glinted in spots from the moonlight. It looked old, and he couldn't quite make out the pattern on the surface. He hadn't seen it earlier, but then again he'd been too caught up to notice.

"Whatcha looking at, city boy?" Maggie's southern drawl held a sexy gruffness, and it stirred Liam back to life. Jesus, he couldn't get enough of her.

Raising his head to look into her eyes he said, "I'm just looking at my very sexy woman and wondering if she might have it in her to go again."

She smirked and rolled her eyes. "Technically, I don't believe we've finished the last one." Then in a softer, almost whispered tone she asked, "Am I your woman?"

Pulling one of his arms out from underneath her, he ran his thumb along her high cheekbone and let his eyes scan every part of her face. "Well, Miss Rivard, I do believe I've fallen for you. And the weird thing is I didn't try very hard to stop."

Maggie's eyes filled, and a tear leaked out the corner of her eye and Liam wiped it away. Watching emotions play across her face, he waited to see what she would say. When nothing came, he tried to cover his disappointment with reason. "I know it might be too soon for you to feel this way. But I can wait, Maggie. I just know this feels right, and I don't think I can go back to the life I had before you. So you take your time and let me convince you I'm not making empty promises." Dropping his head, he kissed her, showing her the passion he felt. They spent the rest of the night wrapped up together as Liam tried to prove his love for her.

17

When Liam woke up the next morning, he felt like a million dollars. His limbs were loose, and his body sated from the many pleasures he had both given and received. Waking up with Maggie draped across him was like winning a lottery. Her scent was on him, and his stubble marks smudging her skin made him feel like he'd claimed her. He was sure if he checked his back, he would find scratch marks. Just thinking about how he'd gotten them made him want her again.

Getting out from under her was tricky, but he managed it without waking her. She turned over and hugged her pillow to her body and stayed asleep. Kissing the top of her head, he slipped into the washroom. Once done, he pulled on some running shorts and a T-shirt, then walked over to the fridge. Opening it, he peered in at its meager contents. How did she survive on coffee creamer, orange juice, a half jar of olives and some butter? *Did this girl ever eat at home?* He caught a whiff of bacon and followed the scent to the door that led downstairs. Looking back over at the bed, then at the closed door, he felt a moment of guilt. But then again, a man's gotta eat.

Opening the door to the landing, he stepped out and closed the door behind him. Taking a few tentative steps, he felt another moment of guilt when Margaret called out,

"Come on down here and get yourself some breakfast Liam. Figure I'd better feed ya cause she doesn't keep much up there."

He smiled as he entered the kitchen. Margaret was wearing dark-blue pants and a floral blouse, with a bright green apron to keep the bacon grease off her clothes. Her hair was up in a bun. She reminded him of his own grandmother.

She turned to look at him, and a smirk appeared. It was so much like Maggie's grin it startled him. "Good morning, sunshine. I take it you had a good night's sleep." She winked at him and turned back to the stove. "How do ya like your eggs?"

Liam knew he was blushing from her comment, but decided not to say anything except, "Over easy, please."

She smiled at him and said, "So polite. I appreciate a courteous southern man. Over easy it is." Margaret puttered away while Liam's eyes landed on the newspaper. He picked it up and scanned the headlines, not interested, just enjoying the companionable silence in the kitchen.

Margaret set a platter-sized plate in front of him. It overflowed with eggs, bacon, homefries, a small dish of cheese grits and four slices of thick toast. His stomach let out a growl.

Laughing, Margaret said, "Sounds like someone worked up an appetite. Dig in, I've got plenty more."

Not waiting for any further encouragement, he dug in. Margaret placed a cup of coffee and a glass of orange juice in front of him, and he mumbled his thanks around a bite of homefry.

Almost reaching maximum stomach capacity, he stopped and sat back, letting himself digest. He picked up his orange juice and for the first time realized that Margaret had taken the seat across from him, watching him with a smile that warmed his heart. "I love to see a man enjoyin' my cooking. I wasn't sure when you would come up for air."

She laughed and sat back, sipping her coffee. "My son used to eat like that. He was a big, strong man, and I used to love watching him with Maggie. Lord, how he loved that child, and he used to spoil her rotten. But she was always a good girl. And he loved her mother something fierce. I wasn't sure about her in the beginning, but she won me over. I could see how much she loved him and she was in love with Maggie."

Margaret was quiet for a few minutes, then said, "The day they died, my heart stopped and a piece of me died with them. I got a call and rushed over to the hospital and just fell apart when I was told. The only thing that kept me going was Maggie. She kept me from spiraling into despair, and I knew I had to hold it together for her. Oh, she cried and cried and my heart broke all over again, but I told her I'd take care of her. Her mother's parents lived far away, and they didn't know Maggie. And even so, I would have fought for her. She was mine, and there was no way I would let anyone else take care of her. Maggie was my everything, still is, but she's getting older and needs to get on to the next chapter." Taking another sip of her coffee she said, "Did she tell you what today is?"

Liam shook his head and she nodded. "Today is the anniversary of their death. Twenty-four years ago, a part of my world ended. But that young girl pulled me through, and I can never repay the happiness she's given me. Oh sure, she's tried my patience over the years. She has a stubborn streak the length of the Mississippi, but I couldn't have asked for better. Now she fusses over me and I pretend to dislike it, but I love that she cares. I would give anything to see her happy."

Liam knew that last part was directed at him. She wanted to make sure he understood what Maggie deserved in her life. She said nothing further and before he could respond she continued, "I'd love for you to join us today. We take flowers to our family crypt. Then we have ourselves a visit and take a walk around seeing who else has joined our afterlife community. Are you available to join us today?"

Taking a moment, Liam wondered how Maggie would feel about this. He had pretty much declared himself to her last night, so why not take the next step in becoming involved in her life to prove he was serious?

"Yes ma'am, my schedule is clear."

* * *

Maggie opened her eyes and listened to the murmur of voices. She'd slept, but she dreamed again. At least this one hadn't caused her to scream herself awake, or pounce on Liam like a sex-crazed teenager. She let her mind drift back to the dream.

She was a young girl sitting outside of a church. People were crowded all around her, weeping and crying. Her heart was heavy with grief having watched her parents die during their trip to their new home. She felt empty, like the despair had hollowed her out. She had no emotions left, and she stared out at a devastated crowd with no will to live.

A man came to stand before her. He knelt and her eyes focused on him. His dark, creamy skin had lines around his mouth. His long-lashed brown eyes had a blue-silver ring around the edge. He had perfectly formed lips; everything about the man was beautiful. She'd seen no one with skin that color before, and she should have felt scared, but something in the way he looked at her made her feel safe.

"Odette, come over here and take a look. This one looks like a lost soul. What's your name, *Cheri*?" His voice was smooth, his tone kind. Before she could stop herself she whispered out, "Césarine." She'd learned some English before they left her homeland. Before the British had forced her and her parents to leave. And now, with their deaths, she had no one.

He smiled and said, "Now, isn't that the prettiest name ya ever heard, Odette?"

She looked over to see a young woman standing beside the man, and she had the most enchanting eyes. They were a light amber color and her smile stood out as her white teeth shone against her dark skin. She bent over at the waist and said to her, "Are ya all alone, child?"

At that, Césarine cried, and as Odette bent down further to comfort her, the man pulled her up to stand and wrapped his arm around her. "Come along home, *mon bijou*."

They walked away from the church and the man held her close as they made their way along the street. She heard Odette say in a hushed tone, "What are ya doing Benoit? Why are ya bringing her with us?"

She glanced up into this man's beautiful face and as he spoke to his sister, he stared into her eyes. "Something in my soul tells me I need to take care a her." A small piece of her heart, way down deep, healed, and she knew that whatever happened now, she was his.

Maggie rolled over and thought about the dream again. She had been Césarine. That was when Benoit had taken her away from the death of her family and given her a new life. She was grateful that Emeline told her about why she was dreaming. It was still strange, but at least now she knew.

Stretching, she heard her grandmother laugh, and she smiled knowing the Liam must be downstairs with her. She lay there a few more minutes and decided she better get downstairs soon or else her grandmother would pull out the photo albums.

She went to the washroom and pulled her hair into a high ponytail. Pulling on her nightgown from last night and a matching dressing gown, she went downstairs. Just as she took the last step, she heard her grandmother as she said, "And look at this one. Oh my goodness, she had puddin' everywhere. I had to rinse her off with the hose before we could leave."

It was too late; the photo albums were out. She stepped into the kitchen to see Liam and her grandmother sitting side by side, flipping through the pages. She was sure that album held pictures of her between the ages of five to eleven. Geez, how long had she been asleep?

"Morning, Magpie. How'd ya sleep darlin'? Like a log apparently since you're sauntering down here at nine o'clock." Her grandmother was always a laugh riot.

Mumbling her good mornings, she shuffled to the coffeepot and grabbed her mug from the cupboard. It read, *'Of course I talk to myself, sometimes I need expert advice'*. Filling it to the top and grabbing a piece of bacon, she leaned over Liam's shoulder to see what pictures her grandmother was embarrassing her with. When she leaned forward, he turned and gave her a quick kiss. "Morning, babe. Your grandma was just showing me pictures of you when you were little."

Her grandmother smiled and laughed. "Oh Magpie, do you remember this one? You and I went on that road trip to Ashburn, Georgia, because we wanted to eat peanut butter sandwiches beside the world's largest peanut." In the picture, Maggie and her grandmother stood side by side in front of a huge cylindrical brick building. On top stood a large peanut with a gigantic yellow crown, the phase 'Georgia 1st in Peanuts' on the side of it.

She remembered. They'd driven with Pete, one of her grandmother's 'friends'. He was a nice man and had treated both Maggie and her grandmother so good. They had laughed so much on that trip.

"Oh, and here's the one of us at the Big Cow. They had the best ice cream." They'd seen it as they drove and pulled right in for ice cream. Even though money was tight back then, her grandmother always made the most out of every situation.

She took a seat at the end of the table beside Liam and watched as her grandmother spun story after story about the adventures they'd had over the years. It warmed her heart to watch the two of them together, laughing and having a good time. It made her think back to last night and the things Liam said to her.

Maggie knew they had a lot to talk about, even beyond what they had brought up last night. But right here, in this moment, she didn't want to spoil it. She was enjoying just seeing the two of them together.

"Magpie, I hope it's all right with you, I invited Liam to

come along to the cemetery with us today." Trying to keep the shock from her face, she didn't answer right away. No one except family had ever come with them. Looking at Liam's face, she could see the disappointment from her silence. It was the same look as last night when he told her he was falling for her and she'd said nothing. That look twisted her stomach into knots.

Liam looked back at the album and said, "Hey, it's no big deal Maggie. I can just call a taxi to take me back to the hotel."

Her eyes flicked over to her grandmother, who was frowning at her, disapproval clear on her face. The last thing she wanted to do, today of all days, was to make her grandmother sad. Reaching over, she took Liam's hand and smiled at him. "It would be great if you'd join us today. Please come." And then to solidify her point she added, "I want you to."

He smiled back at her, then lifted her hand to kiss it. She loved to see him smile, and she was glad to wipe that sad look off his face.

* * *

Forty-five minutes later they turned in between the tall stone pillars at the entrance to the Metairie Cemetery on Ponchartrain Boulevard. They slowed their speed and drove around looking at the tombs. There were over seven thousand tombs here, and it covered an impressive amount of acreage. There were many famous people buried here, and Maggie was always in awe when they came to visit. She liked to think that her ancestors were living their afterlife beside some of New Orleans' rich and famous.

Driving a little further, Maggie told Liam to pull over to the side to park. Her grandmother had already purchased some flowers, and as soon as they exited the car, they walked off toward their family tomb. It was a beautiful day, the sky a bright blue, and the breeze held its normal humidity, but wasn't stifling.

Grandma was in good spirits as they walked through. Liam was holding on to her arm as she pointed out tombs and sculptures to him. Maggie could tell she enjoyed having someone to tell all her stories too.

"Liam, did you know this cemetery was once a racetrack?" When Liam shook his head, Grandma smiled and said, "Back in 1838, I believe it was, it was originally the Metairie Race Course. It was the place to be back then. However, during the Civil War, the owners had to sell the racetrack as it wasn't bringing in the amount of revenue they needed. They sold it and in the 1870s they converted it into a cemetery."

They finally stopped in an area with a few trees, and the name 'Rivard' was on the tomb in front of them. It wasn't a huge tomb. It had four spaces to inter their loved ones, and Maggie always felt sad when she looked upon the names. Seeing her mother's, father's and grandfather's names always gave her a lonely feeling. Only her and her grandmother remained in her family unit. They had other family, of course, but the two of them had been a pair for years. Lonely souls, her grandmother would sometimes say, both with holes in their hearts from loss.

As they stopped in front of their family tomb, she and her grandmother placed flowers and some water in each of the concrete vases. When she looked up, she could see two small stone angels looking down, as if watching over their loved ones.

Stepping back, she felt Liam's heat behind her and leaned into him. He placed his hands around her shoulders and leaned over. "They were so young," he whispered and wrapped his arms around her. She nodded and said, "Too young."

They watched as her grandmother fussed around the tomb, pulling out a few weeds and brushing off some leaves, humming as she worked. Maggie helped her most of the time, but she knew her grandmother loved the task, so she let her fuss. Plus, her heart was heavy and having Liam hold her felt good. She was glad he was there. But it worried her that the next time she came, her mind would float back to this moment. Maggie hoped he meant what he said about not making empty promises.

Having completed her inspection, her grandmother walked over to Maggie and took her hand. Feeling the older woman's frail hand in her own, she was reminded that the years before she would be coming here alone would come all too fast. She lifted her grandmother's hand and kissed it. Looking over, Maggie said, "Looks like the place is holding up pretty well."

Seeing tears in her grandmother's eyes, she squeezed her hand. Just then Liam turned his mouth to her ear and whispered, "I'll go for a walk." He gave her the briefest of kisses, unwrapped his arms and walked off to look at the other graves. With her arms now free, she hugged her grandmother and felt the fragile arms come around her, seeking her comfort.

"You'd think by now it would get easier. It's not like I don't come here throughout the year too, but knowing today is the anniversary, it makes my heart break all over again." She could hear the watery sniffle and reached into her pocket for some tissues. Pulling back, she handed her grandmother a few, and the smile spread over her face.

"I always think I'm gonna be stronger than I am. But here you are always taking care of me. They'd be so proud of you. So beautiful, kind and caring; you amaze me all the time. I couldn't have asked for a better person to be part of my life, Baby Girl. Oh no, here comes more water works." And now Maggie's eyes were tearing up. She pulled a few more tissues from her pocket and dabbed her eyes.

Looking around, Maggie could see Liam taking his time checking out the tombs. She turned back to find her grandmother looking at her. "I spoke with Emeline yesterday after you left her place. I can't tell you how happy I am you went to see her. She talked nonstop about what a great visit you had." Her hand raised up and touched the pendant Emeline had given her, her grandmother's cool fingers brushing against her skin. Her grandmother's smile warmed her face. "I see she gave you a present."

Maggie nodded. "Yeah, she made me a *gris-gris* bag too, that I put over my door. She's supposed to be coming tomorrow to meet with Liam and I. Did she tell you?"

"Yes, she told me. There's more she could have said, but I know enough. She also said you're worried about how to tell Liam?"

A low chuckle came from Maggie. "I don't know how to bring this up. I tried broaching the subject, but it didn't seem to head in the right direction, so I stopped. Then I wasn't sure how to start again. I swear if I blurt out the truth, he'll think I'm nuts and run for the hills."

A frown appeared between her grandmother's brows and she looked deep into her eyes. "Now I will not assume I understand all of what is happening here, but from what I do know, I can understand how this might seem... unbelievable. But watching him today, the way he looks at you... my goodness, does he look at you, and that's not just lust in his eyes, Maggie. He might not know what's going on, but his soul is telling him you're special. And I'm sure if you ask him, he's most likely having some of his own dreams, same as you."

Maggie looked back over to see Liam still wandering along the path. His broad shoulders and dark hair made her stomach do a flip. She hoped her grandmother was right and that he too was experiencing dreams. It might make it easier for her to explain if she started by asking him that first.

Turning back to her grandmother, she said, "I hope you're right. I'll talk to him tonight after dinner."

Liam meandered down the path away from where Maggie and her grandmother were standing in front of her family's tomb. He was glad he'd come. When she'd leaned into him and let him hold her while she dealt with her loss, it made him want to protect her. As her grandmother stood by Maggie, he knew he needed to leave them alone to share their grief.

It amazed him at all the famous names he recognized as he moved along the rows. Some tombs were beautiful. Ornate statues of the Virgin Mary, stained glass windows, winged angels, and wrought-iron gates at the entrances of some tombs. He'd heard tales when he was younger of a flaming tomb of a bordello mistress and another about an apparition of a man in a police uniform who seemed to patrol the cemetery. People swore they'd seen it, but he wasn't sure about any of those claims. Liam knew all too well that tall tales abounded in New Orleans, as the saying goes, '*never let the truth get in the way of a good story.*'

As he moved along, he saw the name Guidry carved into a stone mantel of an old tomb. The tomb had a gold plate engraved with a crest with a bow and arrow on it. Underneath the crest, the word 'Chasseur' had been etched in thick font. His French was minimal, so he wasn't sure what it meant. He thought perhaps it meant chase or follow. Anyway, the tomb was fancy and Liam could tell how prestigious the Guidry family was.

Looking at his watch, he walked back to Maggie. He made his way over and noticed that they were still talking, but there were no more tears. As he moved closer to their family tomb, he noticed there were other marble name plates on the side. He could see a sentence written in French along the top. Maggie walked over to him and asked, "Whatcha looking at?"

"I was just noticing a sentence here. It looks like French. Do you know what it says?" Liam looked down at Maggie, and she shrugged her shoulders.

Just then Margaret walked over and said, "Oh, that's written on the Rivard family crest. She leaned in and read the sentence out loud, *'Les gens de la riviere'*. I believe it translates into 'people coming by river' or something of that sort."

Liam thought about that for a moment. It seemed somewhat familiar, but he couldn't quite place it. Before he could puzzle it out, Maggie took his hand and pulled him towards the car. He took Margaret's arm again because she was unsteady walking on the grass. Maggie whispered that her grandmother was tired, and they should head back home.

Driving back to the house, Maggie was deep in thought while Margaret was nodding off. Liam wondered how it must feel for the two of them reliving the loss. He considered how lucky he was, and hoped, if he could, he would bring some happiness into Maggie's life. The more time he spent with her, the more he wanted that.

Once they got back, Maggie told him to head upstairs. He made his way up and went to the fridge to get something to drink. Just then his phone rang, and he answered without checking the name, "Kavanagh here."

A male laugh came over the line and said, "Dude, so formal. It's just me." Liam could hear Owen's voice come across the line and he smiled.

"Hey, man, what's going on?" He'd always loved talking with Owen.

He could hear noise in the background, like his cousin was with a bunch of people. "I wanted to know if you were still up for beers tonight?"

Liam winced, as he'd forgotten about the invite from Owen. As much as he wanted to hang out with him, he wanted to be with Maggie. But he hadn't seen Owen much at the barbecue, and he wanted to see him. He could always go out for a beer, then come back. Maggie would be cool with it. He would be back by nine o'clock, nine-thirty at the latest.

"Sure, I wouldn't miss it. But I can't stay out too late though. I know you have the day off, but some of us have to work." He could hear laughter and then Owen said, "Sure man, no problem. How about I swing by and pick you up? What hotel are you staying at again?"

"Oh, I'm at Maggie's place right now. Can you pick me up here?"

Owen let out a whistle. "Did you stay overnight there, lover boy? Looks like Liam has himself a girlfriend. Walker was telling me about your date the other night, too. Have you spent any nights at the hotel?"

He didn't want to talk about this with Owen. His feelings were in a bit of turmoil, and he was sure that Owen would not want to hear him talk about his relationship. He decided against telling him. "Yeah. How about you pick me up here at seven and we go for a beer?"

They agreed, and just as he was hanging up, Maggie stepped into the apartment. She had a container of something frozen in her arms. She set it on the counter.

"I have a surprise for dinner! How would you like to have my grandmother's out-of-this-world shrimp gumbo? Her gumbo is renowned, you know. Ask anyone, she's won ribbons for this gumbo. And you are about to be served this mouthwatering delight. Sound good?"

Liam had already pulled himself off the couch and was striding over to where Maggie stood holding her hands out as if the container was on display. He pulled her in with a tender kiss. In a low seductive whisper, he said, "It sounds amazing, but even more so if you wear those tiny pajama shorts. Mmm, I like those."

She laughed at that. "Sorry, city boy, I think if I wear those we might not get to dinner."

Kissing along her neck and pulling her close, their bodies

brushed, and he started wondering if he even needed to eat at all. Perhaps he could just have her to fill his appetite.

Once again, his stomach betrayed him and growled. Damn his stomach! "Oh man, that beast is something else. Just give me like twenty minutes and I'll get you fed." She stepped back and patted his stomach. He took her hand and placed a kiss in her palm.

He moved over to the table so he could sit back and watch her work. "Oh, I hope it's OK, but Owen is going to pick me up around seven. He asked me yesterday to come out for a beer. I figure I won't be out too late."

She'd been busy pulling out a pot when she slowed her movements. He noticed she didn't look over at him, and wondered if she was upset that he was going out. Then she went back to her pot search and said, "Oh, sure. Yeah, you should see him."

Her voice sounded high and almost robotic. It was like she was trying hard not to allow any emotion into it. But before he could ask, she continued, "At least you still have time for dinner. I wouldn't want you to miss out on this."

Liam decided not to ask. Knowing how much she valued having her own space, she would understand. Besides, he would be back later. He wanted to come back and lose himself in her body again. He'd also grown very used to falling asleep with her in his arms.

18

Maggie lay brooding on her sofa, staring at the ceiling. It was now twelve forty-five, and she'd not heard a word from Liam. Pissed off and disappointed, she couldn't believe she'd thought he differed from the other guys she had dated before.

Dinner was great, and he'd raved at how good the gumbo was. Conversation flowed easily, and she almost mentioned Emeline, but watching the clock she realized there wasn't enough time. Owen had picked Liam up at seven, so she would talk to him after he came back. But as she lay there fuming about how he hadn't called, she realized she'd missed her opportunity.

She'd have to call Emeline and ask her to hold off one more day. Maggie knew how important it was for them to talk about everything, and now they wouldn't have a chance. Not that she wanted to begrudge him going out with his cousin. He should spend time with his family. But he said he would be back no later than nine-thirty, and that was over three hours ago. It reminded her of all the relationships she'd had and how those guys had disregarded her feelings.

Deciding she couldn't wait up any longer, she shut off all the lights and locked the door. He was out of luck if he showed up now. She would not sit around waiting for him any longer. She had to get up for work in the morning and if he thought she would let this slide; he was dead wrong.

Maggie was just pulling up the covers when she noticed the dream catcher he'd given her hanging on the window blind by her bed. He could be so sweet. If she was honest, she'd lost a piece of her heart to him that day. Looking away from it, she snuggled under the covers when her phone rang. She wanted to roll over and let it ring, but it might be the hotel. Picking it up, she sighed when she looked at the screen. Since he'd left her waiting all night, she should ignore his call altogether, but this might be her only opportunity to tell him not to come here, because there was no way she wanted to see him now. Clearing her throat, she said, "Hello."

She could hear the thump of music and loud laughter of whatever bar he was in. He called her and expected her to have to yell over top of the noise in the background. The music and voices quieted and then she heard his deep sexy voice. "Hey, Baby." Maggie could tell he must have had well over one beer as the two words came out like one. She decided not to answer.

There were some shuffling noises, and he said, "Baby, are you there?"

Taking a deep breath, she answered, "Yes."

"Oh good. I thought I called... dropped... dropped your call... I mean my call... the call. So I glad I didn't cause I reeeaaallly wanted to hear your voice." She stayed silent and waited for him to continue.

"So, we ended up staying up longer, and I wanted to call you sooner, but I didn't know how late it was. So then Owen ordered some shot rounds... um, shots of rounds, and we were watching the game, and we won! Then it was now and so I am calling you, Baby."

Oh great, just want she wanted to hear. "I see. You shouldn't have bothered calling. I'm in bed, Liam. I have work in the morning."

She could hear traffic and horns blowing and then Liam yelled into her ear, "Hey asshole, I'm walkin' here, t-trying to talk to my girlfriend, ya dumb ass!" Then, he said, "Geez, some people are such asses... holes."

Closing her eyes and shaking her head, she said, "Ya, I noticed that. Look Liam, I have to get up early so I gotta go."

"Wait... wait, don't go, Maggie. Baby, wait ... please don't hang up on me, Maggie. I want to be with you right now. I have to be with you. Mmm, I want to smell your hair and taste your skin and touch you. Oh man, I want to touch you." His words ended in a weird growl.

Furious, she said, "Let me get this straight. You leave me waiting here all night, and now you're making a booty call? Is that what this is? How classy! Well, Liam, you have a lovely hotel room to go back to, so make use of it."

His voice grunted and she could hear someone else in the background calling his name and the peel of high-pitched laughter. He sounded sad as he said, "Please don't make me go there, Maggie. I need you, baby."

Off in the distance she heard a girl call out, "Hey handsome, if she doesn't want you, I do." Then someone, most likely Owen yelled out, "Hey Liam, come on we gotta go, the Uber is here. We're going to Trudy's place."

Maggie's heart broke and her voice was thick with tears as

she said, "Sounds like your ride is leaving Liam. You better go."

"No Maggie, wait Baby, don't hang up. I'm coming right now."

A girl's voice sounded close, and Maggie listened as she heard, "Come on. Come to Trudy's. I'd love to get to know you a lot better."

White-hot anger flashed as she said, "No, Liam. Apparently, you have somewhere to go and someone else to be with. Do not come here." Then she hung up. The pressure behind her eyes led to tears sliding down her face. As she lay the phone down on her nightstand, it started ringing again. She picked it up and turned it off. There was no way she could go through another phone call like that.

All she'd wanted was to talk to him tonight about this curse and prepare him for Emeline's visit. She would have to call her in the morning to cancel. Hell, maybe he wasn't the 'one' after all. She could put this entire thing behind her for now. Maybe if her luck kept going this way, she might never fall in love. Sitting up, she pulled the leather cord over her head and threw the pendant on her nightstand, hearing it land then slide to the floor.

Rolling over, she hugged the pillow close to her. The smell of Liam surrounded her. His scent was everywhere, and it made her ache to call him back and tell him to come. No, she wouldn't do that. She was worth more than to be his booty call. But she buried her face in the pillow and cried until she fell into a fitful sleep.

* * *

As she hurried around the jazz club, picking up empty glasses and wiping down tables, she stole a look at the stage again. The saxophone player was pouring his soul into the song, and she couldn't help but swoon. Summertime *was one of her favorites. His name was Nolan Johnson, and he was dreamy. He'd come down from northern Louisiana with the dream of making a name for himself in New Orleans. He'd been playing here for a little over a week, and already people were asking about him.*

She'd learned to keep her distance from men, but there was something about Nolan. The soft brown hair, the perfect lips and the dark-blue eyes just made her stomach flutter. She hoped he'd stay awhile. And tonight she would make sure he knew she'd been thinking about him.

Tearing a page out of an old receipt book, she wrote her phone number on it. The note she scribbled there read, 'Let's get a drink sometime, Becca'. She kept it in her pocket until she took drinks up to the band. It was a bold move, but she didn't care.

When the set was over, she was right there with the drinks. "Hey there, pretty lady, is one of those for me?" She turned to see Nolan staring right at her and she felt weak in the knees.

She smiled and looked up into those dark-blue pools and said, "Sure is. Got your tonic water and lime right here."

Placing it on a table beside the stage, she placed it on a coaster and put her note underneath, making sure he'd see it sticking out when he went to get his drink.

Weaving between tables back to the bar, she watched as Nolan grabbed his drink and then stopped to pull out her note. She watched the smile spread across his face, and then he was searching the crowd. When his eyes landed on her, he held up the note and winked. She was on cloud nine.

Rebecca was finishing her shift when Nolan made his way over to her, saxophone case in hand. "You finished your shift?" He was smiling, a little dimple winking out at her from his left cheek.

"When I wrote that note, I didn't mean tonight, I meant when we're both free." She returned his smile, putting her hand on her hip.

He looked away, blushing, and her heart sped up. "I know you didn't mean tonight, but I thought maybe I could walk you home. We could figure out what day would work."

"Okay, just give me a minute. I'll be right out." She rushed into the back, told Tula, the other waitress, she was leaving and grabbed her purse. Just as she was about to push through the kitchen door, a hand came around her arm. It brought her to an abrupt stop, and she looked over to see who it was. Sammy tightened his grip on her arm as he said, "Why you rushing off, Doll Face? I was hopin' you and me could spend some time together tonight."

Sammy Matranga was the owner of the club, and she avoided him as much as possible. She knew he wanted her, but she'd been refusing his advances. She couldn't risk losing her job by getting involved with her boss. She and her mother were struggling as it was, and they didn't need to be out on the streets.

"Sorry Sammy, I've got a lot of stuff to do for my ma tomorrow. Gotta get up early, you know how it is." She hoped she was keeping the grimace off her face as his touch was making her skin crawl.

He grinned at her. Her stomach rolled with nausea as he leaned closer, his breath pungent with the stench of cigar smoke and garlic. It took all her willpower not to yank her arm out of his grasp. "You know one of these nights you'll have ta come up to the flat and hang out with me and the boys. We'd love to get to know ya better."

She pasted a smile on her face and nodded. "Yeah, one of these times, when I'm not too busy. Thanks for the offer though, Sammy." She hoped he didn't notice how she bolted out of the kitchen.

Picking up the pace, she walked over to where Nolan was waiting. Looking back over her shoulder, she could see Sammy watching her leave with Nolan, and felt a shiver down her spine. She knew how possessive men could be, and she hoped she hadn't just put herself in a terrible position.

The cool air washed over her face as they stepped out onto the street. The evening was pleasant, and as they made their way to her apartment, they talked about everything. She couldn't remember a time she'd enjoyed her walk home so much.

Standing outside her door, she waited for him to say good night. The streetlight caused a shadow to cover half his face. Staring at each other in silence, he moved in to cover her lips with his own. His lips tasted like citrus and spice, and she could feel herself leaning into the kiss.

Pulling away, he smiled, and his dimple showed. "Monday night, then? I'll take you out for dinner." Bringing his hand up, he tilted her chin and ran his thumb across her bottom lip. "Good night, Rebecca."

As he walked away, she looked across the street. She could see a man standing in the shadows. He stepped out, and she recognized him as one of Sammy's friends. Feeling the cold tingle of fear crawl up her back, she knew he would tell Sammy exactly what he'd saw. She also knew she'd regret it.

* * *

Maggie woke with a start, the tingle of anxiety still lingering on her skin. She let her heart rate settle and wondered what happened to Rebecca. If the past kept repeating itself, then she was sure it was something horrible.

Turning her head to her alarm clock, she had about fifteen minutes before it went off. She thought back to last night and her conversation with Liam. Closing her eyes, she didn't want to think about it again. Her heart was heavy and it would do her no good to dwell on it first thing Monday morning.

She heard a knock on the inside door of her apartment. She called out, and her grandmother peeked in. "You can come in Grandma, Liam's not here." She sat up in bed and swung her feet over the edge.

Frowning, her grandmother said, "Where's Liam? I thought you had plans last night?"

Maggie laughed, but there was no humor in it. "Apparently his two-beer limit with his cousin turned into a dozen, and then he actually had the nerve to call me after midnight for a booty call. Three hours late and he thought I'd welcome him with open arms. I told him he could either go to the hotel, or find someone else's bed to land in." She could feel the surge of emotion and pushed away from the bed to fuss in her closet for something to wear to work.

Her grandmother remained quiet, and she wondered if she should have kept all that to herself. The sound of slippers shuffling across the floor, then warm arms coming around her waist made her smile. Her grandmother always knew what she needed.

"I can see you're angry, Magpie, and no woman on the planet would say you're not justified to be. But let me tell you a little something about men. They screw up, all the time, but that don't mean they don't care. And I haven't spent a lot of time with Liam, but I'm sure he was probably pretty upset you turned him away."

Maggie looked at her annoyed, so she rushed on, "And rightly so. But I'm sure it upset him. And as for landing in someone else's bed, he wouldn't be that foolish. Not when he has you. My gosh, girl, I've seen men fall over their feet trying to get a look at you, Liam included. Try not to think the worst. It was probably just a boy's night out that got outta hand. I'm sure he feels bad for causing you any heartache."

Shrugging, Maggie leaned over and kissed her grandmother's cheek. "Thanks, but he hurt me and I just don't want to think about it anymore this morning."

A resigned smile spread across her grandmother's face. "Well, it's always a woman's right to stay mad when she wants to." Then she continued, "And I'm sorry I intruded this morning, but I have a problem. I tried starting my car and it won't turn over. Franklin next door came over to look and said it will need to go into the shop. My dilemma is I'm supposed to watch Little Mags and Spencer this morning for Delilah. I'm hoping you can let me borrow your car. I need to run some errands as well."

Maggie smiled and said, "Sure. Give me a few minutes and we can head out."

Her grandmother grabbed her travel mug off the counter as she walked by. "I'll get this ready for ya while ya get dressed. I'll also make something for breakfast so you can eat in the car. And don't say no cause ya need to eat."

Twenty minutes later, they were on the road, her grandmother at the wheel and a toasted bagel with peanut butter in Maggie's hands. Pulling up in front of the hotel, she hopped out and told her grandmother to come back around four to pick her up.

The valets must have been busy because no one was out front, so she walked in through the front doors. The place was a hive of activity with people checking out. The concierge, Josiah, was busy talking to some guests about going to The Ruby Slipper for breakfast. Porters and bellboys were busy with luggage, and guests were getting ready to depart. Everyone was occupied, so she decided she would check in with the staff later.

Going about her morning routine, she booted up her computer while she made a coffee. She'd checked her phone on the ride over and saw over two dozen text messages from Liam, all of which she ignored. No texts from Nelson or Maxon, so everything must have gotten straighten out. Remembering her conversation with Leticia on Friday, she pulled out the mail from the insurance company file. She'd call her later to discuss.

Just as she was getting ready to head over to see Nelson, her cell phone rang. If it was Liam, she'd let it go to voicemail as she was in no mood to deal with him. But as she checked the screen, Damon's name appeared. She connected the call.

"Morning, Damon, how is Baton Rouge?" She hoped he was in a pleasant mood. No one needed to deal with a grouchy Damon first thing on Monday.

"Morning." His greeting was brisk, and there were no pleasantries shared. "I heard the security cameras are down."

Puzzled, she wondered why she hadn't received a message from Nelson about it. "I'm sorry, I wasn't aware they were down. I just got in. Let me check with Nelson and I'll call you right back. Did Nelson call you?"

She heard a huff on the line. "No, I haven't heard from Nelson. As the owner, Maggie, I get alerted by the security company when such things happen."

Her face heated from his condescending tone. "I didn't realize that. We've never experienced this issue before. But I can assure you that if there is an issue, Nelson is on top of it." Or at least she hoped he was, and that was the reason she hadn't gotten a text.

"Well, I just spoke to a technician, and he thinks he knows what the problem is. I tried calling Nelson in the security office, but he must be elsewhere in the building. I thought perhaps, if you're not too busy doing whatever it is you do on Monday mornings, you could go down to the basement and click the reset button on the main panel. Unless you don't want to get your hands dirty. I'm sure I could call the company back and have them drive over to the hotel. Then they could charge us a for a service call."

Wow, someone had woken up on the wrong side of the bed. Trying not to grit her teeth, she said, "It's not a problem, Damon. I'll go down and hit the reset button. I'll call you back as soon as it's done."

She could hear the grin in his voice as he said, "No need to call back, I'll just stay on the phone with you until you get it done. I want to make sure you don't get sidetracked."

She held the phone out from her ear and gaped at it. Did he think she was that incompetent? What an asshole! If she didn't love this place so much, she'd tell him to kiss her ass and shove this job where the sun didn't shine. Instead she said, with just a hint of sarcasm and the thickest southern drawl she could muster, "Ab-so-lutely. I'll just pop down there and handle it... Sir."

Getting up from her desk, she headed for the door, almost forgetting to grab the utility door keys. Locking her office, she marched down to the back hallway. Unfortunately, there wasn't a single person in the hall she could ask to fetch Nelson. Phoning Nelson would have been her priority in this situation, but since she couldn't get Damon off the phone and he had made her feel like an incompetent idiot, she'd just go take care of it herself.

There was a stairwell down at the end of the hall which would take her to the basement. She hated going down there. Under normal circumstances, she'd have asked one of the male employees to go down or have one come with her. But since Damon was impatient, she was just going to have to suck it up.

The stairwell had two landings, and on each landing were small utility rooms. She wished she could have been lucky enough to have the main panel in one of those, but it was at the bottom in one of the back rooms.

She flipped on the light switch and just a single bulb came on; two others were out. Great, just what she wanted; to enter the basement in the semi-dark. Maggie must have voiced her last remark out loud as Damon said in a low tone, "What's the matter."

She turned at what she thought was the sound of a voice coming from somewhere behind her. Going down into the basement was giving her the creeps. "It's nothing Damon, I must get Colin from facilities to come down here later and change the bulbs. There are a couple out." There was no response from Damon.

Maggie started down the steps and made it to the first landing, which was still lit. The rest of the stairway was dark. Walking down into the inky depths, she made it to the second landing and going further would be very difficult with the lack of light.

"Wow, it is dark down here. I'm hoping when I get to the bottom, the other lights work. If not, I might have to find someone to fix them first."

Taking the first two steps, she paused as she heard something. She was turning around when she was shoved from behind. Arms and legs flailing, she could find nothing to grab onto. She heard her keys clang as they hit the metal railing, but she was nowhere near it to grab on. Damon's voice came over the phone, calling out her name, alarm in his voice. Her phone smashed on the stairs. Trying to lessen the damage, she pulled her body into a tuck. However, pain in her shoulder, elbow and tailbone made her tense up. Then, her head struck the floor at the bottom.

Laying there, she took stock. The pain radiated through her head and body. The sound of shuffling feet echoed in the enclosed space. They rolled her onto her front, as a pair of rough hands put a blindfold over her eyes and a piece of extra wide tape across her mouth. Next, rope was being tied around her hands and feet before she could pull away. She thought she heard two pairs of feet moving, but she couldn't be sure, as her head was pounding.

Her captor pulled her along the cold concrete floor, grunting with the effort as Maggie struggled to get free. She wasn't sure where they were going; all she knew was whoever had tied her up was not likely to put her anywhere people could find her. She received a sharp kick to her ribs, and she stopped moving as her side throbbed. As the ache spread, she found it hard to take in a full breath without discomfort.

She heard the jangle of keys and a hushed voice said, "In here." The voice was too low and quiet to make out.

After several minutes, they dropped her on the floor and a gruff voice said, "Stupid bitch. I think it's time you went for a little nap." As she turned towards the voice, something heavy smashed into her head and she was out.

19

As light fell across his face, Liam squinted to keep out the muted sunlight and wondered why his mouth tasted like he'd chewed on a dirty sock. Trying to turn in any direction made his head pound and his stomach rolled like it was considering ejecting all its contents.

He struggled to pinpoint where he was. Taking in as deep a breath as he dared, he couldn't pick out any specific scent. However, one scent was missing. There was no magnolia perfume. Why would that be? Maggie's apartment always smelled like her. He took another deeper breath. Nope, no perfume.

Then it all came rushing back. Raising his head, he immediately stopped the motion and groaned. Oh God, what the hell? Pain shot through his head, and he broke out in a cold sweat. Yep, his stomach was on an evacuation mission. Bolting from the bed, he had a disoriented snapshot moment and realized he was in his hotel room. He stumbled and slid, holding his hand over his mouth, barely making it to the toilet.

He thought he would never stop. Wave after wave of vomit and bile rocked his body. Even when he was empty, he still went through the motions. Once it was over, he made his way to the sink for a wet facecloth. Slumping back beside the toilet, he rested his cheek on the seat.

What the hell had happened last night, and why was he so sick? Liam remembered getting into an Uber. He had a vague memory of coming into the hotel and seeing Albin, the bartender, and asking him to open the bar back up so he could have another drink. Oh God, did he say anything about Maggie to Albin?

Cringing, he recalled saying something about not having her warm, sexy body in his bed, so he might as well drink. Shit, his foggy brain remembered Albin saying he'd drink too if he had a chance with a girl like her and had messed it up.

He couldn't even remember what he drank. Albin said something about giving him the best hooch from his private stock. The asshole had given him moonshine. But by that point, Liam could have been drinking lighter fluid and he wouldn't have cared.

It was all Owen's fault. Damn his cousin for buying shots. Gagging, he couldn't even think about those vile tequila shots without heaving again. He remembered some of Owen's friends showing up with a bunch of girls. One was trying hard to put the moves on him, but he tried to let her down easy. She was a pretty girl, light brown hair, blue eyes and a nice figure. But she was no Maggie.

Liam remembered talking to Maggie when that girl came over and said she wanted to get to know him better. The tears he heard in her voice as she told him not to come over had gutted him. Calling back and texting was useless as she must have turned her phone off. He'd fucked up and now he was here, alone and sicker than a dog. And he deserved it for making her cry. Now she was thinking he was like every other asshole she'd ever dated.

Deciding he would need to take something to stop the pounding in his head, he dragged himself to the counter. Digging through his toiletry bag, he found a bottle of pain relievers. Shaking out three tablets, he turned on the tap and grabbed a glass from the counter. Saying a silent prayer that the pills would stay down, he drank another glass, then shuffled back to bed. The clock read six-fifteen.

Picking up his phone, all he wanted to see was a text from Maggie. Looking at the screen, the only text he saw was from Owen. It was time stamped three in the morning, asking if he made it to the hotel. Owen also asked if Liam would mind if he gave his number out to some girl. Groaning, he texted his cousin back telling him, hell no, he was not to give out his number to anyone.

He lay back on the bed and wished he had a cold pack for his head instead of the lukewarm facecloth. At least the nausea had stopped. But he'd received no texts from Maggie. He knew she'd be awake and would have seen all his messages. If she bothered to read them. Maybe he should be thankful she hadn't texted to tell him to go screw himself. The thought broke his heart in two.

No, he wouldn't think about it. He would make this up to her and it would all turn out okay. He just needed more sleep to get back on his feet. After that, he would beg. He wasn't too proud to grovel and plead for her to forgive him. Nothing was too much for her to ask. He would find her later and give her the moon if she wanted it.

* * *

Over three hours later, Liam opened his eyes and felt relief that the headache was just about gone. Sitting up, he took stock of his body and felt not too bad. Not one hundred percent, but much better than when he first woke up. Shuddering, he made a vow to never drink like that again.

Deciding a shower would make him feel even better, he went to the bathroom. Grabbing his shampoo and body wash he paused to look at the bottle. His sister bought him the toiletry set for Christmas. She'd picked it up in some fancy store in Montreal when they'd gone to see some friends. He liked the product, and it was running low. Reading the label, the brand was from New Zealand called Hunter. He flipped it over and saw a sticker on the back in French.

He stopped when he read it. Written on the label was the word 'Chasseur' along with some other information in French. It was the same word written on the Guidry tomb at the cemetery. Something in his brain struggled to puzzle out what his subconscious was telling him, but he couldn't tease it out. Shaking his head, he decided the sooner he took a shower the better.

As he showered, he thought about how he'd hurt Maggie. Why hadn't he called her sooner? He'd left her waiting for hours and then called her because he'd wanted her so badly. Yep, it had been a total dick move. He missed her smiling face, the smell of her perfume, and he definitely missed having her warm soft skin pressed against his body. It was official; he was a complete idiot. How could he have been such an ass to the most beautiful woman he'd ever know? All he wanted now was to pull her to him and breathe her in.

Dressing quickly, he needed to find her. He was about to grab his phone to head downstairs when it rang. Looking at the screen, he saw it was Damon, so he connected. "Good Morning, Damon, how is your trip going?"

There was a bit of a muffled sound on the other end, but Damon said, "Not too bad. I'm heading out on the course today to work on my handicap. But that's not my reason for calling. I wanted to let you know that I've changed my mind on the direction I want to go with the hotel. This market isn't as lucrative as I'd hoped, so I'm just going to sell. Financially it makes the most sense."

Liam's mind raced with the idea that Damon would sell the hotel. It would devastate Maggie. "I'm sorry to hear that, Damon. I thought the hotel was a profitable business."

"I'd hoped so, too. I haven't mentioned it to anyone. I'm sure it will upset the staff, but hopefully I can sell it to another chain hotel. If everyone is lucky, they might keep their jobs. I'm sure Maggie will give them all stunning recommendations." Damon's mocking tone annoyed Liam.

He was just about to ask what he meant by the comment, when Damon continued. "I'd appreciate you not saying anything to Maggie about this. I know how close the two of you have gotten over the last week. Have you even stayed at the hotel at all?"

He definitely heard something in Damon's voice, and it pissed Liam off. "I don't think that's any of your business, Damon. Maggie has been professional with me during business hours and whatever we do after hours, is between myself and her."

"Now don't go getting all upset, Liam. She's a beautiful woman, all that gorgeous hair and exotic eyes. No man would fault you for wanting her. Hell, if she was a little more... in my social class, I'd have taken her too. But it would never have worked out. I know she wanted there to be something, but I just couldn't associate with someone so far outside my circle."

Liam saw red as his anger rose. What a fucking prick. He squeezed his cell phone so tight he thought it might crack. "Damon, she's worked her ass off for you and that's the things you say about her? You know what, people around here are right, you *are* an asshole."

There was a lengthy pause, then Damon cleared his throat. "I can see this conversation is over. I would appreciate you leaving the hotel before I return, Liam. And you can pay the full bill for your stay before you leave." Then the line went dead.

What the hell just happened? How had that conversation spiraled into a steaming pile of shit? The guy was a certifiable douche and if Liam ever saw him again, he'd punch him in the face for saying what he did about Maggie. Then he remembered what Damon said. He was going to sell the company. Liam needed to see her.

Just as he was slipping on his shoes, he heard his phone chime and an email was sitting in his inbox. He thought about leaving it, but just in case it was an email from his boss, he better check. It would be just his luck that Damon would've contacted his boss, and he was getting reprimanded.

As he opened his inbox, he saw that it was an email from Maggie. The subject line was empty.

To: Liam.Kavanaugh@WDSEngineering.org
From: MagGRivard23@yahoo.com
Subject:

> Liam, I'm sorry, but I think it's best if we don't see each other again. Please don't make this any harder than it is. I just don't think I can pursue a relationship with you. We're just too different and I can't be with you.

Maggie

Liam stared at the screen. If it was possible for an organ to break, then his heart just cracked in two. No way was this happening. A breakup by email?! Not after what they'd shared this last week. He meant something to her, and she sure as hell meant something to him. That wasn't just sex they had, no way. It was something more than that.

For him, it had been much more. Holding her, kissing her, loving every part of her while she moaned her pleasure; that was not just sex. But was it more than that for her? He thought back on every moment they'd shared. The way they'd moved together, the soft caresses, the way she cried out his name. Shaking his head, he knew it was more. Holding her in his arms while they slept, laughing, talking and enjoying each other's company, the way her eyes sparkled when she talked about Little Maggie and Spencer. The whispered pillow talk and the way her breath felt on his skin while she slept.

Maggie better think again if she thought for one damned minute he wouldn't fight for her. She was everything he'd ever dreamed of. He would march downstairs right now and apologize for being a complete jerk. Then he would tell her he loved her and that he would move back here because he couldn't live without her.

Liam stopped in his tracks. He loved her. Holy shit, he really did! He'd never felt like this before. And he would fight her tooth and nail until she admitted she loved him too. If his company couldn't transfer him, then he'd find a new job. As long as he could come home to her every night and wake up with her every morning. Then someday she'd have his babies and they could sit on the front porch with Margaret and watch them grow. But before he got too far ahead of himself, he needed to convince Maggie first.

Heading towards Maggie's office, the one person he'd hoped never to run into again was standing in the lobby; Officer Kenny. *Great, just what I need now, a run in with Officer Asshole!*

Looking around, he made his way forward, but before he could slide by, Kenny said, "Hello Mr. Kavanagh. How goes the review? You still here for a while?"

Turning towards the officer, he pasted on his best smile. "I'm meeting with Mr. Guidry tomorrow to go over some of my findings." Only a small white lie, but this jack off didn't need to know his business.

The Officer's eyebrows rose. "You're finished then? Bet you'll be glad to get back up north. I hear those New York women are wild."

Kenny was baiting him, but he knew how to play this game. "I've met a few wild ones in my time, but it's too much drama for me. To tell you the truth, I'm looking into starting a business with my cousin right here in New Orleans. So, I'll be moving here for good." He wasn't lying, he and Owen had talked before the shots started flowing.

Kenny just frowned, moving closer to him. "I think you should just head back to New York and stay there? Maggie and I have a history and I want to have another chance with her."

He could feel the rage crawl straight up his spine and it took all he had not to wrap his fingers around Kenny's throat. Assaulting an officer was not something he wanted to deal with today. His smile was razor sharp as he looked into the officer's eyes. "Well, Kenny, that's not gonna happen because she's not interested in you. And I have no intension of leaving town. I'm happy right here. If you think I'll step back, you're out of your mind. I'll be staying, *Officer*, and there isn't a goddamn thing you can do about it. Now, if you'll excuse me, I have a meeting to get to."

Liam strolled towards Maggie's office. Nelson was just walking towards him, and he frowned. "Everything all right between you and the officer? He looks kinda like he might taser you."

Liam grinned. "He'd love to taser me, or beat me into a gooey puddle, perhaps dump me in the Mississippi with a brick around my ankles, but he won't. He's just pissed I'm still here, and he wants Maggie. Poor bastard can't take a hint. But that's not my concern unless he pushes." He looked at Nelson and nodded towards Maggie's office. "Did you just come from seeing her?"

Nelson shook his head. "I went to see her. We always check in on Monday mornings, but she's not there. I was just going out to see if she was with anyone else right now."

They headed towards the main lobby. As they entered, Nelson said, "Her car isn't there." Turning, he walked over to the reception desk and called over to Rosie, "Hey Rosie, have you heard from Maggie this morning?"

Shaking her head, Rosie replied, "No, it was a zoo out here earlier and I didn't get any messages. I texted her a few times, but didn't get a response, which is weird because she always answers. I hope she's OK."

He thought back to the email she sent him. It didn't seem like something she'd do. But maybe she'd stayed home so she could avoid him. No way. She'd never jeopardize her work. Something felt off about this.

Turning to Rosie, Liam asked, "Do you have Margaret's cell number? Maybe we should check in with her to see if she and Maggie are OK." He didn't mention the fact that Maggie was angry at him, or that she'd sent him a breakup email this morning. He'd keep that to himself. If he had his way, he'd have this entire thing straightened out soon.

Rosie looked at him and said in a low tone, "Weren't you with her last night?"

Clearing his throat, he said, "No. I was out with my cousin. I came back here." She nodded and pulled out her phone. He and Nelson watched as Rosie scrolled through her contact list and hit her screen. The wait took forever until Rosie smiled. "Good morning, Mrs. Rivard, how are you this morning? It's Rosie from the hotel." The two men waited as Rosie continued, "Oh, that must be nice for you. Yes, they sure are growing up fast."

Liam could feel his patience thinning, but he resisted grabbing the phone. Rosie was listening to Margaret and responded. "I know she sure loves those kids. And speaking of Maggie, Mrs. Rivard, do you know if she's planning on coming in today? We haven't ..."

Rosie's voice faded off, and a frown creased her brow. "Oh,

that would be why we didn't see her car this morning. And what time was that? I see, well, let me just check in with the other employees and see if maybe I just missed her coming in. Great, you have a pleasant day, Mrs. Rivard."

Rosie hung up the phone as she said, "Margaret has Maggie's car today. She said she dropped her off here around eight."

Liam glanced at his watch. That was four hours ago, and no one had seen or heard from her? That was just too strange. Liam turned to Nelson. "Can we check her office?"

Already in motion, Nelson nodded. "You read my mind, son. Come on."

He watched as Nelson pulled his big ring of keys off his belt. Opening up the office, Nelson stepped in, followed by Liam. Looking around, they saw Maggie's flip flops on the floor and her purse and briefcase on her credenza. Nelson wiggled the mouse and the password screen appeared, which meant she had turned her computer on when she came in.

Nelson was just reaching for the door when Liam noticed the paperwork sitting out on Maggie's desk. "She must have been in here for a little while. It looks like she opened some mail."

Liam glanced at the pile lying on the desk. He was about to walk away when something caught his eye. It was a letter from an insurance company, Liam recognized the logo. There was also a file on the desk with other insurance papers enclosed. Liam was just about to move towards the door when Nelson said in a hushed voice, "What in the world is that about?"

Holding the paperwork out to Liam, he could see the beneficiary name stated as Mr. Damon Guidry. Nelson pointed to another letter. "What does that one say?"

Liam picked it up and flipped to the beneficiary page and said, "Guidry Corp."

Looking up at Nelson, he could see him looking at something else. "This change took place last Monday. Now why would there be recently changed insurance papers with a new beneficiary? Something smells fishy." Thinking back to the day when he saw Damon with those two guys, he got a weird chill up his back. "Nelson, how well do you know Damon?"

Nelson shrugged. "I know just enough to know I don't like him. He took over running this place just over two years ago. It was his father who bought the place sometime back. Now, there's a man you'd like. A tough negotiator, and a shrewd businessman, but he's fair to his employees. Damon couldn't care less about us. If it wasn't for Maggie, this place would have lost a lot of good workers. She is amazing to work for and Damon relies on her to do it all. I've never liked the way he looked at her either. But she's way too smart for him. Maggie saw right through him and stood her ground. He stopped looking at her after a while."

Anger surged through Liam at the thought of Damon watching Maggie. Just thinking Damon would eye her up made him want to punch him in the face. And to think Damon had said she wanted to be with *him*. She was way too good for that pompous snob.

Nelson continued, "I remember reading something before he took over here about how he'd gotten into a bit of trouble. Lost some big investments and a few of his businesses had gone under. I also heard his father was furious. I think he put him to work here to help build up his credibility. But this hotel isn't Damon's. It's owed by Guidry Corp. I signed some papers for the security company recently, and they listed the company as Guidry Corp. and the owner as Robert Guidry, Damon's father."

He glanced down at the insurance papers and then back to Nelson. "Do you think Maggie was questioning this? Maybe she went to the head office to find out what was going on?"

Frowning, Nelson said, "It seems unlikely she would. She doesn't have her car, and her purse is there. Except I don't see her phone anywhere. Let me make a few calls to see if I can locate her. I don't want to panic until we have something to panic about. It could be she walked down the street to get herself one of those fancy coffees she likes. Let me check with René to see if he has seen her. Might be that she had other meetings to go to and he hailed a cab for her."

They left the office and Liam watched as Nelson went off to make his calls. None of this seemed right. Standing there alone and worried, he wasn't sure what to do. He'd been eager to see Maggie, but now he was at a standstill until they found her. Liam decided he would go back up to his room. Maybe keeping himself busy would help rid him of the anxiety he was feeling.

* * *

Maggie's first thought was how cold she felt. She was numb straight through to her bones. Next, she realized she was lying on concrete. Struggling to think about why she would be on the floor caused a sharp pain in her head. Over the pain lay a thick fogginess, and she couldn't remember where she was.

Taking stock of her body, she figured out other things were wrong. There was tape over her mouth, her hands and feet bound, and she wore a blindfold. She tried to roll over, but with her hands behind her she couldn't go over without lying on her hands at a weird angle. Her ribs throbbed, and she lay still for a few seconds to stop the pain. Letting her body relax, she focused on other things.

It smelled like old mildewed fabric, rubber and dust with just a hint of lemon cleaner. Where had she smelled that before? Her mind felt thick, but she took her time pulling at threads of memory. Then it came to her; she was in the basement of the hotel. Her skin prickled with the thought of being down here. But she let that thought go. She needed to figure out how and why she was on the floor of the basement.

Wiggling around, she tried to find anything she could lie on. The cold was making her teeth chatter and her muscles ache. Her head brushed against something. Maneuvering closer, she could tell it was an old piece of carpet. It smelled like disintegrating rubber and mold, but she didn't care.

She squirmed and shimmied on to the rug as best she could then lay still catching her breath. She felt the knot of the blindfold at the back of her head. Rubbing it against the carpet, she felt it loosen. It took some time, and a few hairs, but she managed to pull it off, her head throbbing the entire time. Opening her eyes, she could make out the bottom of a door, a very faint light coming under it.

Maggie struggled to get her hands in front of her, but the ties were so tight she'd have to dislocate a shoulder to do it.

However, laying on her side and bending at the knees, she tried untying her feet. Her ribs gave out a sharp stab, but she focused on what she needed to do. After more struggling, she made a mental note to do some serious yoga when she got out of here; if she ever got out of here.

Shaking her head, she scolded herself. She was a Rivard, and she could do this. All she needed was to keep her head on straight. Nodding, she continued with the rope around her feet. Little by little she got the knot loose, and in another few minutes she untied it enough to get it over one foot.

Her head was still foggy, but images were coming back. She had come to work. But why was she in the basement? She could feel bruises on her arms, ribs and head, and thought she must have hit something, or someone hit her. Yes, someone had hit her, and her elbow ached like an abscess tooth. She remembered falling down the stairs. No, she didn't fall, someone had pushed her. But who?

Shuffling around, she sat crisscrossed. Moving over to lean on a wall, she used it to get herself into a standing position. Her legs felt shaky, but they held as she walked towards the light coming from under the door. She listened, pressing her ear against the crack. There was no sound except for the hum of electricity. Turning her back to the door, she grabbed the handle. Locked. Crap. She rubbed her arm along the wall knowing a light switch was there. Suddenly the lights in the room came on. She slammed her eyes shut as shooting pain blasted within her skull from the piercing light. Her stomach gave a roll, and she thought she might vomit.

Taking in some deep breaths, she turned her head so she could slowly introduce light to her eyes. As she opened them, she could see blood on the front of her purple blouse. Lifting her head, she realized she was in one of the storage closets in the basement. Stacks of old chairs and door mats lined the walls. There were also some dusty plastic plants in the corner. Damon thought they would be great for the lobby, but she'd convinced him to go with real live plants.

Damon! She'd been talking to him on the phone. Maybe he'd called someone when they'd gotten cut off. She must have made a noise as she fell, right? But if so, why was she still down here? If he'd called, then surely someone would have come down here to check already.

She moved across the room and shifted stuff around on the floor with her feet. Perhaps there was something useful she could use to cut the ties on her hands or to pry the door open. Just as she was about to give up, she saw a broken chair leg. It had been bent, and the metal had compressed at the broken end. Crouching down awkwardly, she grabbed it in one hand and made her way back to the door.

Sticking the broken chair leg into the crack of the door, she began trying to pry it open. It was awkward as hell with her hands being tied behind her back. Just as she felt like she might get somewhere, she heard voices in the hall.

20

Liam wasn't good at waiting. In between pacing, he checked his emails and finished the report he was now *not* doing for Damon. He still couldn't understand the call this morning. Why would Damon bother hiring his company to start an assessment if he wasn't serious? It's not like it was a cheap undertaking. Billed hours and travel costs weren't exactly chump change. It made little sense. Unless Damon wanted it to *look* like he was trying to improve the hotel. From what Liam had observed and gathered from the employees, he didn't think Damon wanted the hotel at all.

He wanted to see Maggie, to tell her what Damon had said. Screw Damon if he thought he would keep it from her. At least telling her would prepare her for when Damon dropped the news. And he'd love to do it if only he knew where she was.

"Where the hell could she be?" Liam said this out loud, his frustrated voice echoing off the walls of the room. Pacing around the living area, he was getting more restless by the minute. He didn't even know where to look for Maggie, but he couldn't handle just waiting.

Making the decision to head back down to the lobby, he heard a faint noise over by the window. Looking over, he saw

Suzanna, her translucent figure floating two inches off the floor. She stood still, hands clasped in front of her waist and a look of concern on her pale face. Liam waited as she stared at him, but she didn't speak. Liam got a weird chill up his spine and he asked, "Where is Maggie, Suzanna?"

It may have been just a trick of the eye, but he could have sworn she moved closer. He knew this was silly, but he said, "Please tell me."

Suzanna stared at him as she moved her arm to point her finger over at the corner of the floor. In a haunting other worldly voice, she said, "In danger. The gilded hunter in the dark place."

Shaking his head, he said, "Maggie's in danger? Where is the dark place?" He was getting frustrated when she said nothing further. Then something clicked in his mind. "The gilded hunter. Do you mean her boss, Damon Guidry?"

Her eyes seemed to widen as she nodded slowly. She repeated, "In the dark place, with the angry man."

What did that even mean? The angry man? Liam didn't understand who that was or where the dark place was. He was just about to ask her again when he realized she was fading away. Her last few words sounded as if she was saying them in a tunnel. "In danger. Find her in the dark place."

Then she disappeared. He stood there a moment and then pulled out his phone. Hitting the redial on Damon's number, it rang and rang, then went to voicemail. Something was very wrong, and a sense of foreboding came over him. He needed to find Nelson.

* * *

Maggie brushed against the light switch and plunged herself into darkness once again. Moving as quickly as she could, she huddled behind the stacks of chairs in the corner. It wasn't brilliant cover, but there weren't very many places to go in this room.

With the jangle of keys and the turn of a knob, the door opened, and a figure was lit from behind with the muted light from the hall. She could tell it was a man by the size and width of the shoulders. Then the light clicked on and again the stabbing pain of her head had her turning away.

"Well, well, well, I see the princess is awake." Damon's voice sounded smug.

Her immediate emotion was relief; however, she realized from his words that this wasn't a rescue mission. She glanced over to see him, all decked out in his usual suit and tie. His hair combed and styled, his gold cufflinks winking as the light glinted off the little rubies embedded in them. Shoes shiny, and she was sure if he smiled the light would reflect off his overly whitened teeth, too.

He stepped into the room and closed the door behind him. Damon looked at her, and her blood ran cold. There, just on the edge of his suit jacket sleeve, was blood. Glancing down at the front of her bloody blouse, she was sure if they compared the DNA of the two it would match.

Damon looked at his sleeve as she looked away. "I know, right? Now I'll have to have this dry cleaned. How dare you bleed on this? It's a twenty-five-hundred-dollar Armani suit! I'd say you'd have to pay for it, but I don't think you'll be here much longer, so I'll just let it go."

She froze. What did he mean she wouldn't be here much

longer? As he approached her, she didn't want to back down, but he had the upper hand. Maggie flinched away as he grabbed a corner of the tape and with a quick pull, he ripped it off, taking what felt like five layers of skin with it.

She cried out from the pain. Taking a few breaths, she said, "Damon, what the hell are you doing? Why would you do this?!"

His laugh was disdainful as he latched on to her arm, pulling her out of her hiding place and shoving her to the floor. Pacing as he looked down at her, he said, "Ah, Princess, let me tell you a little story. Not too long ago, my father told me if I didn't straighten out my life he would take this hotel back from me. It seems he doesn't think I have a good head for business."

She couldn't help the little huff that came from her at his comment. Damon grabbed her by the hair and pulled it, positioning her head so he was staring right into her face. Her scalp burned, but she didn't make another sound.

"Careful, Princess, or I won't tell you the rest of the story. Where was I? Oh right, my asshole father. He thinks he'll take this place away from me. So to keep the business and show him I could, in fact, handle my business affairs, I used my entrepreneurial skills to branch off into other business... areas. You know, diversify my assets and show him what a keen investor I was. But alas, I seem to have run into a bit of a snag. Now, in all fairness, I wasn't given full disclosure on the businesses they were and the nuances of such ventures. Things may not have been on the up and up, but the risks were worth it. However, now I come to find out those investments need to have another large influx of cash and I'm left with some hard choices."

Maggie watched as sweat beaded along his upper lip and his very prim appearance was not as unruffled as it first appeared. He squinted his eyes and continued, "I asked my father to let me sell this place and he flat out refused. He said it was an important part of his portfolio and the entertainment sector was big dollars in New Orleans. This meant I needed to do some re-evaluation. I needed him to think I would commit to the hotel. That's why I hired the engineering firm. Thought it would look convincing to spend the money on the evaluation. My alternative plan was going well until you had to stick your fucking nose in it."

She cried out in pain as he pulled harder on her hair, but she croaked out, "What are you talking about?"

Gritting his teeth, he almost spit in her face as he said, "You think I don't know that you saw those insurance papers? I have my spies here, you know. Or at least I did until he grew a pair and I had to take care of him."

Her eyes grew wide with fear, and she gasped. Damon just rolled his eyes. "Carlos had only been here about two months, Maggie, so I'm sure you didn't know him that well. I had to fake his credentials to get him a job in the kitchen, but it was worth it, at least in the short term. He told me what I needed to know by getting in good with the staff. Then he started saying how he didn't feel right about prying. He said how great everyone was and that he liked it here. I couldn't have him telling you what my plan was, could I? So, I took care of it. He'd outlived his usefulness, anyway."

She remembered Urbain saying Carlos hadn't been as

good as his references had said, but he was getting better and he was a good kid. He seemed like a sweet guy, always timid and shy, but kind. Oh God, now he was dead. Tears slid down her face.

Damon took his other hand and brushed a tear off her cheek, almost tenderly, but when he spoke again it was with a layer of ice in his tone. "You just had to look at those papers, didn't you Maggie? Did you show them to anyone else?"

"No." She would not reveal that she'd sent them to Leticia. A picture of little James in his sailor outfit flashed through her mind, and there was no way she would do anything to destroy his world.

"Are you sure, Princess? You better not be lying to me." His tone had turned to steel and anger flashed in his eyes. It was almost as if he wasn't himself at all. Like something had changed him.

She tried to swallow and said, "I swear, I didn't show them to anyone."

He narrowed his eyes on her. "I hope that's true, for their sake. Anyway, let's get on with the story shall we. My father said no, and I needed a solution to a very sticky problem. Then the insurance claim from a few months ago popped back into my head and it was a perfect way to handle this... predicament."

Maggie still couldn't figure out how this would solve anything. The only way it would solve a problem was if something happened to... "No." It came out as a whisper, and her voice trembled. "No, Damon, don't do anything to the hotel. Please don't. There has to be another way."

Damon shook his head and yelled, pulling her hair harder

still, making her scalp ache from the pressure. "There is no other way, Maggie! He's left me with no choice. If anyone is to blame, it's him. He put me in this position. But don't worry, I'll make sure everyone is out of the hotel before it blows up. I'm not a monster. Well, all except for you I'm afraid, Princess. And if you think anyone will come down here and find you, you're wrong."

His eyes took on an almost anticipatory gleam as he said, "I've got a guy who knows all the tricks of the trade for this security system. No one saw you come down here, and no one will save you, especially not that asshole, Liam. I may have hacked your email and sent him a sad dear John note letting him know you're no longer interested in him. It's too bad, too. When I spoke to him this morning, he got nasty with me when I said a few things about you. I think he liked you a lot. It's a shame you won't be around Maggie, he could have been 'the one'." He did an air quote when he said the last word, his fake frown mocking her.

Fear raced up her spine as she struggled to pull away. He just held her tighter. "Yes, unfortunately Princess, you'll be blown up with the place. It's just too bad. What a waste."

His eyes roved lasciviously down her body and hovered on her breasts. "Yes, too bad indeed. I almost wish I had the time to have you right now. It seems such a tragedy to let you die never having the pleasure of being between those amazing legs."

As he bent his head, Maggie realized he wanted to kiss her, and she struggled to pull away. He held her head tighter and forced his tongue into her mouth. She almost gagged from the force of it. Before she thought better of it, she bit down.

The metallic taste of his blood filled her mouth as Damon's scream reverberated off the walls. Loosening his tight grip, she was able to pull back and get a small amount of relief for her scalp. Looking up, she could see blood dripping from his mouth onto his almost pristine suit.

"You. Fucking. Bitch!" He punched her twice so hard her head flew back and cracked on the concrete floor. Pain seared through her head as her vision blurred. She heard Damon shuffling around, cursing and spitting. Something slammed into her side several times, and the metallic taste intensified. She realized it was her blood this time. A searing pain seemed to split her head open as a blunt object hit her in the temple. Her stomach rolled, and bile now mingled with the blood in her mouth.

Pressing her head to the cold floor, she heard the door open and Damon yelled out, "The place you love so much will be your tomb. Enjoy your stay at the fucking Colonial Hotel, Maggie."

The door banged shut and the jangle of keys meant he was locking her in. She struggled to keep her eyes open, but the extreme pain seemed to pull her down. Her last thought was of Liam's handsome face and how she'd never told him how she felt. The curse had taken her in this life, too.

* * *

Liam took the stairs down two at a time, sprinting into the lobby. He needed to find Nelson. Just as he was making his way to the security office, he saw Margaret come through the front doors, followed by another woman.

Margaret spotted him, worry lines etching her face. His

eyes moved to the lady beside her. She was a beautiful black woman; tall and thin, with a spine straighter than a soldier. Looking at her profile, her skin was radiant and his were not the only eyes drawn to her. There was just something about her that seemed almost otherworldly. She turned her head, and the full force of her eyes hit him. The dark honey amber eyes almost glowed against her dark skin.

He slowed his steps, almost coming to a stop as he looked at her. Somewhere off in the back of his mind, he thought he recognized her. But then he just shook his head and continued towards the two women.

"Margaret, what's the matter? I thought you were looking after the kids today?" Taking her hands in his, he could feel her tremble.

She nodded her head. "Yes, I was, but Delilah's home now. I was just about to run some errands when Emeline called me."

Liam gripped her hands tighter and said, "What's going on, Margaret?"

She looked into his eyes but said nothing at first. Liam's eyes drifted to Emeline's hands and recognized the necklace that Maggie had been wearing.

Looking into Emeline's face he asked, "Why do you have Maggie's necklace?"

Emeline's tone was somber as she said, "I was to meet the two of ya at her place this evenin'. There are things I needs to tell ya. I gave her this necklace on Saturday. When I arrived at the house to set up, I saw it on the floor by the bed."

Frowning, Liam didn't understand the significance, and he needed to find Nelson. But before he could say anything, Emeline continued, "This pendant is a protection charm. I asked Maggie to wear it. I'm not sure why she took it off. But ever since I woke up this mornin' I've had a bad feelin'." He looked at the charm again and wondered if Emeline's grim feelings were the same as his.

Margaret shook his hand. "I've been thinking about the call I got from Rosie earlier and it's been bothering me ever since. Then Emeline called, and if a mambo says she's having an unpleasant feeling, that's not something you ignore, ever. Where's Maggie, Liam? Have you seen her?"

Looking into Margaret's eyes, he could see the unease and he didn't know what to say. Clearing his throat, he said, "No, I haven't seen her. I was just coming back down to see Nelson to find out if he'd located her. I needed to tell him what I saw..."

Emeline stepped closer to him. "What did ya see Liam?"

Shaking his head, he pulled one of his hands out of Margaret's grasp and scratched his head. "Well, this might sound crazy, but I saw... a ghost. She spoke to me."

He watched Emeline, and she didn't look phased by that at all. "What did she say?" Both Emeline and Margaret leaned closer, their gazes intense on his face.

"She said Maggie was in danger and I needed to find the gilded hunter. She is in the dark place with the angry man?" The last part came out as a question because the entire thing made little sense.

Emeline nodded and turned to Margaret. "She must be more in love than she let on. The curse is coming upon her fast. We needs to find her quick. Liam, does any part of what the ghost said make sense to ya?"

His mind picked up on Emeline's words. Two words

played in a loop in his head. Love and curse. It took a few seconds for his mind to focus on the rest of what Emeline had just asked.

"Um, I think the gilded hunter is Damon Guidry. I saw his family tomb yesterday when we were at the cemetery and the word on that tomb means hunter. The ghost also looked like she was pointing, but I couldn't understand to where. She was pointing at the floor, but over..."

Liam tried to mimic Suzanne's movements. "She said the dark place twice. I don't know where that is. I don't know if she means it's dark because it's in a place with no light, or is it a dark place because it's evil and dangerous? And I don't know if Damon is the angry man or if there is another angry man."

Just then Nelson came into view, and Liam almost yelled out his name. Seeing them, Nelson rushed over, followed by Maxon.

"Liam I was just coming to find you. I think there might be an issue with the cameras. It's the weirdest thing. I looked back through the recordings to see when Maggie had come out of her office, but when I did, there was nothing there except for a continuous loop of empty hallway. We checked a few other recordings, and there are at least three others which were on a loop as well. Besides her office hallway, the back hall, the front entrance and the back entrance were on loops. We have it fixed now except the back entrance. That camera has gone offline completely." Nelson looked at the two women, and his eyes went wide.

Liam reached out and grabbed Nelson's arm, forcing the man to look at him. "Suzanna came to see me in my room. She said Maggie was in danger, and she was in the dark place with the angry man. Do you know what that might mean?"

A deep crease formed on Nelson's forehead. "Where have I heard that before? Angry man... angry man in the dark... it might be the ghost I told you about in the basement."

Liam nodded as he remembered the story now. He turned to Margaret and Emeline. "I'll check the basement." Turning to Nelson and Maxon, he said, "Nelson, let's go down. Maxon, I think the reason the camera is offline is that someone needs it to be. I think the area should be checked out. We should also call the police. Rosie can call while we split up."

They were just about to head for the basement when the fire alarm rang out. Everyone covered their ears. He looked over at Margaret, Emeline and Nelson.

Raising his voice over the intermittent ringing, he yelled, "If this is legit, you'll need to get guests out. I'll look. Make sure that Rosie calls the police. I don't think this alarm and Maggie's disappearance is a coincidence."

He could tell that Nelson wanted to go with him, but then he took a ring of keys from his larger one and tossed it to him. Turning, Nelson escorted Margaret and Emeline to the front doors. Before they got too far, Margaret turned to him and yelled, "Find my baby girl, Liam, please find her."

He nodded and turned, running for all he was worth to find his Maggie.

21

Holding Julien's head in her hands, she brushed his hair back from his face. She watched as her tears fell, mixing with the blood, and dirt streaked across his cheek. Julien weakly grabbed her hand and pressed it to that same cheek, pulling a sob from her. He was fading fast and there was nothing she could do. His lips trembled, the wet sound in his chest rattled as he said, "I love you Belle, d... don't forget it. But I'm cursed. I should've known I couldn't have... you are the light, Belle, a light I couldn't hold..."

His eyes closed, and a coldness gripped her heart. The sharp wail of sirens filled the night...

* * *

Maggie's mind felt thick, and her limbs were heavy. She couldn't pinpoint the reason. Was it the loss that had her mind feeling foggy? She pictured Julien lying on the ground, a knife protruding from his chest. He'd tried to save her from that life. That horrible life of strange men treating her body like she didn't matter. Like her life didn't matter. Struggling to reach back in her memories, everything faded away. Maggie couldn't pick out the details until the face disappeared altogether.

Trying to drag in a breath, she tasted copper in her mouth.

A stabbing pain in her head brought her back to the present. She was lying on the floor, her muscles so stiff it was painful to move. Maggie winced as she focused on the sound. Was that a siren? The high pitch buzzing sound was unfamiliar. The noise drilled into her skull making her brain feel like it would explode.

Rolling over as best she could, she tried to pull away from the noise. And then she remembered what that sound was; the fire alarm. Tears stung her eyes as she realized what it meant. Damon had left her down here to die alone, and no one was coming to save her.

A sob built in her chest as she thought about her grandmother being alone. The pain in Maggie's chest had nothing to do with her head, bruises or the cold in her muscles. It had everything to do with the heartbreak she felt at leaving her grandmother. She'd never have the chance to tell her how much she loved and appreciated everything she had given to her. It wasn't fair for her to have another loved one taken from her life. Maggie thought of Delilah and Eric and the kids, the new baby on the way. Lola and Gladys. Rosie, Genevieve, Nelson, Urbain, and all the people she loved like family. She prayed they'd make it out of the hotel.

Liam. Another sob racked her body as she thought of what might have been. Maggie longed to be in his arms again, feel his warm chest against her cheek and hear his heartbeat. She wanted to see those denim blue eyes and sexy smile, to feel his breath on the back of her neck, as they drifted off to sleep. What she wouldn't give to hear his deep laugh and see his heart melting grin. God, she loved him; she knew she did, but she was too stubborn to tell him. And now it was too late. The curse was once again pulling them apart.

She cried as her head throbbed, pulsing with the sound and the pain. Maggie felt as if she would shatter from the loss and heartbreak. All of it culminated in a sphere of cruel reality that she couldn't pull away from. It was all over. She never told Liam how she felt. She should have let him come over last night, but she was stupid and jealous. And, if she was lying here, that meant he loved her too.

Maggie realized that something was wrong with her head. There was too much pressure. Every move made her feel nauseous. She had to stop crying because it was making everything worse. Oh God, how many blows to the head had she taken? How many hits on the concrete? She had to stop thinking; it was making everything ache.

Trying to clear her mind, she lay still. That's when she thought she heard something over the shrill. Was she just delirious or was it a voice? Oh no, what if Damon changed his mind and killed her before he blew the place up? She tried to move but everything hurt, and she knew she wouldn't be able to save herself.

Maggie heard a voice for sure this time calling her name. Someone was calling out and she didn't care who it was if it meant they were coming to get her. She tried to call out, but her dry throat only allowed a whisper to come out. Wetting her lips, she tried again, but still only a whisper came out. Wondering what she would do if whoever was looking for her left, she drew in as much breath as she could. Struggling against the pain, she screamed out, "Here!"

That's all she had in her. She couldn't call out again. Maggie felt the cold and pain pulling her back under. It would feel good to just let go. She was tired, so very tired. If she could just be somewhere warm and rest, she'd be fine. As the moments ticked on, she thought she heard a jingling sound and a deep muffled voice calling her name.

The door flew open and the high pitch alarm got louder. Maggie tried to move away from it just as she heard the shuffling of feet and a warm hand touched her arm. She felt weak, and try as she might, she couldn't open her eyes. Arms were slipping around her and everything hurt, but she could do nothing more than whimper. Then she felt lips on her forehead and heard the sweetest voice ever. "I've got you, Baby."

She felt weightless as she listened to him breathing and she could feel warmth from his chest as he cradled her. She was with him and even if it was too late, as least she wasn't alone.

Then a loud shot rang out, and she was falling... falling.

* * *

Liam felt the burn of the bullet in his shoulder as he fell back, Maggie still in his arms. He shifted so his back took the impact, keeping her head from hitting the floor or wall. He looked up the stairwell and could see a man at the top of the stairs.

His shoulder and arm pulsed with pain, and he could feel wetness covering his sleeve. Liam pulled Maggie tighter and dragged them both back around a corner. He waited, holding her close while trying to hear any sound coming from the stairs. He needed to do something. Kissing her forehead again, he whispered, "Baby, I've gotta put you down. But I'm right here."

Laying her down as gently as he could, he crawled around on the floor until he found a long piece of pipe that was lying against the wall. It was about four feet long and two inches in diameter and felt solid and weighty in his hands. Stepping around Maggie, he leaned against the wall.

Seeing the hint of a shadow on the floor, he tried to guess how close the man was and if it was Damon. Holding his breath, he counted to three then swung out. He could make out Damon's face in the dull light from the emergency lights, but he wasn't as close as he needed. The throbbing in his arm hadn't allowed him to swing as hard either. The pipe hit Damon on the upper arm and he stumbled back, but didn't lose the gun.

"Fucking asshole! You just had to come and find her, didn't you? Looks like I need to put a few more holes in you to make sure you get the message." Liam shifted as he felt another bullet graze the same shoulder that was already hit. He cried out in pain.

Lurching back, he moved away from Maggie. Gripping the pipe again, he was about to tackle Damon when he realized the gun was pointed right at his head. Liam stopped, as Damon sneered. "I hope she was worth it Liam, because she just cost you your life."

Then a gun sounded, but Liam didn't feel any pain. He watched as Damon's face went slack and blood pulsed from a hole in the side of his head. His body crumpled as he hit the floor. Taking a step back, Liam watched as a deep red pool spread around Damon's head.

Looking up, he could see Kenny standing on the stairs, his gun pointed at Damon's body. Liam let out a breath, then stumbling, he turned to Maggie. As he struggled to pick her up, his shoulder screamed in agony, but he needed to get them out of here. He didn't know what was wrong with Maggie, but she wasn't waking up and his fear for her life consumed him. Why wasn't she waking up? Gritting his teeth, he hauled her up against his chest, and almost fell back as the pain shot down his arm.

Liam was half dragging Maggie around the corner as Kenny reached the bottom of the stairs. "I'll take her from here, Liam." Kenny reached for Maggie.

"Like hell you will. Move." Liam's arm throbbed, but he wouldn't let her go.

"Damn it man, you can barely hold on to her, how in the hell are you going to climb up all those stairs. Don't be an ass. Let me help her."

Liam knew he was right as he was already struggling to hold her. She needed help and so did he. Hating that Kenny was right, he nodded as the officer scooped her up and started up the stairs. Liam followed slower and his feet felt weighed down.

Kenny yelled over his shoulder as he made his way up. "We got an anonymous tip that there might be a bomb on the premises."

He looked up at the sound of more voices. Other officers were coming down the stairs towards him. Flashlights glanced off the metal railings and it blinded him for a moment as they pointed one at his face. He felt an arm come around him and looked to find another officer helping him up the stairs.

"Let's get a move on and let the bomb squad do their thing." At the word bomb a second time, Liam dug down deep for strength and moved as fast as he could. Apparently, it wasn't fast enough, as another officer got on his other side and hustled him up the stairs.

Emerging out the back door of the hotel, the light seared into his eyes. The two officers hadn't let go, and they seemed to run for miles with him in their grip. He opened his eyes just in time to see people lined along the street. There was an ambulance, and they took him straight to its open doors. Just in front of the doors he saw Maggie on a stretcher, still as death, and he struggled to get away from the officers. They let him go, and he stepped towards her, just as they lifted her up to go in the ambulance.

"Wait!" Liam yelled out and stumbled forward just as they were closing the doors.

Kenny stepped into his view and said, "Liam, they have to take her to the hospital. Another ambulance is on the way for you."

He pushed Kenny out of the way. "I don't want to go in the next one. I have to be with her." Tears stung his eyes as he looked at Kenny. The officer looked like he would refuse, but Kenny turned and yelled out before they closed the door, "Jared, you got room for one more?"

Jared, the paramedic, stuck his head out the door, took one look at Liam's bloody shirt and pleading eyes and said, "If you're OK to sit then we've got just enough, but get a move on, and put that seat belt on."

Liam didn't need to be told twice. He scrambled forward and Kenny helped him onto the bench opposite Jared. Then

Kenny slammed the doors shut. The ambulance pulled away from the curb, sirens blaring.

Shifting forward, Liam took Maggie's hand in his. Jared was checking her vitals and hooking her up to a bag of fluid as he yelled things out to the driver. Liam squeezed her hand as the tears flowed. Clearing his throat, he said, "Hey Baby, you stay with me now, you hear. It'll be fine. We're going to the hospital and they'll fix you right up."

Maggie lay motionless, and he squeezed her hand again. He looked up at Jared and said, "Why won't she wake up?"

Not stopping what he was doing, Jared answered. "As near as I can tell, she has no external wounds, except for some bruising. I think we're dealing with possible head trauma or internal bleeding. If it's head trauma, that means her brain could be swelling and we need to relieve the pressure. If she has internal bleeding, then she'll need surgery. How long was she down there?"

Liam shook his head. "She's been missing since this morning."

Shifting on the bench, Liam almost slid off. Jared's eyes shifted to Liam as he said, "Buddy, you're bleeding pretty bad from that shoulder, just let me finish getting her hooked up and then I'll look at you. And get that seat belt buckled."

Shaking his head, Liam said, "Don't worry about me. You just focus on her. She's all that matters now."

Bringing his hand up to her face, he tried to caress her cheek around the breathing mask and wipe away blood and dirt from her beautiful skin. He took her hand in his again and watched her face for any sign that she would wake up, but she was so still. He couldn't lose her. Damn it, he'd just found her.

His arm throbbed, and he leaned back as a wave of dizziness moved through him. He tried breathing through his nose, but the smell of antiseptic and blood made his stomach pitch. A sheen of sweat broke out over his skin and black spots appeared in his vision. Looking towards his arm he could see the whole sleeve soaked through with blood.

"Hey, Buddy, are you doing OK over there?"

He heard Jared's voice, but it sounded far away like he was calling to him down a tunnel. His tongue felt thick and no words would come out of his mouth. He was floating but weighed a thousand pounds at the same time. It felt like the only thing that tethered him to the earth was Maggie's hand. Staring at their joined fingers, the last thing he heard was Jared's disembodied voice saying, "Jack, I think we got ourselves a situation here. Better call ahead and tell them to have a stretcher ready. Lean back, Buddy, I don't want you falling over face first."

Then everything went black.

* * *

Liam could feel cool fingers and warm wetness on his skin. Tingles of numbness and pain shot through his shoulder as he winced. Then a soft voice said, "Hello, handsome. You gonna wake up for me?"

He opened his eyes and standing beside him with her hands on his shoulder was a short Latina woman with dark eyes and a lot of blond streaks in her hair. She was older, dressed in blue scrubs with paw prints on them and a name tag that read "Carla".

Trying to swallow, Liam struggled to sit up, but pain shot down his arm and he ceased the movement. Carla placed a hand on his chest to make sure he laid still. "Take it easy. You lost a lot of blood. Just sit back and relax."

Before she could move away, Liam grabbed her wrist. "Where is Maggie? Is she OK?"

Carla took his hand in hers and patted it. "So that's the name you've been mumbling all this time. I thought it was Mary. Is Maggie your girl?"

Liam nodded. She smiled and said, "I'm not sure, but I'll try to find out for you. My colleague Patty is going to be some upset when I tell her you have a girl already. She sure was hoping you were single. You just relax and let the medicine do what it's meant to."

He watched her leave and leaned back into the pillow. He felt like he'd been in the ring with a heavyweight champ. Reaching up, he felt a bandage on his forehead. He hadn't hit his head at the hotel. Why did he have a bandage there? Closing his eyes, all he could think about was Maggie. He needed to see her, touch her and make sure she was all right. What was it that paramedic had said? If her brain was swelling, they needed to release the pressure. Had they gotten to the hospital in time? Why couldn't he remember getting here? He couldn't remember getting out of the ambulance either. How long had he been here?

So many questions, and no way to get answers. His frustration was making his head hurt. Carla was right, he needed to settle down. Taking some deep breaths and relaxing his limbs, he could almost feel himself drift off. He quickly opened his eyes, not wanting to fall back asleep. Liam decided he needed to find Maggie. Looking at the intravenous pole beside him, he figured he could maneuver it.

Lifting off the covers, he realized he was wearing a hospital gown and no underwear, but he didn't care. He needed to find his Maggie. Moving his legs over the side, he was thankful to see the pole was on wheels. He reached over and shut off the monitor. He hoped that would not send an alarm to someone who would race down here. Next, he removed the clip from his thumb, which was measuring his pulse.

Undeterred by the tiredness that pulled at him or the possibility of being caught, he lowered his feet to the floor. Grabbing the pole and holding the back of his gown closed, he shuffled his bare feet to the door. Leaning out, he saw the coast was clear. A wave of dizziness came over him as he started out. Breathing deep, he moved slower and leaned on the wall when he needed it.

He peaked into three rooms before he got caught. And of all the people to catch him, it had to be Kenny. Shit. "Liam, what do you think you're doing? Are you trying to get another blow to the head?"

Liam looked at him, puzzled. Kenny nodded. "Oh, that's right, you don't know. Well, in case you were wondering, champ, you passed out in the ambulance and hit your head on Maggie's stretcher on the way down. Poor Jared had to drag you out of there by himself. You may have given the guy a hernia."

Reaching up, Liam touched the bandage. At least now he had an explanation. But he still needed answers. Moving as if to pass Kenny, he held out a hand, and didn't care if he was flashing anyone behind him.

"Move, Kenny. I've gotta find her." He took two steps, and the dizziness threatened to take him down. He leaned into the wall. Kenny grabbed his arm to steady him.

Shaking his head, Kenny said, "Dude, you need to get back into bed. You're not ready to be moving around on your own." Searching, he mumbled under his breath, "Where is a nurse when you need one? Oh, there's one. Hey Joanne, can you bring me over a wheelchair before Mr. Kavanagh here takes a face plant on the floor?"

A wheelchair appeared, and Kenny sat him down. The nurse, who he couldn't see, started wheeling him back towards his room. Panicked, he yelled out, "No, I need to see her! You don't understand, I need to know she's OK!"

He could feel the tears in his eyes as the nurse stopped. Kenny stood there staring at him like he'd lost his mind. And maybe he had, but he didn't care. Kenny's eyes moved from him to Joanne as he said, "What room is Rivard in?"

The crisp voice from behind him said, "She's just come out of surgery and they allow in no one but immediate family."

"By the looks of this guy, he'll keep risking his life to see her. I suggest you let him. If anyone deserves to see her, it's him. He saved her life." Kenny looked at him and gave a slight smile. Then looking back at the nurse, he gave her a grin as he said, "Come on, Joanne; just give him a quick look. Then you can get him back in his bed."

Kenny didn't move, just waited to hear the verdict. Liam heard a huff from behind him and then the crisp voice said, "Fine, but just a quick one then back in your room. You're lucky you didn't fall and break your damn neck. She must be something if you're willing to risk that."

Liam nodded and could feel a sob working its way up his throat as he said, "She's everything."

Joanne wheeled him to ICU and as he looked around, he could see glass walled rooms all open to the nurse's station. Then he saw Margaret beside Maggie's bed. The woman looked like she'd aged ten years and his heart broke. It was bad; he knew it.

When Margaret saw him, tears were running down her cheeks and she gripped the used tissue in her hand. As soon as he was beside her, he wrapped his one arm around her as best he could. She sniffled and then pulled back. Brushing a hand over his cheek, she said in a tear-strained voice, "You found my girl for me, Liam. You found her and brought her back. I can't thank you enough."

He gripped her hand in his and looked at Maggie. She looked so small and fragile. Tubes and hoses were linking her to electronics and monitors. He tried to hold it together, but seeing her helpless, he let a tear spill down his cheek. The shattering of his heart and the devastation hit him like a wall. Then he remembered that Margaret was here, and he pulled himself together. Gulping in air, he leaned towards Margaret and said, "She's a fighter, Margaret. She'll make it."

Margaret was rocking back and forth in her chair and looked at him, as she smiled a sad smile. "My dear boy, there's so much you need to know. Emeline will tell you everything. It's the only way we can save her." Patting his hand, she moved so he could be closer to Maggie.

Liam gently took her hand in his. It was lifeless, but warm.

Pressing it to his cheek, he let a few more tears fall. He didn't understand what Margaret was talking about, but if it would help Maggie, he'd do anything.

He heard a male voice behind him. "There are way too many people in this room. Immediate family only."

He kissed her hand, letting his lips linger on her soft skin. He reluctantly let it go as Joanne backed him away from the bed. Margaret nodded and said, "Emeline will be here soon, Liam. She'll tell you everything."

Liam's eyes lingered on Maggie. What he wouldn't give to see those beautiful grey-green eyes again. To hear that sweet voice and that laugh that filled his heart like a song. As they took him back to his room, he only nodded, and muttered a thank you to Joanne once they got there.

Joanne was a tall, muscular woman who had him back into bed and hooked back up to his monitor in no time. She adjusted his IV and fiddled with a few things as Liam tried to get comfortable. When she was done, she gave him a faint smile and told him to stay put. He just nodded and looked towards the window.

The sky outside was fading from deep pink to inky blue and it reflected the growing heaviness in his heart. All he wanted was to be with Maggie. To hold her in his arms and tell her how much he loved her. Tell her how he was planning on staying here and how much he wanted to build a life with her. Her beautiful smile... her gorgeous eyes...

It was getting harder and harder for him to keep his eyes open. Damn it, Joanne must have given him something to help him sleep and make sure he stayed in bed. But he didn't want to sleep. What if Maggie woke up and he could see her?

Struggling against the drugs just seemed to make it harder to stay awake. His last thought as he watched the night close in was that if they made it out of this he would marry her as soon as he could.

22

As if looking through smoke, indistinguishable faces floated in and out of focus. Their nearness unnerved her, making her feel exposed and on edge. To add to her disorientation, she couldn't pinpoint where she was. Every time she tried to think back to where she'd last been, a pain would pulse in her head, until she stopped thinking about it. Her body felt detached, not floating, but not tethered to anything. There was ground under her feet, but the smoke was dense which made it hard to make out where she would next step.

Reaching out in front of her, she swept her arm back and forth. A few more steps and her hand encountered something. Gripping it in her hand, she pulled whatever it was closer. Then a face came into focus only two feet from her own. She didn't know who it was, but she seemed familiar.

A young girl with long blond hair and grey-green eyes stood before her. She smiled and whispered, "Cela se produit encore." *And Maggie knew she'd said, 'It's happening again'.*

Maggie wondered what was happening, and tried to back away, confused that she could see nothing. Before she could step away, the girl seized her hand.

"La malédiction de Delia est à nouveau sur nous." *Maggie*

felt the girl squeeze her hand and then the words seemed to translate in her mind, 'Delia's curse is upon us once again.'

Shaking her head, Maggie tried to fight the girl's hold. Before she could pull away, the young girl looked deep into her eyes and said, "La prêtresse est la seule qui puisse nous sauber maintenant. Le seul..."

Maggie watched as the girl faded away, her words rendering in Maggie's mind, "Your priestess is the only one who can save us now. The only one..."

* * *

Liam opened his eyes. He wasn't sure what had awoken him, but he remembered where he was. The beeping of the monitor and the smell of antiseptic filled the room. He heard whispering and moved his head to see Carla, the nurse from earlier, and Emeline in a conversation. They were arguing, and he wondered what was going on.

The room was unlit except for the lights behind his hospital bed. He could see the profile of Emeline's face and watched as the lines around her mouth formed deep creases as she frowned at Carla. As if sensing his eyes on her, she turned and gave him a tight smile which didn't reach her eyes.

She moved towards him and put her hand on his arm. Just like the first time, her light amber eyes mesmerized him. Emeline rubbed her hand back and forth on his arm as she said, "How are ya feelin' now, Liam?"

He went to speak, but nothing came out. Clearing his throat, he said in a raspy whisper, "Better."

Emeline nodded and said, "That's good. Margaret told ya

I was comin'?" Liam nodded and felt the warmth of her hand on his arm.

Looking solemn, she said. "I don't have a lot of time to tell ya the story ya needs to hear Liam. You're just gonna have to put your faith and trust in me." She swallowed and continued to rub his arm.

"I know it's gonna be hard to believe but we were family once, many lifetimes ago. We've all lived many, many times. And Maggie has been a part of all of those lives."

At the mention of Maggie's name, Liam leaned closer to Emeline.

"Long ago, in another life, you and Maggie were Benoit and Césarine. The two of ya fell in love. A love so deep and so strong that no one could tear ya apart. Unfortunately, a Santero priestess named Delia was also in love with Benoit. The love between the two of ya enraged Delia, and she cursed ya both. Not long after that, ya both died. Tragic, horrific deaths. The curse she placed was very dark and strong. She phrased the curse so that the two of ya would be born again and again, falling in love with each other in every lifetime. But ya would also die young in every lifetime because of that love. I've been researching this for a long time, Liam. I'm gonna try my best to stop this cycle of love and death. It needs to stop. It's not fair for ya both to bear such a horrible curse."

Tears brim her lower lids as she held his gaze. Watching her, he didn't know if what she said was the truth, but her reaction to the telling of this story made him trust her.

"I'm sure you've been having dreams, Liam. These aren't just dreams, but glimpses of your past lives. You've been remembering the lives you've lived before with Maggie. I believe the spirits have been trying to tell ya something is wrong. And that is the reason I'm here. We needs to break this curse. And I need the two of ya together to break it."

Emeline motioned to Carla and said, "We will take ya to see Maggie. If we do nothing, Maggie will die. I know in my heart it will happen. I've spoken to the elders and they've told me it is so. We needs to move fast. Every minute the two of ya are under this curse, the more dangerous it is. Carla, you will help us, won't you?"

Carla looked like she wasn't on board with the plan, but she nodded. The next thing Liam knew, Carla disconnected his tubes, and he was being wheeled out of the room.

The halls were quiet as they made it down to the doors of the ICU. He could see another nurse at the doors. She wore blue scrubs and waved them in. Emeline walked ahead and gave her a quick hug.

"Thank you, Adela. I appreciate your help. We needs to make this fast. We'll try to stay out of the way." Turning to Liam, she said, "Adela has been watching over your Maggie."

The doors opened into ICU, and the quiet of the outer hall ended. The beeping of monitors and the hum of equipment surrounded them. Wheeling him into Maggie's room, Carla and Adela pulled a curtain to block others from seeing.

Emeline pulled a dark brown cloth bag out from under Maggie's bed. From it she pulled bowls, bottles and vials of things that she would need. Adela came over and helped Emeline settle things on the bed. They spoke in hushed whispers, so Liam couldn't hear what they were saying.

His eyes focused on Maggie. Even hooked up to machines, with dark shadows under her eyes, she was beautiful. He wheeled himself closer to the bed and took her hand. It was still limp in his hand, and it felt colder now. He knew it wasn't a good sign. Cupping it in his, he rubbed it, hoping to infuse some warmth and life into it. The steady peeping of her machine assured him she was fine, and he hoped it stayed that way.

Looking over at Emeline, he watched as she pulled a knife out of her bag. She laid it on the bed and picked up a bowl, emptying the contents of one vial in it. Emeline looked at him, then at Adela. Glancing over her shoulder, she nodded to Carla who was standing over by the door.

"I know we can't have open flame in here, so I'm just gonna light this out in the hall. I only needs a few embers. Now as long as we don't have the smoke alarm go off we should be all right." Both the nurses looked concerned but didn't stop her.

Emeline lit whatever was in the bowl. When she came back to his side of the bed, a small spiral of smoke rose from the bowl. Blowing on it gently, she set the bowl on a rolling table. Turning, she took up another vial then looking Liam in the eyes she said, "I needs you to focus on Maggie. It's important ya think of her and your love for her. Concentrate as best as ya can. I needs ya to hold her hand. I needs blood from ya both. It's essential to lift this curse. Delia was powerful, and this curse was meant to last."

Emeline grabbed the knife and held it under where Liam and Maggie's hands were clasped together. Taking one of Maggie's fingers, she ran the blade over the tip. It must have been sharp, as it took no pressure to slice into her skin. Blood immediately pearled along the cut and dripped into the bowl. Emeline applied pressure and a few more drops fell.

She looked at Liam and he held out his finger and watched as Emeline guided the blade over his finger. He felt the slight sting of pain from the cut and watched Emeline squeeze his finger. Blood droplets fell into the bowl, mixing with Maggie's. The smoke in the bowl wavered with movement and Emeline added a few more items from the vials on the bed.

Reaching over, Emeline laid her hand over Maggie and Liam's joined hands and closed her eyes. Liam closed his eyes too, focusing on everything he felt for Maggie. All the love that he felt for her and the life he wanted to have with her. Their future and all the generations that would come from the two of them. He thought about how she made him feel and the lightness she brought to his life. She was his everything. His reason for breathing, being and living. Liam would give anything and everything to save them both from this curse.

When Emeline spoke, her voice was strong and commanding,

A curse long ago was placed,
Out of vengeance and jealousy.
We must lift this curse,
Its tormented souls released.
Love should never be punished,
For it is a divine gift of God.
Anger and hatred have no place in love,
It celebrates only joy and tenderness.
Lift the curse to see these souls liberated,
Free to live and love and be.
Lift this curse and set right the path,
Taken off course from its destiny.

Unshackle these souls from their burden,
And let them rise into the light.
Make right what God intended,
Let his love guide them.
As witnessed by our ancestors,
Set them free, so mote it be.

At the last of Emeline's words, a heated pulse entered his hands and climbed up his arm. It entered his body, settling in his chest where it warmed his core and spread throughout his limbs. It made him feel lighter, as if someone had lifted a weight off him. In his entire life, he'd never felt so... whole. Keeping his eyes closed, he heard Emeline speak again, "Thank you for spreading your light. I give you my undying gratitude and love."

Liam opened his eyes and looked up at Emeline. Her face looked tired, but she smiled down at him. As she lifted her hand off their joined hands, the machine beside Maggie shrilled with an alarm as her body convulsed. Shocked, Liam held tighter to her hand until someone grabbed the wheelchair from behind and pulled him away. Losing her hand felt like he'd severed a limb, and he yelled her name as he was rolled into the main area of the ICU.

He watched as doctors and nurses raced into Maggie's room. They were calling out to each other, as they wheeled a cart into the room. Paddles appeared as they exposed Maggie's chest. Liam sat forward as he heard the word, "Clear" and Maggie's body gave a small jolt from the shock. The flat tone of the machine had him frozen in place, his brain unable to process what was happening right in front of him. Another

"Clear" and he held his breath waiting to hear that beautiful rhythmic beat. More movement and he looked on as they administered needles into her IV and another person rushed in with what looked like a bag of fluid.

Behind him he felt Emeline's hand on his shoulder, but her voice seemed to resonate in his head. "Dear Lord, please say we released it in time. Pray for her Liam. Pray for you both."

As Liam watched the devastating scene in front of him, a tear ran down his cheek. It was like watching a horror movie, only it was real life; his life and as he looked on, he was watching it slip away.

* * *

Maggie walked along a riverbank, feeling the warmth of the sun through the breaks in the branches above. As she looked out across the water, the wind rippling the top as the birds dipped and splashed. She laughed at them as they looked to be having fun. Turning to speak, she realized she was alone. Why did that feel wrong? Wouldn't she be with someone in such a beautiful place?

Glancing around, she could see the branches hanging down over the water, heavy with Spanish moss. As she listened, she could hear frogs and bugs, their croaks and whines a chorus of sound.

A figure approached, picking her way along the bank, careful not to step on anything sharp. The figure's feet were bare and coated with mud. Pulling her gaze upward, she could see it was a young girl, her white dress pulled up so as not to touch the muddy water. Just before she reached Maggie, her head lifted, and Maggie gasped.

It was like looking in a mirror, only a decade earlier. Dark hair waved along this girl's shoulders, glossy and rich. Her skin was creamy porcelain with high cheekbones and dark pink lips. Promi-

nent brows over thick lashes drew Maggie's eyes, then she stared. Grey-green eyes peered back at her and she almost put her hand out to see if this young girl was real.

They both stood staring, unsure of what to say. The girl was smiling at her, but a worried line appeared between her brows. Seeing the concern, Maggie felt the need to comfort her, but who was she? The young girl reached out a hand taking one of Maggie's. Looking down, she could see their hands together, but it felt as if she was wearing a glove, keeping the heat and touch dulled.

The girl spoke to her in a soft voice, which seemed more inside Maggie's head then coming from the girl's mouth. "I'm glad I made it this time. I never get this far before it's too late, but not this time. I made it."

Maggie must have looked puzzled, so the girl continued, "You need to turn back. It's not safe to come any further. Someone is helping you, so you need to go back, before it's too late."

The girl glanced over her shoulder at the trees. She seemed nervous now, but Maggie couldn't understand why. "Maggie, you need to go back before she comes. They're waiting for you. You've gotta chance now, but only if you go back."

"Go back where? I don't know where I am. How can I get back?" Maggie looked over her shoulder and saw only the riverbank and trees. It didn't look like any place she'd ever been.

"If you keep on this path it's gonna be too late, and I can't fail again." The girl was looking frantic. She took Maggie's hand in both of hers now and squeezed. The pressure felt strange, like a pulse of energy had come from them. The energy ran straight up her arm and into her chest. She felt her heart flutter with the sensation.

Maggie tried to pull away, but the young girl was stronger. "Do you feel that energy, Maggie? They're trying to get you back, you need to go."

Maggie shook her head and said, "Who is trying to get me back? This is all so confusing."

Letting go of her hand, the young girl cupped Maggie's face and said, "Believe me when I tell you I've been waiting here a long time. This all started because I fell in love. I don't know if I would go back and change it because I love him so much. But it should have only been our burden to bear. She cursed us all for eternity, and it's too much. They removed the curse, but her power still exists here on this side. You need to wake up. You're safe there. Your family needs you."

Tears filled Maggie's eyes as she said, "Césarine?"

The young girl nodded as she wiped away Maggie's tear as it breached the edge of her lid. "Yes Maggie, it's me. Now I need you to make me one promise."

Maggie nodded, and Césarine smiled. "You need to live. Live and love and don't hold back. You're meant to be with him. My Benoit is part of his soul, and he needs release. We need to move on and the only way to make that happen is for you to set us free."

A pulse came through Cesarani's hands again and Maggie could feel it spread through her body. Césarine nodded and backed away, letting Maggie's face go. Just as she was about to turn away, the sky turned dark and the wind whipped the branches back and forth. The birds on the water took flight, as their frightened calls had Maggie backing away from the water's edge.

Césarine came towards her, raising her voice to be heard over the gale. "You need to go, she's coming Maggie. Please go."

Placing her hand on Maggie's chest, there was another pulse of energy and this time it felt more powerful, and she felt herself stumble. She turned and began to run, the moss hanging from the tree almost becoming tendrils, trying to hold her. The path was shifting and she struggled to run. Then she tripped and as she fell, she could hear a scream of anger and Césarine turned, shielding Maggie as she yelled, "It's over Delia. You can't hurt us anymore."

Maggie stared back at Césarine. As the young girl took a last look at her all she said was, "Keep your promise."

Then a black figure swept her away and Maggie fell into a swirling darkness, so cold and painful it took her breath away.

23

The muted light in the room pulled her from sleep, and she took in her surroundings. There were pale-blue walls, devoid of anything except a kitschy flowerpot painting in a white plastic frame. The smell of antiseptic stung her nasal passages as she realized she was in a hospital. She could hear a monotone voice paging a Dr. Marshall to come to the Neurology Department over the intercom in the hallway. The breathing tube resting along her top lip was cool as it forced air into her nose. There was an IV tube taped to her left hand, which was connected to a bag hanging beside the bed. She could see the monitor, her vitals displayed in numbers, while the green blips bounced like a metronome keeping her hearts rhythm.

Shifting her gaze, she saw Liam hunched over with his cheek lying on the bed. He held her hand as his lips pressed against her fingers. Dark shadows bruised his stubble covered face. Even with his hair disheveled and lines creasing his skin, he still looked amazing.

As she lay there taking in all the tiny details of his face, her heart filled with hope and love for him. They were meant to be together. Staring at him now, she could feel the rightness of it. And if he was here, perhaps he felt it, too.

Thinking back to Césarine, she remembered the promise

she'd made. Watching Liam sleep, she knew she would do all she could to keep it. She would live, and love, and grow old with Liam, if that's what he wanted. They could be together and share all that life offered; and she knew she would treasure every minute.

Squeezing Liam's hand, he opened his eyes and sat straight up. He winced with the movement and she realized that he was wearing a hospital gown, his shoulder and forehead bandaged. Before she could say anything, he was out of the chair and cupping her cheek in his hand. Her name sounded like a whispered prayer on his lips. "Maggie." He took in every inch of her face before he kissed her, his warm lips gently caressing hers. His breath on her lips was something she would never take for granted again.

Pulling back, he stared into her eyes. Running his thumb over her bottom lip, his voice choked up as he said, "I thought I lost you."

Moving so he could take her hand again, he cupped it against his face. He closed his eyes, and she felt the burn of her own tears. In how many lifetimes had that gesture happened? Just looking at his closed lids, she felt an overwhelming sense of completeness. This time they would make it.

Clearing her throat, her voice came out as a whisper. "I'm right here."

He kissed her palm and then moved to sit on the edge of the bed. She glanced at his shoulder and then back to his face. He looked away, avoiding her eyes. Maggie could tell he didn't want to talk about how he ended up getting hurt, but she wouldn't let him off that easy. "What happened? Why are you bandaged up?"

Liam shook his head, still avoiding her stare. "Let's not talk about that. It's better if you just rest now."

Maggie frowned. "I'm fine. I want to know what happened with everything." He was quiet for a long time, until she said, "I'm a big girl Liam. I can handle it."

Looking back at her, Liam smiled and kissed her hand. "You're my girl."

"Nice deflecting, and we'll get back to that comment in a minute, but I deserve to know what happened." She wanted to get back to the 'my girl' comment, but for now she needed the whole story of how she got here.

Fidgeting and settling back in the chair, he looked at her. "Fine, but if I see you getting upset, I will stop." She nodded, and he told her everything.

Damon's plan was to blow up the hotel for the insurance money. After everything with Maggie and Liam had transpired, they found out that an anonymous caller had tipped off the police about the bomb. The squad found an explosive device in a basement maintenance room wired with a remote. Damon had hired some guy by the name Jack Chi to wire the hotel. Police took him in to custody and he rolled on Damon the moment the heat was on him. They linked Jack Chi with the murder of Carlo Benetti, the kitchen hand. They found his body in a dumpster behind his apartment building. Carlos was getting information for Damon and when he decided he didn't want to be a spy anymore, Damon paid to have him killed.

Maggie interrupted the story to ask, "Where's Damon now? Is he in custody, too?"

Liam squeezed her hand as he shook his head. "He's dead,

Maggie. Kenny shot him. Damon shot me in the shoulder twice when he saw that I'd found you. He was about to shoot me a third time when Kenny took him down."

Maggie gasped, her taped hand covering her mouth. Damon was dead. She wasn't sure how she felt about that. He'd killed Carlos, planned to kill her, ruin the hotel, and would have killed Liam, too. She should feel relieved he was gone. But knowing he wouldn't have to live with the consequences of his actions just made her feel empty. Thinking about all the chaos Damon caused just so he could prove something to his father was just distressing.

Liam was watching her face as she said, "Thank you for saving me. The last thing I remember is Damon in the storage room with me. He tried to kiss me, and I bit his lip. He went into a rage, and he punched me. My head hit the floor and everything is fuzzy after that."

She could tell by the set of Liam's jaw that he was angry. He reached up and stroked her cheek, the bruised skin still tender. Liam told her the remaining details from that day, about the fire alarm and getting her to the hospital, and then they fell silent. She felt overwhelmed by all the information, but she was glad he'd told her. Maggie didn't know what the future of the hotel would be, but she would do whatever she could to help keep it running smoothly.

As her eyes met Liam's he smiled and said, "I met Emeline, and she's quite something. She lifted the curse, Maggie. We're free of it, for good. I watched it happen, experienced it, and then I had to sit on the sidelines and watch as the doctors worked to bring you back to me."

Seeing the pain in his eyes made her heart ache. She could

only imagine how hard it would have been for him to go through that. But they were free of the curse, and that news filled her with hope and eased her mind. "I wish you hadn't had to witness that. But I'm here now. And thanks to Emeline, we are free to live our lives any way we want."

He was watching her, and a smile spread across his lips. "From the story Emeline told me, it seems as if fate pushed us together. Maybe we need to see this thing through, you know, to see if the theory is true, that we were meant to be together."

She smiled as wide as she could, without causing herself pain. "Maybe, or if you wanna go back to your big city life I'd understand." Waiting a beat, she watched to see what his reaction would be. God, she hoped he didn't say he wanted to leave. She would never forgive herself.

He turned his head and looked out the window. He seemed lost for a few minutes, like he was contemplating her idea. She was just about to say he better not even consider it when he spoke.

"Maggie, it's not every day someone walks into my life and falls at my feet. That day was the start of something neither of us could have guessed would be this big. I saved you once and then again, and I would do that over and over forever if I had to. I've been waiting my entire life for you. And I will give up everything to be with you, because without this love between us, there is nothing in this world for me. So, you better brace yourself, Ms. Rivard, because I'm here to stay."

As he spoke, tears pooled in Maggie's eyes and spilled over. "Liam, time and a horrible curse has torn apart our souls. All those lost lives and their love tortured makes a part of me ache inside. But let's make this one the best it should have been for all of them. I never want to let you go."

Their lips touched again and this time Liam deepened the kiss. Her heart expanded, and it filled her with overflowing happiness. He leaned in further and she could feel her skin flush. Just as he was digging his fingers into her hair, the alarm on her heart monitor scared them both.

A nurse rushed in the door and looked at the two of them as she hurried over to the machine. Turning it off, she glared at Liam. "Mr. Kavanagh, what are you doing back in this room?! I told you she needed to rest, yet I find you in here yet again, and this time you've woken her and spiked her heart rate. What am I going to do with you?"

Liam smiled his sweetest smile and with absolute sincerity he said, "You could always pretend you saw nothing and hang a do not disturb sign on the door?" He popped out his bottom lip, giving his best sad face.

Shaking her head, the nurse said, "I'll give you ten more minutes with your lovely lady, Mr. Kavanaugh, then it's back to your own room. You both need to rest."

As the door closed, Liam turned his face back to her. "Guess she is immune to the sad face. Ten minutes isn't near long enough."

Maggie laughed. "No, ten minutes isn't enough, but technically we've got years ahead of us now."

Smiling, they pressed their lips together one more time and enjoyed the thought of a lifetime of kisses to come.

Epilogue

Maggie strolled into the spare room. Actually, it was more like waddled, with hands braced on her back. The dull, throbbing pain she'd been feeling all day seemed centered in her lower back. She almost wept with relief when they put the finishing touches on the baby's room this afternoon.

She and Liam had married over a year ago and they were expecting any day now. Maggie still couldn't believe how fast time had gone. Realizing the apartment in her grandmother's house wouldn't be big enough for the two of them and their soon-to-be plus one, they'd bought a house right down the street. Maggie worried that moving out would be hard on her grandmother, but that hadn't been the case.

Her grandmother ended up renting the apartment out to a friendly lady who worked at the library. Her name was Clara and she and her grandmother had hit it off. Now every time they went over to see her, the two of them and Gladys, were out on the front porch having a grand old time. It made Maggie happy to know she wasn't alone.

Stopping in the doorway, she leaned on the frame and watched as Liam re-angled the camera that connected to the baby monitor. He'd been fussing over every minor thing the last few days. She was glad he'd wrapped up work earlier than planned so he could be home with her for a couple of weeks.

Liam's boss in New York hadn't taken the news about him wanting to leave all that well. Instead of letting him go, the company had come back and made him an offer he couldn't refuse. They wanted to open another branch anyway, so with Liam's agreement, they expanded to New Orleans. They also allowed him to be part of all decisions and when they suggested expanding into restoring historical buildings, Liam had told him all of his brilliant ideas. They loved it, and since then he'd been doing more of the things he loved.

As he turned, she smiled at him. "How many times are you going to fiddle with that camera? It's been perfect every time you've touched it."

He smiled back, sheepishly. "I know, I just want everything to be perfect."

Laying the screwdriver on the dresser, he walked over and wrapped his arms around her. He was careful not to squish her and buried his face in her neck. He kissed her behind the ear and slowly kneaded his hands into her lower back. It felt so good she moaned.

"Mmm, does that feel good, Baby? You want me to do more of that? I can make you feel fantastic." Liam's sexy tone had her feeling a tingle in her lady parts. Then she remembered how hard it was the last time they tried to make love. With the way her back hurt, there was no way she wanted to attempt that again.

"Are you seriously trying to get me going right now? Do

you not remember the fiasco the last time? Besides, I feel like a beached whale right now." She leaned back and saw the heat in Liam's eyes.

He smiled as he continued massaging her back. "I don't know what you thought the problem was. I loved every second. And as for the way you look, you are more beautiful than ever."

Shaking her head, she said, "You like making love to my gargantuan body, do you?"

"Hey, don't say that. I love your body right now. Every time I look at you, I want to beat my chest and yell, 'Look at my beautiful wife, see how virile I am; I made a human!'"

Liam dropped to his knees in front of her and placed his hands on either side of her burgeoning stomach, placing a kiss right in the center.

Maggie rolled her eyes, "Yeah, *you* made a human. I apparently had no part in this creation at all."

Liam stroked her stomach and spoke to it. "Now, little one, I hope after you arrive your mommy's sarcastic attitude doesn't rub off on you. I'll try my hardest to help you, but I can only do so much."

They both laughed and Liam said, "I can't believe we'll be holding a little Emeline Margaret Rosalie or a Benjamin Curtis Lucian soon. It just seems amazing."

As she looked down, he kissed her stomach one last time and then got up to place a soft kiss on her lips. Looking into those dark denim eyes, she felt overwhelmed with love and anticipation.

Sometimes she felt like she was in a dream and had to pinch herself so she knew it was real. Liam was the most amazing man. The life they were making together was better than anything she could have imagined. So much had happened since the day they left the hospital after the incident at the hotel.

Damon's father had taken over the running of the hotel again and had given her full reign over managing every aspect. It was running smoothly, and the staff were thrilled. Between her additional responsibilities and Liam's new job, it was a wonder they'd even had time for making babies. Oh, who was she kidding, they went at it like rabbits every chance they got.

Her back throbbed again, and pain rippled low in her belly. Hmm, that was weird. The sensation seemed to compress and wrap around her. She held her breath, trying to relax. Liam had returned to kissing her neck, and she stood still, waiting to see if the pain would return.

He was kneading her back again, which didn't feel as good as before. "Hey, are you sure I can't persuade you to come to bed with me one more time? I can massage your back. I'll have you bend over on your hands and knees like last time. Then I'll rub my..."

Before Liam had time to finish the sentence, Maggie felt a sharp pain and a wetness between her legs. Gasping, she pushed Liam back as she glanced down.

"Babe, I don't think we'll be going back to bed for a while. My water just broke!"

* * *

Many, many hours later, as the last of the well-wishers left the hospital room, Liam sat on the side of the bed and watched as Maggie held baby Emeline. Their baby girl was more than he could have dreamed. Soft brown downy hair, creamy skin and a perfect little bow mouth. His heart swelled as he looked at both of his girls.

Maggie smiled as she stared at the baby in her arms. "I thought Emeline would use up an entire box of tissues when we told her what we named her. Without her none of us would be here; we owe her so much. Liam, isn't she the most beautiful baby you've ever seen?" Then looking down, she said, "You are the most beautiful baby girl, my little Emmy."

Liam moved in closer, looking down at their baby, then up at her. "She takes after her mother."

When Maggie smiled, his breathing stopped and, in that moment, he couldn't have been any happier. Maggie was right when she said that without Emeline they wouldn't be here, living this wonderful life together. He would never need more than this in his life. Every dream he'd ever had was coming true.

As he looked on, Maggie shifted Emeline, placing her tiny lips against her breast and watched his baby girl suckle. Pride overwhelmed him, and he knew she would be an amazing mother. Looking deep into her grey-green eyes, Liam asked, "Are you happy, Baby?"

Laughing, she smiled as she said, "I don't think I could get any happier than I am right now."

Lifting his hand to cup her cheek, he said, "We deserve to be happy, Maggie. And although it's taken many life-times, we can now live the life they all should have had."

Tears glistened in her eyes as she whispered, “I love you, Liam.”

He kissed her lips and then pressed a soft kiss on Emeline’s head. “I love you both so much.”

The End

Acknowledgements

The idea for this book arose during a visit to an historic sugar cane plantation, just over an hour's drive west of New Orleans. As I stood in the reconstructed slave house on the property, the air seemed heavy still with repression and abuse.
I looked upon the long list of names of the slaves, and I wondered about the people behind them. Those enslaved souls who laboured and died to line someone else's pockets. I tried to imagine how love and passion could possibly bloom in this setting. Then I thought about lovers throughout history caught up in wars and perilous violence. What carried them through and how did their love thrive in the face of such devastation? I left the plantation that day with a plan for capturing these glimpses into past loves in terrible circumstances through a novel set in the modern world.
It's not surprising to me that New Orleans would end up being the setting for my second novel. It has always been on my list of places to see and experience. Visiting this city and the surrounding areas, steeped in its rich mysterious past, was amazing. The people, the music, and the stories surpassed my expectations.

This is why I need to say a very special thank you to Christine Cairns, who invited me to come on the trip that gave rise to this book. Our Bourbon Street crawl, the boozy, musical night out at the Spotted Cat and the Natchez Steamboat cruise at sunset will forever be etched in my mind. Gin Blossoms on me next time!

I also want to send my gratitude and thanks to:

My talented friends at the Writers Community of Durham Region, whose encouragement and creativity inspire me to keep writing!

My beta readers, Lindsay Smith, Tara Ashley, and Christine Cairns, for insightful and inspiring feedback.

Copy editor, Sarah Stokes, who provided both thoughtful suggestions and a keen eye.

Cover designer, Nadia Morel, for her ability to pull my random thoughts together to create something captivating.

My friend and neighbour, Susan Stanton, who provided additional editorials and perspectives on writing.

My friends and colleagues for their continuous support – through late night texts, copious messenger chats, lengthy phone calls, and in the year of 2020, many virtual tea dates, cyber wine nights, and socially distanced get togethers. I am forever grateful.

My family and extended family, who love and encourage me to pursue my passion.

My sister Cheryl, who is always there for me, and niece Robin for all her love and support. Love you both so much.

My husband, Darren, for keeping me grounded and always having my back as we share life, love, laughs, and a teenage son.

My son, Kevin, and my best work to date. Thanks for supporting me. Love you to the moon and back.

My Mom. You have been gone for fifteen years, but never a day goes by that you're not present. Still living my dream, Mom.

My father. This book is dedicated to my dad, my biggest fan, who died a year ago. His unwavering love and devotion provided me with the courage and strength to go after my dreams. He always pushed me to succeed and I couldn't have asked for a better foundation.

Lastly, I want to express my appreciation to everyone who believes in me enough to pick up this book and take another literary journey with me.

So, to phrase it in New Orleans terms, let's pass a good time.

About the Author

Lana lives in beautiful Northumberland County, Canada, with her husband, son and crazy yellow lab, Mater.

When she's not writing, she works as a finance and administrative officer. By day she diligently crunches numbers. Her free time is spent writing and fulfilling her passion as a storyteller. Her bookshelves are filled with romance, mystery, fantasy and young adult novels. She is currently working on a young adult fantasy trilogy.

Lana's love of romance combined with the mysterious necromancy of New Orleans, Louisiana, evolved into her romantic suspense novel, Love Tormented. This novel was her second Nanowrimo writing project in 2017. She has also self-published a romance novel, Rewriting Love, released in 2018.

You can follow Lana on Facebook and Twitter, or at her website.

Facebook: https://www.facebook.com/LanaJPickering/
Twitter: @LanaJP
Website: http://lanajpickering.ca

If you enjoyed this story, check out
Rewriting Love by Lana Pickering.

Years after the tragic death of her husband, writer - Julia Witmore decides to start a new life with her son in Heritage Falls, Illinois. Moving from the heart of the big city, Julia struggles with the intrusive nature of small-town life and opening her heart to new possibilities.

Jake Vincent wonders if there will ever be more to life than raising his two girls and dealing with his crazy ex-wife. He's looking for someone who will not only be the perfect role model for his girls, but a woman who can help heal his bitter heart after years of searching.

A chance meeting brings Julia and Jake together and gives them both a second chance at love. Neither of them knew passion and sex could be this hot, but every encounter is steamier than the last. The chemistry between them sets off fireworks.

With true feelings growing between them, will a dark secret from Julia's past end both their stories, or will they have a chance at rewriting love?

CPSIA information can be obtained
at www.ICGtesting.com
Printed in the USA
BVHW040443270121
598810BV00007B/29